Also by Matt Bondurant

The Wettest County in the World
The Third Translation

THE
NIGHT
SWIMMER

A NOVEL

☙❧

Matt Bondurant

SCRIBNER

New York   London   Toronto   Sydney   New Delhi

SCRIBNER

A Division of Simon & Schuster, Inc.
1230 Avenue of the Americas
New York, NY 10020

First Scribner hardcover edition January 2012

SCRIBNER and design are registered trademarks of The Gale Group, Inc.,
used under license by Simon & Schuster, Inc., the publisher of this work.

For information about special discounts for bulk purchases,
please contact Simon & Schuster Special Sales at 1-866-506-1949
or business@simonandschuster.com.

The Simon & Schuster Speakers Bureau can bring authors to your live event.
For more information or to book an event, contact the Simon & Schuster Speakers Bureau
at 1-866-248-3049 or visit our website at www.simonspeakers.com.

Designed by Carla Jayne Jones

Manufactured in the United States of America

1 3 5 7 9 10 8 6 4 2

Library of Congress Control Number: 2011005575

ISBN 978-1-4516-2529-5
ISBN 978-1-4516-2531-8 (ebook)

For Stacy

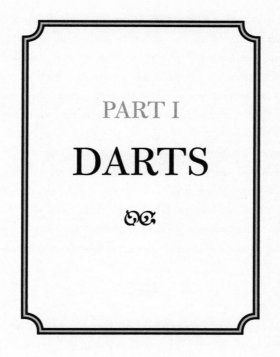

PART I

DARTS

Sitting in a chair on the stones before the house drinking Scotch and reading Aeschylus, I think then of how we are gifted. Of how we have requited our appetites, of how we have kept our skin clean and warm and satisfied our various appetites and lusts. I would not want anything finer than these dark trees and this golden light. I read Greek and I think that the advertising man across the street may do the same; that given some respite from war and need the mind, even the mind of the ad salesman, inclines to good things. Mary is upstairs and I will have my way here, very soon. This is the sharp thrill of our mortality, the link between the rain-wet stone and the hair that grows from our bodies. But it is while we kiss and whisper that the children climb onto a stool and eat some sugary sodium arsenite that is meant to kill ants.

☙❧

The most wonderful thing about life seems to be that we hardly tap our potential for self-destruction. We may desire it, it may be what we dream of, but we are dissuaded by a beam of light, and change in the wind.

The Journals of John Cheever

Prologue

Now, in calm weather, to swim in the open ocean is as easy to the practiced swimmer as to ride in a spring-carriage ashore. But the awful lonesomeness is intolerable. The intense concentration of self in the middle of such a heartless immensity, my God! who can tell it?

Herman Melville, Moby-Dick

It began with a dart, a pint, and a poem, three elements that seemed to demonstrate the imprecise nature of fate. When Fred stepped up to the line, the dart held loosely in his hand, you could see in the way he carried his body the assurances of a man who was well prepared. Fred was always lucky, but to say that now seems to remove something essential from him. In fact it is Fred who should be telling you this story, as he was the one preparing for this all along. Not me.

The judges in green suit jackets stood by with clipboards and the rest of us, the other contestants, the wives, girlfriends, family, and other various hangers-on, quietly drank our free pints of Murphy's in a cavernous pub in the city of Cork, Ireland, 2002. There were thirty candidates in the first round, drawn from thousands of entrants. The contestants seemed all cut from the same mold: all men, between the ages of twenty-five and forty, with that bearing, look, and attitude you see in bars all over America and the world; a sort of studied nonchalance, an ease with the environment of drink and bar sport, the verbal acuity, the ability to hold drunken court. Average, unaffected attractiveness, most a bit on the portly side. Roughly manicured facial hair. The kind of men who excel at giving toasts at a wedding. Fred loved to give a toast almost more than anything. He coached me through one I gave for my father's retirement party.

Under a minute, Elly, that's the key, he said.

We devised a simple recipe of amusing story, then heartwarming anecdote, finished with a touch of personal sentiment. Neat as a pin: laugh, cry, cheer.

The Murphy's contest was a sort of dilettante's challenge, which suited my husband. Fred moved between interests like an errant housefly, but he had a focus of attention that was astonishing and exasperating, like the boy so enamored by the spider that he doesn't feel the rain. The first prize was a pub in Ireland, title and deed.

It was a common enough dream for young Americans of a certain set: by moving into a mostly imagined past, represented by Europe, we could recapture something we so desperately wanted in the present. Or simply a way out of the meat grinder of the suburbs. We named our place in Burlington Revolutionary Road, a joke that no one got as far as we could tell. It was Fred's idea. Fred always wanted to admit our hypocrisy and failings. He could have been a champion medieval monk, so adept he was at self-flagellation. Fred felt if we got it out in the open, acknowledged our defeat, then it wouldn't turn out so badly for us.

By the time he won the contest Fred was nearly crushed by the six years he'd worked in corporate training. When he started at the company, fresh out of graduate school, they were still using paper handouts and the same binders on memo writing they had used in the 1970s. Fred came into the Burlington headquarters with effective ideas and churned out a few PowerPoint presentations, and in a year he was the senior consultant in charge of product development, creating a new line of seminars, communication presentations, and short talks on effective e-mail writing strategies. We bought a house near the lake in Burlington and settled in. I got a part-time teaching job and spent most of my time swimming in Lake Champlain. I'd come up the road from the lake and Fred would be out on the deck mixing a pitcher of margaritas, some kind of meat sizzling on the grill. It was a good life. We should have considered what it was we were giving up when we moved to Ireland.

One evening Fred's father called us from a seaplane, circling over our neighborhood. He was looking for a place to land.

Anyplace to get a steak in this town? he shouted over the drone of the engine.

Fred was half in the bag, crouched by the fireplace with the phone contemplating building a fire while I lined up a couple shots of Patrón with salt and lime. This was the year before Fred won the contest, and it was a night when it felt like the world was going to sleep, a sensation as calm and benevolent as stretching out in a length of warm salt water.

Dad? Fred said into the phone.

I need landing coordinates, his father shouted.

We could hear the whine of the seaplane outside as he banked above the lake, coming low over the trees. Too low, it seemed, and for a moment I thought of the providence of power lines, water towers, other tall structures.

You've got to be fucking kidding me, I said.

Fred waved me off, a slice of lime in his hand.

Do you see the marina? That's your best bet. We'll pick you up in fifteen minutes.

I was always amazed how Fred would spring into action whenever his father called. He had taken to spending most nights wearing headphones hunched at his computer for hours in a kind of priestly attendance to solitary ritual, listening to obscure Internet radio stations, typing whatever came into his head. Fred was a big bear of a man, but at his desk he looked like a little boy sitting in a tiny chair, surrounded by tiny furniture, a tall pint glass of bourbon on ice beside him. He swayed with his eyes closed, tapping away at the tiny keyboard, composing long strings of nonsense.

Like automatic writing, he would say, flushed and grinning, massaging his sore ears. Like Yeats. *The Order of the Golden Dawn.*

We did the shots of Patrón and slipped on our raincoats. It was October, and the cold was coming down from Canada like whitewater, and the lake effect spiked the moisture content. In another few weeks it would be snow, and by December the lake frozen in the shallow bays.

Better bring the bottle, Fred said.

It was pouring when we reached the marina and the lake was flat and oily black, perforated by the fine mist of rain, and I considered the possibilities of hurling myself into that darkness, the weight of my coat and boots, the flight and suspension, my hands dividing water.

Hamilton Frederick Bulkington Jr., or Ham, as everyone called him, was coming in too fast. The plane sashayed across the water toward the dock, the back end swinging around, spraying water in sheets. Fortunately, the marina was empty of people, but the slips were still full and the gas dock had a few boats tied up. At the last possible second Ham spun the plane around and blasted the engines, then killed the motor and coasted in. By the time the tail section bumped on the dock, he was climbing along the pontoon, a leather valise in one hand and a massive hard-sided gun case in the other. He shook hands with Fred then handed him a line to tie off. He had gained weight since I saw him last, and the flesh was loose around his chin and ears, but he still looked like a man cut away from the stake. His charcoal pin-striped suit hung on him like a sweater on a dog. He turned and smoothed back his thin swatch of hair, the rain pouring off his face, and addressed me.

Elly. You look fit as ever.

Fred hefted the gun case.

What's this?

Thought we'd do a bit of duck hunting, Ham said. First thing in the morning we'll knock some down.

You can't leave the plane just tied up here, I said.

This is a hell of a spot, Ham said, addressing the dark expanse of the lake.

Ham wanted dinner so we hustled off to the truck and Fred drove us into Burlington, to a new eco-friendly café built into the cavernous exposed brick cellar of an old timber warehouse.

Ham set his valise on the bar and took off his coat as we waited for a table. His shirt was stained down one side with something brown and fetid. He ordered us single-malt scotches, something Fred and I hated, and we clinked glasses with the somber formality of a doomed business transaction.

When'd you get the plane? Fred asked.

A guy I know lets me borrow it.

Do you have a license? I asked.

Not needed, he said slowly, in this kind of situation.

What kind of situation?

Ham waved his arms at the scene around us, as if to say, *this*.

He put his hand on Fred's shoulder, something I'd never seen him do, and looked him straight in the face.

I've got something for you, Ham said, grinning. Something for my son, Hamilton Frederick Bulkington the third. And for the next Bulkington to come along, eh?

Fred blushed, surprised and clearly uncomfortable. For years Ham had barely taken an interest in Fred and now he was lobbying for progeny? We all looked away and took a swig of our drinks. Ham rattled the ice in his glass, trying to get the bartender's attention.

We got a booth by the wall. Our waiter, a young woman with dreadlocks erupting from her head stood by with her hand-whittled pencil stub, her eyes glistening and shot through with crimson. Ham perused the menu with obvious disdain. It was printed on triple-recycled paper with root ink, making it hard to read.

What's *this* shit? Ham said.

I got it, Fred said, and ordered a few rare grass-fed porterhouses, curried potato salad, and a bottle of heavy merlot. Ham was trying to light a cigarette with a packet of damp matches. Fred rapped his knuckles and pointed to the no smoking sign that was carved into the golden maple table in six-inch letters.

I've got decisions to make, Ham said to me. But first, the ducks. Four a.m. You have a suitable dog, yes?

No, I said. No dog.

Well, Ham said, with a note of asperity in his voice, *someone* is going to have to go in to retrieve. You up for it, Elly?

Fred laughed. I didn't see the humor and I put the toe of my Wellington into his kneecap, making the recycled silverware jump on the table.

Ham frowned and reached over to stroke my forearm, something he liked to do.

My favorite newt, he said, our family amphibian.

I'd like to see you get in that water, I said. You haven't the bottle for it.

Ham drained his glass and nodded.

Right you are there, Elly.

He ran his fingers along my skin. His eyes were like pinpricks of black, star-shaped and sunken.

That's why we need you.

I have skin like a walrus. I have a condition called congenital hypodermic strata. Essentially it is a thin, even layer of subcutaneous fat deposits under the skin all over my body, all the way down to my fingers, giving my skin a dimpled surface. This fat layer makes my total body fat around 32 percent, which is quite high for a woman of my weight, and my body density is precisely the same as seawater, which gives me loads of natural buoyancy. I'm no Lynne Cox, but I can stand water most people can't. Lynne Cox swam from Alaska to the Soviet Union in 1987 with no wet suit, five miles in forty-degree water. There is only one other known person who can survive water that cold, and that is an Icelandic fisherman named Dahlen who in 1963 swam a mile to shore from his capsized boat in Baffin Bay.

For everyone else, anything near forty degrees Fahrenheit without a serious wet suit would feel like a million burning shocks in every pore. After five minutes your limbs would begin to lock up, the blood retreating furiously into your heart. Your lips would draw back, your mouth convulsing for air, and the exposure could cause your teeth to freeze and shatter in your skull. A few more minutes and you would enter accelerated hypothermia, your heartbeat going adrift until you went into full ventricular fibrillation, your heart literally tying itself into a tangled knot in your chest.

I guess I'm lucky that the fat layer is thin and spread so evenly. You couldn't tell unless you touched me, and I am told that it doesn't feel unpleasant, just like someone with goose bumps. For the first few weeks we were together Fred thought I was always cold, and I let him believe it, playing along and shivering with what I thought was charming, girlish delight. I couldn't pull that off for long, especially after the November afternoon when on a dare I dove into a lake in Massachusetts, Fred standing on the dock in his sweater and boots. But he came to love my skin, the feel of it, the same way I came to love the swatch of hair on his chest and his oniony smell.

My skin has helped to make me a good swimmer, as does being six feet tall with the wingspan of an albatross, but I can't say I'm glad to have it. I have coat-hanger shoulders, my deltoid muscles like loaves of bread. Fred always liked to stroke the striated fibers of flat muscle that spread from my waist, like butterfly wings, he said. Of course I wish things were different.

By the end of dinner and our fourth bottle of wine it was clear that Ham and Fred were planning on drinking straight through to morning. They ordered dessert and then pulled out the bottle of Patrón. I abstained and asked the waiter to bring over four liters of distilled water with a wedge of lime. When she brought the water in carafes I stood up and chugged each one without stopping, making my stomach and bladder swell like a frog. Then I went to the bathroom to pee and wash my face and get ready to drive the Land Rover home. In the bathroom mirror my face looked hard and dry, my nose and cheeks inflamed, my pupils spinning disks. I dunked my head in the sink and tied my wet hair back in a ponytail. I was about to turn thirty, and so much about our lives was going to change. I closed my eyes and thought of the lake.

Anyone who has swum in a pool understands the palpable difference between the sensations of swimming in a few feet of water and in twelve feet or more. It shouldn't feel different, but it does. It is the knowledge of that vastness beneath you that cannot be shaken or forgotten, something about the drastic proportions and ratios involved. To be nothing more than a speck, a mote of flesh, traversing a vast expanse of water, a long line of horizon, and to feel at once buoyed by the bubble of elements, hundreds of feet from the bottom, is a sensation that I think must be close to flying, like a great soaring seabird, wide-ranging and steady above the clouds.

I had been swimming competitively for most of my life, and for much of that time I harbored a punishing desire to be an Olympic champion, or to seek some kind of greatness on an international scale. It wasn't until I'd burned out two years into college that I discovered that what I really wanted was to be alone in the water. I began to fill the void with open-water swims in lakes, rivers, and ponds, hurling myself into any body of water I could find, day or night: a beach house in the Outer Banks with old high school friends, camping by the shores of a muddy lake with Fred, the springs of northern Florida. My natural state seemed to be damp and clammy, my hair stiff with salt or lake scum. It was my only true source of satisfaction, when I felt most complete. Until I met Fred.

The mornings on Lake Champlain were often windy and brisk, so I took to swimming in the evenings after work. The beach officially closed at dusk, but people still hung about or paddled in the shallows, mothers with small children filling tiny plastic buckets. I was constantly amazed at the willingness of New Englanders to fling themselves into a body of water in often miserable circumstances. In a dead rain, the air temperature at fifty and the water at sixty, there would be a stumpy old man hacking out some laps and a few families with umbrellas frolicking in the water. I would walk out waist deep and stretch my upper body and gaze at the New York side of the lake, the sun setting between the humped shoulders of the Adirondacks. If the air was clear, as it often was, you could see the illuminated pine trees on the peaks lit like tiny hairs on a body. It would be night before I returned.

Lake Champlain was a dream in this way, one of the deepest freshwater bodies in North America, with depths up to six hundred feet in places. That kind of depth comes at you from the black bottom like throbbing psychic waves. On a clear night when it got late and darkness began to settle in, with those booming northern stars and the endless sheets of black, it was like swimming in orbit around the earth.

Back at the house Hamilton rearranged our liquor cabinet looking for scotch, even though we told him we didn't have any. Fred had the music cranked up, some kind of jangly techno, and I was lighting candles. Ham started sweeping bottles onto the floor with lurching movements, grunting like a bull, and finally Fred grabbed him by his arms turned him away and Ham stood there, blinking in our kitchen, the light making his face look positively withered. I poured out a measure of Early Times, our late-night garbage drink, and handed it to him.

I just found this, I said, just some blended stuff, but it'll do.

Ham smiled deeply and held the glass up to the light, the amber liquid sparkling. A half hour later he was sprawled on the couch. The rain had quit so Fred and I went outside on the porch to smoke a joint. I had triple vision and my head felt like cement, but Fred's

music was sounding good. Fred had said on more than one occasion
that one of my finest qualities was my ability to drink like a steve-
dore. Fred brought Ham's gun case out on the deck and opened it up.
There were three guns in there, gleaming with oil.

Jesus, he said, as he hoisted a heavy shotgun.

Even I could tell these were some seriously expensive firearms.
The stock was hand-tooled and embossed with all kinds of engrav-
ings, the barrel gleaming silver, like something a Spanish nobleman
riding a stallion would carry.

Fred passed me the joint and pointed the gun through the white
birch trees toward the lake. The moon was shimmering low, the
color of cinnamon, reflecting on the black water.

I looked back through the glass doors into the living room, where
Ham lay on the couch, bathed in the glow from the television. He
was on his stomach, one leg hanging off with a toe on the ground,
knee bent, like a sprinter exploding out of the blocks.

Well, I am certainly not going fucking duck hunting, I said. Good
luck. I'll see you when you get back. Don't wake me up.

You have to go, Fred said.

My husband turned to me with distant alarm in his eyes, like a
baby waking from a nightmare.

Please, he said.

It was already three in the morning and we were due to climb
in a boat and assassinate some ducks in an hour. This was about the
time I usually began regretting our drinking habits. Fred and I had
become accustomed to cocktails before dinner, something that we felt
was a purposeful indicator of our nostalgic bent and general fondness
for the habits of that earlier generation who populated the works of
John Cheever and other postwar writers. It was a generation who
drank punch bowls full of scotch and water and did obscure dances
on parquet floors, who ate small piles of nuts out of cut glass bowls,
everyone helping themselves to the pyramid of cigarettes that were
laid out on a silver platter, the lighter a heavy, two-handed affair that
gave a satisfying click and a small, efficient flame. As the night drew
on the laughter would increase, and frequently that party would

revolve around an inert form on the floor, always a man, wearing a nicely tailored suit and often holding a hat. In the morning everyone coughed and spat like jockeys into scraps of paper before lighting up the first cigarette of the day, still wrapped in the wadded sheets of the bed, their spouses snoring with a steady, comforting intonation.

In Burlington, Fred and I had parties for my colleagues at the college, early afternoon affairs, a tall pitcher of martinis beading sweat on a wooden table on the back patio. We were the only ones who ever drank it. Our friends clustered like frightened birds, sipping their careful glasses of wine. We stopped stocking any wine or beer in an effort to force these people to have a cocktail but they were undeterred, always trundling a bottle of some shitty ten-dollar Australian red, or a six-pack of some esoteric, locally made beer. They would regale themselves with tales of former exploits, their wild youth, a teenage drunken mission to a suburban strip mall, the rathole hostel in Amsterdam, always with murmurs of amazement and self-satisfaction. Then after an hour or two these people shutting it down to head home, talking about babysitters and papers to grade and early mornings and then it would be ten o'clock and Fred and I standing in our empty kitchen, a half pitcher of martinis left, shouting at each other.

I awoke to the smell of frying meat. In the kitchen Ham was cooking a pile of bacon. It was ten minutes after four. While Fred and I got dressed he stuck the bacon between slices of white bread and wrapped them individually in tinfoil, then set them in the cooler, already packed tight with ice and beer. Fred's johnboat was chained to a tree down at the beach, and we drove the Rover down onto the sand to unload. The sky was still obsidian but I could feel the Green Mountains at our back, casting a cold shadow. The lake had a light chop, the wind low and insistent, pushing the water into neat, angular peaks. With the three of us, the cooler, and the guns, we had about two inches of freeboard. I tried to back out again, but Ham wouldn't hear of it. He was still wearing his pin-striped suit, his hair at odd angles.

We motored out to Crab Island and anchored in a small cove near the shore, close to some overhanging brush. There were birds everywhere, squawking in the trees, lighting out for their morning fly, hitting the water, ducks, gulls, terns, cranes, all kinds of things flying around. We could have swatted them out of the air with tennis rackets.

Mother of god, Ham said, we are gonna get a few.

Ham broke out the guns and I could tell by the way he was fumbling with them that he had only a rough idea of what he was doing. He was jamming ammo in the wrong places. He tried to hand me one, a real beautiful thing that had a kind of lacy scrollwork on the butt depicting mountain ranges, but I told him no way was I going to shoot a bird. He and Fred sorted out the shells and loaded up and got them pointed in the right direction. I grabbed a pair of earphones the size of softballs out of the gun case and clamped them on my head, bringing everything to a low hum.

What are we looking for, Fred said, what kind of duck?

That little fucker right there, Ham said, and swiveled his piece over and let go with both barrels at a fat brown bird that was paddling toward the boat, probably looking for a handout. The water exploded in a geyser in front of it and the bird leapt into the air. Then all the birds in the vicinity let out a collective shriek and took off in all directions, like someone let them loose at a parade. Ham was fumbling for shells that rolled across the bottom of the boat, the sharp smell of gunpowder in the air, Fred waving the barrel of his gun around like a lurching fool.

They went through the ammo in about two minutes. The only things they hit were a couple birds that never got into the air, and now several half-mangled birds struggled on the water at varying distances from us. Fred looked a bit green, gripping the edge of the boat, his shotgun broken open and the barrels hanging in the water. The fat brown duck, the one that Ham had opened up on, was closest to us, only about twenty yards away, and appeared to have been winged; he couldn't get the flight process going. The shotgun pellets had churned up his feathers, soft downy tufts smeared with blood. I was hoping he would get up and out of there. Ham dug around in the case and sure enough came up with two more shells. I took off the headphones and the audible world rushed in.

That fucker there, he said, we are gonna have Peking style.

Fred made a noise, some kind of grunt, as Ham sighted the duck again.

For a moment I saw my hand swinging in a graceful arc, smashing my Labatt bottle across his temple, knocking his lumpy body into that cold water. Instead I decided to say something, some kind of request to let the bird live, but Ham had already let go with one barrel, knocking the duck clean out of the water, a full somersault. The duck righted himself, brayed a bit, and looked at us with something like defiance. Ham brought the gun up again but the duck bobbed his head once and went down, diving under the water in a blink.

We sat there with the water slapping against the hull, the remaining birds clearing out over the horizon as the sun was coming up over the mountains, flooding the lake with golden color. A few minutes went by. I'd seen ducks go down to feed but this guy stayed down a long time. Ham rested the gun across his legs and opened a beer. Fred had his head in his hands, his back humped over and I could tell he was going to be sick.

I've seen this before, Ham said. The blue grip. Happened to me in the Philippines, and once in Missouri.

What? I said. What are you talking about?

When a duck is wounded, Ham said, they sometimes know they will be shot again so they dive to the bottom. Grab hold of something with their beak. They hang on down there, trying to wait us out. It's called the blue grip.

I looked into the water, dark and coppery, the dusty beams of sediment drifting in the unseen currents. We weren't far off the shore, but the water must have been at least twenty feet.

Grab on to what? I said.

You know, Ham said, like a tree limb or something. Something on the bottom.

Fred was retching over the side of the boat, a pitiful sound, and

I wanted to reach across and put my hand on his shoulder, comfort him. But I was on the other side of the boat, with Ham between us, spent shells, the cooler, the gun case all in the way. Fred's vomit spread like a pool of oil around the boat, glossy and rainbowed. Ham was watching the water and trying to light a cigarette with another pack of wet matches. The duck was still down there, clinging to something. I leaned over the side, staring into the water, trying to see to the bottom.

He won't come up, Ham was saying. They hang on down there until they drown.

At first I had the vague idea that I would swim down and save the bird, that maybe I could protect him. But after a few feet the darkness of the water made clear the impossibility of this task. Instead I stayed under and swam away from the boat and down, out toward the middle of the lake, into deeper water, where it remained the same temperature all year round, feeling that strange suspension, the crackle and thrum of that impenetrable, living water, the cold that cuts right through to the bone.

Fred's last job was in August 2001, in Newark. His travel was heavy, but mostly on the northeast coast, New York, Philadelphia, Newark, and occasionally I'd fly out to spend the night with him. I flew in on a Friday evening and we had dinner in the corporate fern bar attached to the hotel, and Fred drank four double bourbons with dinner and he ordered the largest steak they had and barely touched it. Afterward he was clearly disconcerted and seemed unwilling to give in to something, so back in his room we smoked a joint that we rolled with some organic face-oil blotters I had in my bag. The pot was so overpowered by lavender that I don't think it worked at all. I was watching Conan O'Brien while Fred stood by the window, peering through the tall vertical blinds, looking out over the parking lot, muttering to himself.

You don't have to do this anymore, I said.

He turned quickly and regarded me with a shocked eye. I noticed that his beard was lopsided, the bottom trailing off to one side of his neck. The ice maker in the hall outside rumbled. On the TV a woman was whooping like a monkey at sunrise, while Conan duck-walked across his desk.

Quit traveling, I said. Send other people. The business won't collapse.

He relaxed, his shoulders slumping, and he came to the bed and dropped his body across mine. The whine of cars on Interstate 95 made the windows hum like an organ, and I thumbed off his pants and we made love on the rough bedspread, the TV bathing us in the blue-white glow of sleepless midnight.

That next week Fred took himself off the schedule and split his jobs, which consisted of the high-end clients, among the two most senior trainers. The first job he assigned out was a training session at an Italian investment firm with offices on the eighty-sixth floor of the World Trade Center. A man named Duncan Avery, who had been with the company for twelve years, went in my husband's place to deliver a presentation on interoffice communication techniques.

That morning Fred had convinced me to play tennis, doubles, with his friend Martin and his wife. I was terrible at anything that involved a ball or racket, but I wanted to support Fred's decision to stop traveling and to spend time with him.

This was back when we didn't have a TV and loved to tell people this fact. NPR was saying that a plane had crashed into a building in New York City, some kind of accident. Disconcerting, but we walked to the park down the street, Fred with a fresh can of balls, our rackets in hand, silently trying to connect the simple beauty of a morning of casual sport with churning industrial death. I will never forget the clean, fresh smell that came through the pine trees, the light touch of cool air on our faces, the scuff of our tennis shoes on the asphalt.

Martin and his wife were waiting for us, looking anxious and completely absurd in their tennis whites. On the courts a doubles game of elderly ladies was interrupted by a cell phone call, and they gathered together with anguished expressions. I think Martin said something to Fred about the planes, New York City. I remember his wife was looking at me with an expression of condolence, as if I had already personally suffered something.

We agreed to go over to Martin's house to watch TV, and we spent the rest of the day there, Martin's wife whimpering quietly and blowing her nose as we watched the towers fall again and again. Fred was in the kitchen shouting into the phone, pounding his hand on the counter. His eyes were red and his face a mask of rage, and we all left him alone.

Fred's throw looked good from the start, the way he measured the board with a practiced eye and balanced the metal-tipped dart, flexing his elbow a few times, and then with a flick of his wrist let it fly. I'd seen him throw a thousand darts. He was good, but not so good that he could hit the bull's-eye every time. After each throw the contestant's friends and family erupted in a cheer or groan. Fred's cheering section consisted of me, Eleanor Bulkington, his wife of three years.

When Fred's dart hit bull's-eye I roared, spilling my Murphy's all over my hands. Only nine men hit the bull's-eye, which meant they would go on to the next round, the pouring of the pint. The top three would go on to the third event, the poem recital. Fred turned to me with a look of astonishment, a look that said, *this is it, this is really happening!* We both knew the darts portion would be the toughest test for him, and in that second I believe he experienced one of those moments of real joy that come so rarely in this life.

I won't be living in the bar, Fred said. I'm gonna write. Do some sailing.

That water is seriously cold, I said. I'd have to get a new wet suit.

Sure, he said. Whatever you need.

The truth is that from the moment Fred was announced as a finalist I had been mostly thinking about the North Atlantic Ocean. The steep green swells, foaming wave faces, the briny smell, the shock of the cold, the massive depth. The idea of it seized my heart in a cold fist, my skin vibrating with anticipation.

In our bed at night, the snows of Vermont whipping over the roof, Fred used to always talk about—*maybe, someday*—the little cottage we'd have, something with no real address and one of those delightful names like Three Chimneys. Our children would grow up tumbling across the heath and moor chasing a setter, and we would observe the quaint customs of the country, a narrow grassy lane bordered with box hedges, the battered Range Rover, scarves and tweeds and Wellingtons. In the summers we would steep our tea out in the small brick garden, snacking on cucumber and butter sandwiches. Slow afternoons at the local, having a pint. Some willowy brook where I would float like Ophelia.

A couple of kids, Fred said. We could name them Basil and Evelyn. They will grow up with charming accents and a fondness for lawn tennis.

In bed I liked to run my fingers through Fred's chest hair as he talked with genuine wistfulness. It was something he so badly wanted, this other life. There was Fred's father, and my own parents and sister to think of. Could we leave all that behind? And then this happened. We had a chance, and we took it.

This is hard to describe now. I will have to carefully measure the tone. In my mind it is a story without words, only the shrill cry of heartbreak. I think of how much time I spent with my head in the water, swimming long stretches of the lake or the churning green sea. I think of what happened on that windy shore, the broken harbor, a small pub on the edge of the world, and I am ashamed.

Chapter One

Murphy's flew us into Cork first class to sign over the prize, and Fred and I spent a few days wandering the city trying our best to be good tourists. We knew the prize pub was somewhere on the southwestern coast, and after a day in Cork we were glad of it. On the streets of Cork you can witness the struggle that postindustrial towns undergo as they attempt to convert themselves into cities of modern commerce and relevance. The sun never shines directly on Cork, it seemed to me. It is a city in shadow. The pubs play Shane MacGowan all day long while middle-aged men in damp raincoats argue in Irish Gaelic, the TVs showing hurling matches on dirt fields before empty stadiums, or fuzzy horse racing in some unknown, far-off place.

Cork is also where Murphy's is brewed and bottled, so the company representatives took us on an extensive tour of the facilities, where Fred took copious notes, gathering the various packets of information they ladled out to him. The next day an affable Murphy's rep named Albert drove us down to Baltimore and the pub Fred had won. There is no bus service to Baltimore. You can get as far as Skibbereen and then you are on your own.

Not a problem getting a lift, Albert said as we cruised through the countryside in the Murphy's van, just stand on the wayside and hold up a thumb. The scenery was lush, rolling, and green, postcard Ireland.

People always stop, Albert said. Not a problem. Just the same, a car might be wise to have.

Albert was a florid-faced man, narrow-hipped and with a paunch that he carried with some degree of pride. He chided Fred about my height and ginger hair, and called me a natural native, a clear Irish-woman if ever he saw. I didn't have the heart to tell him I was mostly German.

The town of Baltimore tips a finger of land in the southwest corner of Ireland that forms the southern border to the wide rock-filled channel known as Roaringwater Bay. Baltimore is clustered along the gently curved bow of a small inlet surrounded by a sharp set of hills, more pronounced at each end, like a pair of shrugging shoulders. On the edges of Baltimore Bay are steep limestone cliffs, stretching hundreds of feet above the thrashing ocean below. A half mile inland and it is all pasture and grass, muddy roads and lopsided cattle.

Baltimore has the immediate aspect of an isolated, rugged out-post and a pedestrian, quaint, domestic town at the same time, a testament to the amount of time that people have been living and working there. We parked the van in the public lot in the tight little harbor, which consists of a set of concrete piers laid out in a rough semicircle, the northern end dominated by abandoned warehouses, an impromptu boatyard, and the Baltimore Sailing Club shed. Fred was immediately interested in the sailboats.

Takes a hardy type, Albert said, to sail Roaringwater Bay. This is a rough stretch of water.

We walked up the short hill to the strip of a dozen row-house shops centered above the harbor, three pubs, a few restaurants, and holiday accommodations. Our pub was in the middle, the concrete exterior painted a deep garnet with black shutters, a carved wooden sign, The Nightjar, arched over the threshold. The slate roof, with its attic gables, was covered in a patina of blue-green lichen.

The Nightjar had a long, low main room, with the bar along one side and a short passage directly opposite with a pair of bathrooms and a step-down into another small dining room. When we got there the main room was filled with stacked furniture and rusty kegs. The carpet in the dining room was a faded gray-green affair, torn and stained beyond recognition from the multitude of boots and fishing rubbers and a permeating stench was squeezed from the floor with each step.

Fred had done research, consulting with pub owners and reading books about the finer points of preparing and maintaining a business like an Irish pub, and so he trotted Albert the Murphy's representative and his clipboard through the rooms, pointing out things and demanding certain repairs and changes as if he had been running a pub all his life. Fred always was good at this kind of deception.

All the dining room carpets had to go, the hardwood floors had to be rebuffed and treated, as well as the paneled walls. The main bar was still in good shape, a hulking mass of Irish maple covered in a glossy layer of heavy shellac, with an angled armrest running along the top and a metal foot pipe. All the beer lines would have to be replaced, as well as the carbon dioxide holders and primers. The kitchen was in a narrow back room with a utility sink, a squat little steel oven, and an ancient range with gas burners, crusted like a coral reef with the scars of a thousand fry-ups. Soon the kitchen was jammed with crates of bottles and paddocks of beer kegs, packages of napkins and bar straws, boxes of pint glasses and shot glasses, stacking up in the back storage area, the old walk-in freezer, as well as spilling into the main bar. Albert brought a crew in to strip the floors and plumbers were punching holes in the walls to wrench out old pipes.

That first evening I discovered that out the front windows you could see Sherkin Island a mile off to the west and the dozens of small rock islands of Roaringwater Bay. Cape Clear Island was just a smudge a few miles beyond that, only neatly visible on a clear day as the setting sun descends behind it into the ocean.

To stay out of Fred and Albert's way I spent whole days at the old Baltimore Beacon, which stands on a promontory a half mile outside of town, a whitewashed brick thimble on a cliff two hundred feet above the water. In the old days local fishermen called the beacon Lot's Wife. It seemed absurd, a candle in the wild dark, but apparently it kept ships from smashing into the rocks for a couple hundred years. Flocks of gulls screamed and swooped, circling back to the cliff face and then suddenly congregating on the water, deep blue and flocked with foam.

We were temporarily bunking in the rooms above the pub, which were drafty, damp, slope-ceilinged affairs, Fred's stacks of sailing books and pub papers on every surface, books in long rows on the floor awaiting shelving, already warping in the damp, our laundry in an old tin bucket. Outside the windows the intermittent hum and beat of the harbor. In the bar Albert and Fred paced out distances and shouted into mobile phones, pints in hand. By the early afternoon the music downstairs would come on and I would go down and find Fred with the dartboard demonstrating his winning form to Albert.

I was thinking, I said, I could scout out some good spots. The islands are supposed to have the best entries. They have actual beaches.

Fred walked over and put his arms around me and gave me a series of intermittent squeezes, the air wheezing out of my lungs. He was deliriously happy.

Explore the islands, he said. Stay a few days. Come back and tell me all about it.

I wish you were coming, I said.

No, he said, you don't.

Fred knew that long-distance open-water swimming isn't something you can really do with another person. After a few minutes you are consumed with the roar and crackle of the sea, and after an hour you are swimming in the ocean of your mind, alone.

Albert had booked a room for the next six months at a bed-and-breakfast on Cape Clear Island, as a kind of bonus to use until the pub was finished and we had found proper housing. He gave me a map of the island and a ferry schedule.

Have to stay out on Cape Clear, he said, if you want to know the *real* Irish.

There were few points of entry around Baltimore unless I wanted to go in off the docks in front of the small crowds of sullen locals waiting for the ferry. So I packed up my gear in my rubberized duffel, along with a backpack with a sweater, jeans, underwear for a week, my tourist map of the island, small laminated sea charts of Roaringwater Bay, and my hardback copy of *The Journals of John Cheever* sealed in a Ziploc bag.

Sitting on the seawall in the harbor waiting for the ferry I spotted a small dark head in the water just off the pier. A lone gray seal, with its sad dog eyes glossy and deep, quietly watching me. I walked to the end of the pier to get a closer look and it seemed unperturbed by my approach, regarding me with its unblinking eyes, then with a liquid movement it dipped its head and was gone.

I don't mind the term *blow-in,* Stephen shouted to me over the noise of the ferry's diesel engine. The wind brought sea spray over the gunwale and into our laps, soaking my jeans. Stephen, wrapped tight in his parka, didn't seem to notice.

However, Stephen said, I do mind the use of the word *fucking* placed before it. That's what they call you around here: *fucking blow-ins.*

The ferry rocked in the choppy swells, and the other passengers, about a dozen people, most dressed in various kinds of flimsy coats and carrying satchels and boxes of groceries wrapped in plastic, huddled together at the midsection taking refuge behind the pilothouse. I could not tell if they were speaking Irish or just the gravelly, heavily inflected English of West Cork.

Stephen wore a knit cap, his round face bordered with a neatly trimmed beard. He was like a large rotund badger wrapped in human clothes.

Ah, he said, what can you do? It's a beautiful place all the same.

His accent was not Irish, rather pleasantly English. The ferry threaded its way through strands of rock and barren half islands, the green slopes of Sherkin Island ahead, Cape Clear a murky shadow beyond.

You see, Stephen continued, if you weren't actually *born* on the island, then you are a fucking blow-in. Meaning you've blown in on the winds, not a real islander. I've been here for *eighteen years* and I'm *still* a fucking blow-in.

I tried to smile, my cheeks wind-blasted and stiff.

Stephen told me he had a six-acre plot on the northeast side of the island, where he ran a small farm with his wife. A few cows, mules, and hens, nothing fancy, he said. His daughters lived on the mainland. They had come to Cape Clear Island on holiday when the girls were children, and returned many times over the years. When the girls were firmly ensconced at school, pursuing the public school fencing championships in foil and épée, Stephen and his wife purchased a small farm on the island and returned for good.

You a twitcher then? Stephen said.

Sorry?

A birder? Here for the birds?

No, I said, I'm actually looking for some good swimming spots.

Stephen looked askance at me, concerned.

Or I may just hike around.

Plenty of good walking on Clear, he said. Figured you for Irish, what with the ginger hair. You sure got the map of Ireland on you.

As Baltimore and Sherkin Island dropped away astern, Cape Clear loomed up in front of us, brilliantly green and black, rising out of the sea like an unhinged edge of the earth. The swells grew as we left the leeward protection of Sherkin, and at times we weaved through channels bordered by sharp chains of black rock no more than twenty feet from the side of the boat. Looking back and confronting the array of outcrops and peaks in the pitching sea, I realized that I couldn't point out the direction of mainland Ireland if my life depended upon it.

Though there were only about a dozen bodies on the boat, I didn't notice Highgate and his dog until we were nearly in the North Bay of the island. This was the first time I saw Highgate, in his yellow slicker and watch cap pulled down low over his eyes, talking to some of the other passengers sitting in the midsection of the boat, a massive German shepherd sitting between his legs in a harness. Despite his cheerful grin and animated face, there was a somber hue about him, like he was encased in an aura of dull light. Or perhaps that is a trick of my memory, influenced by what I know about him now.

When we chugged into the North Bay of Cape Clear, another ferry was attempting to unload a backhoe on the dock. The boat captain, obscured by the murky glass of the pilothouse, was racing the engines then quickly reversing, the steel loading ramp slamming rhythmically on the concrete boat launch. The driver in the backhoe cab was looking to time the swells. A large wave retreated, drawing the boat back, and the captain gunned the engine and the boat surged forward. The loading ramp slapped down and the backhoe driver raced off the boat and onto the pier, its shovel whipping back and forth like a scorpion's tail. Just when the next swell was about to carry the boat onto the ramp the boat roared back, and in one movement spun its front around and powered out of the harbor.

That'd be Kieran Corrigan at the wheel, Stephen said. That's his backhoe, his construction site, his island.

I don't know where I'm going, I said.

Stephen pointed up the main road that led out of the harbor.

There are really only three roads, he said, and they all connect. If you keep walking you'll be bound to arrive eventually.

The first thing you notice about Cape Clear Island is the wind. It howls mostly from the west but changes directions constantly and never lets up for more than an instant. On Cape Clear you are always leaning into the wind. There are no discernible flying insects on the island, and the native birds tend toward small chattering things that fly low in and out of the underbrush, or large, strong-backed and wide-ranging seabirds, the kind that could carry off small pets. But as Clear is the first landfall for birds coming east over the Atlantic, you are likely to see nearly any species of bird at any time.

I walked up the quay past a few corrugated sheds and prefab

structures and an old stone building perched on the water in the
east corner that was the Siopa Beag, or general store. Just up the
hill the stacked stone remains of a church and a walled graveyard
containing a jumble of worn and slanted tombstones. Cars in various states of decay were parked on the pier and around the harbor,
some with motors running, waiting for passengers. A pub called the
Five Bells stood on the hill facing the docks, a few men standing on
the flagstone patio watching the harbor proceedings, pints in hand.
A reedy young boy with a mound of red curls rode a bike along the
top of the narrow seawall. Other than him, there was a distinct lack
of young people. We were the only people there under the age of
fifty.

The ferry crowd quickly dispersed, Stephen bundling off to the
island cooperative store, where they sold tourist maps, books, and a
paltry collection of island handicrafts, roughly knitted shawls, carved
driftwood, CDs of traditional songs sung in Irish Gaelic, shell art. I
found myself following Highgate up the road. Halfway up the hill
from the harbor he took a detour up an extremely steep path through
hip-deep weeds and brambles, walking with a deliberate step and his
chin into the wind as if he was smelling his way. His German shepherd drove like a sled dog and he lurched up the hill, hanging on to
the dog's harness, until he disappeared over the crest.

I passed the Corrigan construction site, piles of stone, concrete
mixers, twisted nests of rebar, the backhoe already at work clawing
at the ground. The driver was a vast specimen in a canvas jacket,
square-jawed, his face red from wind, the levers like toothpicks in
his hands. The sun was glowing low over the western hills, and all
the road signs were in Irish and impossible to decipher. Albert had
written down "Ard na Gaoithe" on a slip of paper and told me if I
had any problems I needed only to ask for "Nora's place."

The two harbors on the island are separated by about two hundred yards of land, referred to on the island as the Waist as it nearly
bisects the island. Just past the construction site the road descended
to the South Harbor, called the Ineer in Irish, an hourglass-shaped
harbor with a short swatch of rocky beach and stone seawalls lining

the inner bay. I walked along the road that rims it on the eastern side, and even on a brisk September day it was extremely inviting, the water green and surprisingly smooth. The visibility was excellent, up to twenty feet at that hour, with a low particle load, small patches of seaweed and kelp. A few fishing boats rolled gently in the light swells that came through the wide harbor mouth. The eastern side of the harbor had a large stone quay built into the rising hill and a wide set of steps descending into the water, the curve of the harbor stretching out a quarter mile on both sides like encircling arms to the open sea. The sound of wind and water, the hillsides rolling in ripples of green, clean wet rocks, the ocean stretching off to the west over the bend of the blue horizon. It was just the kind of spot that I would expect to be crawling with people. But there was no one there. I sat on the wall for an hour with tears in my eyes. I couldn't have dreamed up such a place. I've often thought that a swimmer views the world as an endless succession of potential entries, and on that day the Ineer seemed to me to have been created for me alone, the entry I had been searching for my whole life.

I followed the signs for Ard na Gaoithe that led up a hill into the island's interior, steep and long enough that my thighs burned. Along the way I met a man coming down, walking a tiny white dog on a leash. He was dressed in jeans and a thin parka, his head bent to the ground, and as we passed he mumbled something unintelligible. In the distance to the east a giant wind turbine rotated silently on a green plateau.

Nora Cotter's place was one of the highest habitations on the island. A small hand-carved sign—*Ard na Gaoithe*—on a low stone fence and iron gate. The wind roared like the sea itself, and I was buffeted as I made my way through the gate. *Ard na Gaoithe* is Irish for "A High Windy Place."

Nora Cotter was a plump, rose-cheeked woman with a pleasant smile. Her B and B was an old farmhouse built in the boxy, concrete tradition of the island, with an additional wing that housed four bedrooms. I was the only guest, the only visitor on the entire island, she said. Nora invited me to sit at the smoldering peat fire in the modest parlor while she prepared some tea and generally made a fuss. This was the reaction I received nearly everywhere in Ireland once I broke through the veneer of indifference; the Irish love a redheaded, freckled American lass, as if the stamp that their people have put upon that faraway land brings them a slice of immortality.

Nora pointed to a framed poster on the wall of an impossibly cute young girl in a green dress with a mound of strawberry curls, "Ireland" emblazoned across the bottom in large letters.

That's my daughter there, Nora Bean. She's in school on the mainland now.

She's adorable.

Yes, she is. And her brother too, Finbar, lurking here about somewheres. You've likely seen him, forever on his bike, hanging about the harbor. He'll be off in another year. The island school only goes up to age sixteen. Breakfast at eight then?

That'll be great, I said. Is there any place to get dinner?

Nora clucked and clasped her hands.

I'm afraid you'll be limited to the pub for that. In the down season there isn't much open. Kieran's pub is due to open next summer and he'll have a full restaurant apparently, but now there's only the pub, sorry. You have a torch? A light?

Nora bustled off and came back with a flashlight.

You'll need it coming back. The way gets quite dark.

My room was simple and clean, the furnishings something like you might see in an old seaside motel along the New England coast.

All payment taken care of, Nora said, handing me the key, courtesy of Murphy's.

Cape Clear Island is the most southerly point of Ireland, save Fastnet Lighthouse which lies four miles to the southwest, perched on a small thrust of black rock. From nearly all points on the island the rock is visible, and at night the beacon flashes on the horizon like a dying planet, an orange-green streak thrown across the southwestern cliffs.

That first night when I descended the hill from Nora's place to the pub I was presented with a spectacular view of the sunset behind Fastnet Rock, the sea shimmering and tipped with whitecaps, and I knew then that if I could get in that water, I could spend a lot of time on this island with little else to wish for.

Chapter Two

There are those who will tell you that the pubs of rural Ireland are these laughing, happy places where strangers are greeted with shouts of good cheer. These people are blackguards, not to be trusted, plainly insane, or just full of shit. Those notions are fantasies. As in any remote outpost anywhere in the world, particularly in the off-season, the reception is decidedly chilly, even hostile, disinterested if you are lucky. Once you are through the door of a rural pub in Ireland every human in the place will do a full-body turn and give you the long stare. You get more than the once-over from the locals if you happen to be an oversize redheaded woman with preternaturally long arms.

The Five Bells had only a few patrons that evening, mostly scrappy gents in builders' clothes, and a woman, Sheila Flaherty, behind the bar. I ordered a Murphy's and inquired about food.

Soup and sandwich?

That'll be great.

Staying the night?

Yes, at Nora's place.

The builders continued to openly give me the up and down, gripping their pints with chipped and cracked hands, beet red in color, the same as their faces and necks. They had the look of old sailors, like the kind you may have seen in the nineteenth century aboard whaling vessels crossing the hemispheres. They wore stained coveralls caked with cement and yellowing long johns underneath. They smoked hand-rolled cigarettes and kept their squinty faces pointed into the dark spaces of the pub.

I took a seat at a small table by the window and shrugged off my damp jacket. The walls were adorned with nautical charts and photos of islanders in an earlier age, boats and cows, narrow, ruddy people, holding on, each photo looking like the aftermath of a natural disaster. Sheila brought my sandwich and soup over to my table.

The birds is it, then?

No, just visiting.

Tough time of the year for it.

Sheila Flaherty wore a man's flannel shirt, untucked, and had the calm, almost sleepy, indifferent manner of a longtime bartender. The soup was rich and oily, with fat-lined hunks of lamb in a thick brown broth. There were no discernible vegetables involved, other than potatoes. The sandwich was made with thick soda bread, black with flecks of hazelnut on the crust, and I fell upon it like a wolf.

I heard a stirring behind me and realized that there was someone else seated at a table in the corner by the peat fire. I heard the plucking of strings and when I turned I regarded a generously fat man fingering a fiddle that he held on his lap. On the table before him he had a spread of papers covered with a cuneiformlike scratching that I assumed was musical notation, which he pored over with a pencil stub clutched in a chubby fist.

When I left the Five Bells, I was thankful for the flashlight that Nora had lent me. The darkness was vast and complete. In the distance there was the throbbing hammer of a car engine, someone winding up a hill on some other part of the island. I eventually switched off the flashlight and walked by moon and starlight. The water in the South Harbor looked smooth, barely a shimmering ripple, but I could hear the steady pound of surf on the rocks below and knew that the swells were still at least a couple feet. I debated for a moment going down the seawall steps to test the temperature but I was already exhausted and turned up the hill to Nora's. The fields stretching off on either side, cut into rough squares by the low stacked-stone fences, glistened with night dew, the hulking shadows of cattle glowering in the darkness.

When I reached Nora's I stood and stretched in the road, looking down into the wide bowl of South Harbor. To the west Fastnet and its baleful eye cast quiet metered slashes across the sea. A single light burned in Nora's place upstairs, another in the entrance hall.

I watched a field a couple hundred yards off where some goats were moving in a mass toward a fence. One animal seemed to rise at the wall, a man, who stepped up and over the wall, continuing on into the next field. The pack of goats remained behind, bleating softly. As he strode across the field with an odd, halting gait, his arms tight to his sides, heading closer to me, I backed into Nora's low wooden gate, trying to keep him in sight. The clouds shifted over the island and the fields darkened for a moment, and when they cleared again he was closer, heading on a diagonal path toward the road where I stood. He neared another fence and I could see his profile, an impossibly long face, the torso distorted and seemingly without arms, the angles of the legs all strange, and when he stepped over the fence I could see his *knees were going the wrong way.*

I was inside the door scrabbling for a lock but there didn't seem to be one. I backed down the dark hall, feeling the wall with one hand, till I reached the last room. I fumbled with the old skeleton key and locked the door behind me. The window was shut and the shades drawn. I could not bring myself to look out. I thought about calling loudly for Nora but instead I sat on the bed in my jacket and hat, and considered what I had seen. It couldn't have been a man. Whatever it was, I was sure it had seen me. It knew I was there. I lay down under the heavy quilts with my copy of *The Journals of John Cheever* and turned to one of the dog-eared pages.

> One does not ask, skating on a pond, how the dark sky carries its burden of starlight. I don't, in any case.

Until that night, I'd never voluntarily spent a single night away from Fred since our wedding. My feet hung over the edge of the nar-

row bed and I curled up and dug myself deeper into the quilts, listening to the winds buffeting the walls of the house. When I put out the
light I knew that I would dream of a white figure walking the cliffs
above the ocean. I fell asleep almost immediately.

In the morning Nora placed a plate of sausages, blood pudding, bacon,
a fried egg, and a slice of tomato on the breakfast table. Another plate
held a stack of toasted white bread, a French press of coffee, a bowl
of heavy cream.

Anything else, dear?

I was alone at the table, facing the window that looked out over
the backyard of the house and up the rising hill of Glenn Meanach,
south to the cliffs and the ocean somewhere beyond. I picked at the
fried meat on my plate with a fork. The egg was crispy and tough
around the edges, just the way I liked it. I worked my way through
the stack of bread and jam packets, a map of the island spread beside
my plate.

The farm across the road out front, that's a goat farm?

Part of it, yes, Nora said. Highgate's farm stretches back this way.

I thought I saw a man, I said, walking in the fields with the goats,
late last night.

Nora cocked her head.

Well, Highgate has some odd ways of doin' things, him and his
woofers.

Woofers?

Volunteers, Nora said. World organic farming something.
Young kids, come from all over to work on the farm. You'll see them
around.

A clear morning, the air bright and the wind salty. Across the road a
pack of goats gnawed gamely on tufts of grass. An old white house,
Highgate's place, was just visible in the distance, surrounded by a
couple of rough outbuildings and old stone barns. Looking down

the road I saw a small flapping form at the bottom of the hill, young Finn Cotter on his bike wearing shorts and an oversize mackintosh, climbing. The hill was at least a quarter mile at a forty-five-degree grade; you could have built a set of stairs beside the road that would have been more serviceable. I waved as we passed but Finn kept his head down, puffing softly, his thin white calves cranking away, moving slower than a walking pace.

I went down to the Ineer, walked to the end of the quay, where a small island called Illaunfaha, or the Giants Island, extended like a stunted thumb into the bay, connected by a concrete causeway. A man walking a small dog, the same man I had seen the day before, circled the harbor edge, heading up to the Waist and the construction site. Under the roaring wind there was the faint thrub of diesel. A few sailboats bobbed in the bay, their stays clinking lightly. Otherwise the Ineer was empty.

The inner mouth of the Ineer is about a quarter mile across, and the water there changes color almost immediately, from jade green to deep blue, then the darker green-black of open Atlantic, all within the space of a few hundred feet. The inner bay itself is thirty to forty feet deep in most places, right up to the walls of rock on either side, like a deep soup bowl with a portion broken off one side. The water in the bay was sparkling emerald green, long brown strands of channeled wrack and other seaweeds swaying with the swells, the shoreline mottled with purple sea cabbage and slick mosses. The visibility was at least twenty feet in the harbor itself. I strapped my GPS to my wrist, powered it up and checked the signal, stripped down to my standard heavy TYR suit and went down the quay steps. I crouched at the bottom and let the waves carry the water over my legs. It felt nice, and I thrust my arm in up to my shoulder to check the reading on the GPS and got sixty-four, which meant no wet suit. I took a long drink of water, put on my cap, slipped on some latex gloves and lubed up my underarms, crotch, and neck with Ultraglide. I stashed my gear bag behind the wall and spat into my goggles as I walked down the steps. I planned to proceed along the southern edge of the bay, staying close to the shoreline, circle around the point, feel out the strength of the current there, and then work my way east along the edge of the island.

I dove off the steps and dolphin-kicked down into the green water, equalizing pressure with my thumb and forefinger on my nose. The bottom of the harbor was nearly uniform black rock, riven with ridges and crawling with scuttling crabs. Turning to face the surface from twenty feet down, I had the sensation of being submerged in a giant cup of green tea, the surface shimmering with light. I relaxed and let myself rise, feeling for the gentle tug and ebb of current, then stroked toward the harbor mouth, keeping within ten yards of the shore, focusing on stretching out and timing the sway of the sea.

At the wide outer mouth of the Ineer I paused to get a sense of the current. I took twelve heavy breaths to hyperventilate my lungs then dove and made the bottom, and grasping a bit of rock I clung upside down, the crabs clearing a circle around me, the water colder here, reading sixty on the GPS, a deep ocean current pushing from the west, curving across the harbor mouth. The color shifted where the massive drop of the continental shelf began, and I looked down into the abyss of the ocean, watching fish and other small creatures spin through the darkening void. This was depth that I had never experienced, and it came pulsing out of the black, waves of invisible power, pushing through my skin until I felt it echo in my spine. When you are swimming in deep ocean water with decent visibility, at first the sea seems wide open and empty of anything, and this creates a strange feeling of suspension, floating in a cavernous void. But that is just an illusion. There is life there. After a while my eyes adjusted and I began to see the multitude of life that occupied the blank spaces of water, the minute, teeming, darting creatures and simple organisms. Then the perspective went; I saw things that could've been a few inches in front of my face, like krill and particle matter, or they could've been the distant images of something much larger, much farther down, the twisting shadows that writhe in the deep. I couldn't tell if they were coming toward me, rising up to my position, or if they were headed in the other direction. I couldn't tell if they were merely swimming away.

I came back to the surface and allowed myself to drift. Bigger seas
would require more care or I could find myself swimming for Spain.
I swam a quarter mile out into the open ocean and looking southwest
saw nothing but the wide bend of the horizon, thousands of miles of
water ahead. Fastnet was a spindled finger in the distance, whitecaps
breaking on its rocky shore. I was suddenly winded, a slow ache in
my shoulders.

Raising my head I saw I had drifted south a few hundred yards,
so I set off back for the point of Pointanbullig on the eastern tip of
the bay, my stroke going into efficiency mode, the long reach, roll,
and pull, giving my heart some rest, till I reached the bay mouth and
the bottom rose up. I did a few laps across the Ineer mouth, another
mile, before coming into the inner bay, reaching the quay steps after
two hours. The bay was still quiet and empty of people and I took a
moment and enjoyed the heavy, blood-rich pull of my lungs as I sat
on the mossy steps, breathing stentoriously, shaking out my arms, the
faint sun warming my skin. Yes, I thought, this is going to work out
well.

After a shower and some tea and crackers in my room, I stepped
out for a walk. Out front a pair of Welsh corgis darted from under
the hedging and bounded about my feet. The corgis led me away
and up the hill to the east, leaping over each other like a circus act,
occasionally checking to see if I was still following. An old crone
stood in a doorway watching us pass, later an old man puttering
around a garden shed raised his head and squinted in our direction.
They returned my waves with quick flips of their hands and stony
faces.

Before we reached the end of the road the dogs took a sudden
turn, slipping through a narrow break in one of the stacked-stone
fences. Across the field rumpled bracken, deep russet and gold, and
the ocean whitecaps beyond. There was a dull, grating sound underneath the roar of wind, and over the next rise I could see the blades of
an enormous wind turbine slowly rotating.

This was the highest point of the island, a place so windy that not
even grass could grow there. The turbine was at least two hundred

yards tall and stark white against the black rock and green hills, a small cinderblock power collection house at its base. The dogs led me right underneath the turning blades, which moved with that terrifyingly deceptive speed of large things, seeming to come slowly from far off, then gaining speed as they neared, until they passed overhead furiously, each tip maybe thirty feet from the ground.

Down to the right of the wind turbine the corgis leapt like salmon going upstream. The ground, dried and blasted from salt and wind, developed a honeycomblike structure, with deep holes and pits hidden under the reddish thorns of the gorse and brambles that eventually gave way to grass again as we came down the undulating hill toward the sea.

The dogs ran ahead and disappeared around a patch of high bramble. I stumbled into a grassy patch, almost stepping on the corgis who crouched low, tongues lolling in the fierce wind, facing the sea. We stood at the edge of a vast drop of sheer black rock that fell away over two hundred feet to the crashing waves of the Atlantic. The cliffs of Cape Clear are like that; they could appear at any time, suddenly, as if the sea was always at hand and the island a continual twisting set of precipices.

The following morning the ferry chugged into the North Harbor on schedule, and I filed on with a half dozen others and took a spot at the bow of the ship. As we cast off Fin Cotter came zipping down the quay on his bike, hair flaming behind. At the very end of the dock he performed a quick stop and twist, spinning in place, and then sprinted back up the quay. The sun hung over the island, shrouded in faded sets of clouds on the horizon, casting Cape Clear in a baleful glow. I told Nora I'd be back in a week, after the Nightjar opened. I knew I wanted to come back and spend time on the island, to get in that glorious water, but mostly I wanted to be back in Baltimore with Fred.

Soon we were past Sherkin Island and into Baltimore Harbor, and I was pushing through the doors of the Nightjar, the tables empty and the floor swept, walking behind the bar to put my arms around the broad back of my husband, who was turned away from me and struggling with the coffeemaker, who turned in my embrace and kissed my forehead, holding a coffeepot in one hand and saying, hey there, E, my sweet, sweet E.

Chapter Three

The Nightjar opened in October to little fanfare. It was a typical West Cork fall day, slate skies running to granite over the hills, a misting of rain, a chill that emanated from the ground. Fred dispersed flyers about town and on the islands, but when he opened at noon there were only two men standing in the street. One was a runty man badly scarred about the face and hands, and the other a strapping, straight-backed American in a Red Sox cap, a fanny pack strapped to his waist, grinning like Teddy Roosevelt. Fred set them up with a round on the house, and it was clear that was what the little fellow was expecting as he set to his glass of Murphy's without a word, wrapping his ruined hands like penguin flippers around his pint. The American's name was Bill Cutler, an ex-marine and now a novelist living on Cape Clear.

Nice to have another Yank here, Bill said, pumping his hand, damn fine.

Bill Cutler was a generous, friendly sort who always greeted you with a hearty bellow and a full-arm wave. The little man's name was Dinny Corrigan; he worked the ferry for his uncle Kieran Corrigan. Dinny seemed to have a certain quiet kind of ownership of all things in Baltimore and out on Clear, as he routinely drifted in anywhere he wanted, helped himself to whatever was available, without so much as a word. He was the kind of person who would be in a room long before you noticed him. His hands were ropy with scar tissue, his ears white hunks of cartilage.

Bill Cutler and Fred set to talking about writing and books while I puttered with the coal pellet fire. Bill had written a novel, a thriller about an illicit trafficking operation that ferried drugs through Cape Clear. He also had a sailboat, *Ceres,* a J/105 that he kept in Baltimore, and soon Fred had bought him another round on the house. The runty Corrigan sniffled when he wasn't included and left the pub without a word.

Don't mind him, Bill said, he's always out for a free one. But a decent chap.

You must come see me on the island, Bill said to me. Most days I'm down at the harbor store in the morning. Some interesting sites on the island; it's the oldest part of Ireland, Neolithic burial mounds, standing stones, the site of Ireland's first church and the birthplace of its first saint. Lots of stories to tell.

Bill agreed to take Fred out for a sail the following day. He finished his beer and arranged his fanny pack at his hip, and strode out the door.

We didn't have a single customer the rest of the afternoon and closed down at ten.

We decided to keep the rooms above the pub rather than move. I knew that I would be spending a good bit of time on Clear anyway, and Fred had set up an office, his garret, he called it, in the spare room with the sloping ceiling that neither of us could stand up straight in. Fred kept the small window propped open and the breeze from the harbor would make the pictures and poems that he taped to the walls flutter like leaves. He had nautical charts, books on navigation, sailing techniques, which he pored over while listening to techno music on his headphones. He was writing a novel.

I'm gonna learn to sail as I write it, he said. Bill's gonna help me.

What's it about?

About us, he said, like *Revolutionary Road.*

He stroked his Vandyke beard and grinned.

Except we actually make it, he said, we follow through and make it happen.

There were two other pubs in Baltimore, the Jolie Brisée, which everyone called the Jolly Brizzy, and Bushe's. Fred and I had been to these other pubs, and each seemed to have its regulars. When it was announced that we were the new owners of the Nightjar, we were welcomed enough, greeted not as adversaries but rather as companions upon a voyage, sharing the hardships. Plenty of business to go around, the other pub owners said, especially in the summer when the tourists show. We were told by Albert the winter season would be scant, and this was reiterated by everyone we met in Baltimore. We only had to survive the winter and come spring, only eight months away, all would be well.

It seemed that in the off-season a regular night might include only a half dozen customers, more if you happened to snare a gaggle of bird-watchers coming or going from the Cape. Fred gave a free round to each new customer, and in those first few days I think every man in Baltimore came through for that free drink; the vast majority of them we never saw again. Bill Cutler remained true, as well as Dinny Corrigan, at least that first week. Bill told us with some regret in his voice that he would not be able to frequent the place once the weather got rough, he needed to stay out on Clear with his wife.

In winter, Bill said, ferry service gets sketchy. I'll be out on the island with the missus, hunkered down, working on my new book.

Fred ordered a copy of Bill's novel, which was out of print, and read it straightaway. I could tell by the way he muttered and shook his shaggy head as he read it that he didn't think it was good. Fred never hid his disappointment well, but he maintained it was a well-conceived suspense novel, adeptly executed. But it was written in the third person, and Fred felt that all the voices sounded too similar.

The trap of omniscient narration, Fred said. That's why I do first person only. It's the true light into the interior of a mind.

My favorite John Cheever stories are invariably in the first person. But the first person also often has a tendency to melodrama, the feeling the narrator is clutching you about the collar and begging for attention. I don't know how Cheever was always able to execute that marriage of tone and emotion. I wish that I did.

In the mornings Bill began taking us sailing, an enjoyable experience despite the banging and slapping of the choppy seas of Roaringwater Bay, and the momentary disasters of tacking in heavy wind. I stayed up on the middle of the boat, rail meat as Bill put it, working from side to side for weight adjustment as the boat heeled over. Bill and Fred rode in the back, where Bill tried to explain the multitude of ropes and sheets that snaked back into the cockpit. It was amusing to see Fred with his handful of ropes, baffled by their purpose, his face wrinkled like a bulldog's. When we returned around noon to open the pub he would be flushed with excitement, and in the evenings he shut himself up in the garret and tapped away at his laptop, building his imaginary universe populated with people very much like us.

The Five Bells pub on Cape Clear was full for lunch the next Friday, the builders with their cash payouts crowding the bar and a clutch of bird-watchers in for the weekend gabbing at the tables, comparing journals and drawings. A young woman named Ariel doled out the sandwiches and soup from the back and washed glasses as Sheila poured a steady stream of beer.

After a bit of screechy tuning the portly fiddler at the next table leaned far back in his chair, his lips pursed, and arranged his instrument under his ample chin. He slowly wandered into a set of soft reels as Ariel brought me my bowl of lamb stew and soda bread. Her fingers wrapped completely around the bowl, extra long at the final joints, like the soft appendages of a gecko. She returned my smile, revealing teeth the color of weak tea and arranged at odd angles. Back behind the bar she plied her flanges into the recesses of a glass with a rag, washing with an absentminded air, her head tilted to the sound of the creaking fiddle. She had the globed, glistening eyes of a medieval Madonna, heavy-lidded, blinking slow and languid.

After a few minutes Ariel began to sing. She had a voice as slender, frail, and ancient-seeming as she was, and it began almost as a whisper, a muted whistling as she dried glasses, her eyes downcast, and the various patrons at the pub quickly went quiet. Everyone began to look away and take their attention elsewhere, as if by acknowledging her singing the spell would be broken. Her voice, clear and precise, slipped in and around notes like wind. The bird-watchers sat in their silent groups, their heads bowed, pawing their journals, Sheila standing at the end of the bar and gazing out the window at the rushing sea, the fiddler rhythmically sawing, boot padding the floor, his eyes closed and a smile on his lips, even the builders in their crusted coveralls set their glasses down with silent care, their faces averted reverently. Then the fiddler seemed to grow weary, or the song was coming to an end and the tune wavered, and Ariel's voice trailed off into silence.

Sheila brought the fiddler a fresh pint and he smacked his rubbery lips in anticipation, his face sweaty from effort. He put his fiddle in a burlap sack and took out a pouch of tobacco and rolling papers. He caught me watching him and grinned, his face flush and ruddy.

'Fraid I can't carry a tune in a bucket.

He bent close to the table, tapping his chest with one fat finger.

Got the heart, I have, he said. But little stamina for it. Some only have a few songs in them. What can you do?

He took a big drink and plunked the glass down.

Well, you aint no birder. Unless pe'haps you a puffin, are ya?

Sorry?

He made wavy motions with his arms, his cheeks bulging as he held his breath.

I seen you swimmin', he said, slippin' off the rocks like a puffin at Blananarragaun. Thought you turned into a seal. And me, sober.

His name was O'Boyle, he said, and he quickly wanted my surname. I told him.

Ah, he said with an air of satisfaction, rubbing his whiskered cheeks, that makes sense it does.

How?

Lemme show ya.

He shifted his bulk, scooching his chair over to my table, pushed my bowl and plate aside and took out a pen from his shirt pocket. He wore enormous floppy rubber boots and the general disheveled appearance of a character from a Balzac novel.

Lemme see that notebook of yours.

I turned to a fresh page in the back and handed it to him.

Okay, O'Boyle said. You've heard of Mary Magdalene, right?

Sure.

Right, we startin' with Jesus. Most think he was crucified and then ascended, et cetera. The truth is that Jesus was a man, a man who simply survived a crucifixion. Nothing so special about that. No floatin' up to the right hand of the father, no supernatural shite. Just a carpenter with some good ideas, follow? So he gets out of there, and he and Mary Magdalene, who was his true love, they run off together, settle in a place in the south of what is now France, called Cathay, right?

O'Boyle started sketching diagrams in a hatched script. He connected his own name, O'Boyle, with an ancient race of traveling musicians, descended from Abel—of Cain and Abel—who entertained the Mongol emperors, and my last name, my maiden name, he connected to an ancient race of Gallic swimmers who swam the English Channel with copies of the teachings of Zarathustra tied to their heads. O'Boyle signaled for more drinks, and we were served by Sheila with a knowing grin. The man gulped his beer like a horse, so I was soon coughing up for another round.

Noah was the life giver, O'Boyle was saying, the new breath of life for mankind, starting fresh after the purge. And God gave him the name Noah, as an illustration of this new breath of life. Listen to it; No——

O'Boyle inhaled deeply as he pronounced the first syllable.

——ah!

Exhale.

Now you do it.

So O'Boyle and I are doing breathy chants of *No-ah* in unison and I notice the place is clearing out, the builders packing it in. When the builders are done, you should be too, in my opinion.

I really gotta get back, I said. It's a good walk you know. You should come to our pub, the Nightjar? In Baltimore?

Aye, O'Boyle said, fixing me again with his queer, apple-shaped eyes.

I gathered the sheets of scribbled paper that O'Boyle had spread across the table and made a pretense of arranging them and shoving them into my bag. I did think that perhaps this would be something I would want to examine later, but upon the light of day I swear it was like another language. In fact, a lot of it was another language, what O'Boyle called Celtish.

O'Boyle's caravan was on the western side of the island, but he walked me as far as the South Harbor, where we would part, I going to the left up the hill to Nora's, he to the right.

You are a seeker, O'Boyle was saying as we walked, a prospector of truths.

This man is insane, I was thinking. But I enjoyed his frank and open friendliness and attention.

O'Boyle pointed off to the right, up the road that led to the western head of the island.

See that stone house there? he said, just beyond that is Lough Errul, the lake, and the West Bog. Follow the path past the lake and to the edge of Coosnaganoa, near Dún an Óir?

I've never been to that side of the island, I said.

Then follow that path, he said, and down inna wad of trees you'll see me chimney poking through. Tomorrow I want to show you something. Unless you have something else to do?

I'm gonna swim a bit, I said. Though that'll be in the morning.

Aye, O'Boyle said, the cormorant needs to dip her wings. Flop out with the sea dogs on Pointanbullig. I'll see you sometime after noon. Bring the husband, eh?

He's gotta run the bar, I said.

Right, some other time then.

You should come over to the Nightjar. We'd love to have you play. Certainly we'd stand you some drinks.

That'd be nice, he said. But 'm 'fraid I don't get off the isle much.

He hoisted the sack with his fiddle over his shoulder and waddled up the road, his jacket flapping in the wind.

On my walk that afternoon I crossed the windmill plateau and went down the eastern slope of the island, wading through waist-high gorse, the trail just a faint trace, stepping over the intermittent stone walls that ribboned across the hillside. Below, at the water's edge, was a small section of beach nestled in a slot of jagged black rock, a place called Coosadouglas, or Douglass's Cove. There was a long concrete boat ramp stretching into the water, mucked over with a rusty coat of algae and mosses. In the gravel lot at the top of the ramp, an old VW beater sat idling, a man behind the wheel.

He was staring straight ahead through the murky windshield, looking out over the water to Sherkin and the mainland. I sat on the stone wall on the hill and for a few moments we both enjoyed the sweetness of the fading afternoon light. A little later the dull thrub of the ferry engine reverberated off the rocks in faint echo and soon the ferry chugged around from the left, heading to the mainland. The man stepped out of the car and walked down the boat ramp to the water's edge. It was the hatchet-faced man with the small dog again. He stood watching the ferry as it rounded into view, navigating a low cluster of rocks, barely visible above water. The man pulled out a Polaroid camera and took a picture of the boat as it showed us her stern, heading east to the mainland along the northern edge of Sherkin. After it receded into the fog of the swelling sea, he walked back to his car, flipping the picture between his fingers, the small panting face of his dog in the front seat, wet nose pressed to the glass, looking at me.

After he left I went down to the beach and picked around the rocks and boat ramp, the plasticky strands of sea thongs and channeled wrack strewn about, almost artfully placed on the rocks. The ramp was slick and pocked with small whelks and barnacles, but with care it could be a decent swimming entry. Sherkin lay about a mile to the northeast and that could be done quite easily if the weather was clear. Nobody had used the ramp in a long time and I wondered why someone constructed it here, on this end of the island.

Walking along the beach to the north I came across a deep canyon at the base of the cliff. A mangled pile of metal and rubber drifted among the glossy rocks, the water sloshing around the tires and fenders of smashed vehicles clearly driven off the cliff. A few molded mattresses wedged among the rubble, a shattered armoire, stacks of Sheetrock, concrete hunks with whiskers of rebar.

The hatchet-faced man with the dog returned to Douglass's Cove every afternoon as the late ferry passed, and every time he took a picture of its stern as it turned to Baltimore. I spent many afternoons there, and I began to enjoy our shared moment, I on the bluff above, the dog licking the car window, the hatchet-faced man and his solitary vigil.

That next afternoon I arrived at O'Boyle's caravan, set down in a crease in the boglands, wedged in a stand of what seemed to be bamboo and elephant ears. His caravan was a faded blue and white striped egg set on rocks, a stovepipe cutting through the roof at a jaunty angle. Under the caravan was a nest of rusted cans, rolls of wire, car parts, and a sleeping black and white sheepdog. A set of oil drums sat by the door, brimming with reddish fluid, a stack of crab traps, a tangled wad of fishing nets. Behind his little grove a square space of earth had been cleared by machine, a kind of foundation dug and two walls of cement block, and the skeleton of a kitchen cabinet set. The caravan rocked as I neared, and O'Boyle came banging out the tiny door, his jostling bulk in a white tank top and black cargo pants, barefoot, carrying a mug, bellowing an Irish greeting.

Projects, O'Boyle said when I inquired about the oil drums and nets, a bit of work I'm doing.

I asked him what his occupation was, besides the fiddle playing, which he told me he did only for free drinks.

Bit o' this and that, he said. Odd jobber.

And the walls?

Oi, that's me new home, he said. Kieran's buildin' it for me. That's our arrangement.

What kind of arrangement?

I does the odd jobs, O'Boyle said, 'e builds the house. Each job is a bit more, you know what I mean? I do a bit for 'em and he puts up a wall, a bit more and perhaps I get a gas range, chest o' drawers, that sort of thing.

O'Boyle led me back on a narrow trail wandering over and around boulders on the edge along the sheer cliffs overlooking Roaringwater Bay. Past the spine of a hill, when we climbed over the last fence, the ground dropped away in a steep, grassy slope to a field of water-slicked boulders covered with lichens and barnacles. The sea dashed itself here in broad strokes, foaming black into small pools brimming with spiny urchins and sea lettuce. A spit of crumbling land led to a grassy plateau held out over the water like a platter, and there perched the remains of a small castle, its interior walls and floors exposed on the island side. The causeway was long gone, and to get to it would require ropes and some measure of rock-climbing ability.

Dún an Óir, O'Boyle said, the Castle of Gold.

The castle was built around 1450 by the Corrigan chieftains, O'Boyle told me. In 1603 attackers hauled their ship's cannon to the hilltop overlooking the castle and pounded it into submission, which is why the land-facing side of the castle is destroyed and the sea side fully intact. The finger of land pointed west to the spire of Fastnet, and it was called the Castle of Gold because of the way the setting sun exploded through it. O'Boyle told me that an alternate legend was that a seventeenth-century Corrigan chief called Finn the Rover hoarded his pirated gold there, but nothing was ever found.

Plenty o' folks been through it with a fork, he said. In the hard times some islanders lived there. It became a refuge for the outcast, you know?

O'Boyle paused and mumbled something in Irish with his eyes closed.

We walked through a set of stone fences, avoiding the cattle that eyed us dully. The cattle gates were the best areas, O'Boyle told me. Perhaps the transition or moving from one field to another brought the cows to some distress, but either way they seemed to defecate an extraordinary amount in the narrow passes between the stacked-stone walls that lined the fields. Most of the fields were empty, and some were even nearly overgrown with gorse and heather. At the first gate we came to the cow patties were numerous and of obviously different ages, some still wet and fresh, and others hardened and sprouting vegetation.

It was these that O'Boyle began to inspect and pick through, his jeans gapping and his shirt rising up to give me a wide view of his plentiful ass. After a few minutes he slapped his knees and then, kneeling, motioned to me.

There she is, he says. It's the nipple that you have to look for.

He held a thin, tender mushroom by its stalk between his second and third fingers. He brushed the top with his other hand, and I could see the small, almost pink protrusion. After looking closely for a few minutes I could see that in almost all the older cow patties in the gateway, sprouts of the very same mushroom swayed slightly in the wind. Across the gate and into the entire next enclosure I could see more of the mushrooms, clustered in small sections. There must have been hundreds.

There's so many of them, I said. Why don't you just gather them up all at once?

O'Boyle winced and rubbed his eyes.

They don't keep. Unless you dry them out, they go soft and nasty in a day or two. Drying them takes out the flavor, and the real power of the thing.

He plucked a particularly tall specimen and stuck it into his mouth. He chewed thoughtfully, as if appraising a fine piece of chocolate.

What do they taste like?

O'Boyle plucked another from its fecal roosting place and proffered it to me.

Tastes like mother earth, that's what it tastes like.

Shouldn't they be washed?

O'Boyle brushed at the stem and cap with his fingers.

There you are then. Clean.

Maybe some other time, I said. But thanks.

He shrugged and popped the mushroom into his mouth like a piece of popcorn, swallowed, then straightened suddenly, coming to attention like a military cadet, his eyes wide, like he was listening intently for something. I heard nothing but the roar of wind mixed with sea.

What?

Sorry, he choked. It's nothing . . .

He looked around wildly, patting his pockets, his lips pressed into a thin line.

What's the matter? I said.

O'Boyle was spinning, like he was trying to get his bearings. He stopped, facing the direction of the Waist, and stared for a moment as if he could glean something from this distance. Then he turned and regarded me seriously.

Do you not hear it? he asked.

He held his chin up, sniffing at the air. The only sound I heard was wind, and I told him so. We stood that way for a few moments.

Sometimes, O'Boyle said, the island is full of wondrous noises. Sometimes I think I'm dreaming. Such . . . beautiful melodies.

His eyes glassed over with tears. He stuffed a handful of mushrooms into my hand, turned and galloped over the field, hurdling the first stone fence with astonishing dexterity, moving like a man possessed. I stuck the wad of mushrooms in my pocket, thinking that Fred would certainly be interested. I walked to the road and started back, O'Boyle now a tiny figure cutting across field and fence at a flat-out sprint, heading toward the North Harbor as if he was being reeled in like a fish.

Kieran Corrigan's new plans for the island included holiday accommodations, a three-story-high staggered line of row houses with

kitchens and full baths. Adjoining this would be a new pub and restaurant and general store. The guesthouses would obstruct the view
of the South Harbor from the deck of the Five Bells and the few
other residences clustered on the Waist, but there was nothing to be
done as Kieran was also the senior member of the Cape Clear zoning
board. A few of the builders were always lurking about, standing
alone at even intervals around the buildings with their hands in their
pockets and smoking, as if they were guarding the site. Kieran had
a kind of bunkhouse built into the complex and for the builders the
construction site, the Five Bells, and the bunkhouse seemed the sum
total of their existence. After work they would come up the road to
the pub for a pint and a smoke, then they dragged themselves back to
the bunkhouse and fell into their beds like drowned men.

Later that evening when I left the Five Bells in the cloaking darkness I heard a pant and the crunch of gravel, and looking toward the
construction site I saw O'Boyle dancing a jig in front of one of the
half-finished guesthouses. He threw his knees high into the air and
stepped widely from side to side, his heavy rubber boots flopping and
slapping against his bare legs, muttering a jaunty tune in Irish. The
backhoe crouched behind him in the darkness like a patient spider. I
made my way up the Waist toward the Ineer.

A rattling Citroën came flying down the hill, the gears whin-
ing as the driver downshifted to slow it, and I stepped off the road
by putting one foot over the ditch and using my hands to grasp the
stone wall. I held myself there suspended, a maneuver I would perfect in my time on the island. The single headlight stabbed at me as I
clutched the fence, then went probing on down to the North Harbor.
When I turned back up the hill I saw a figure moving along the top
of the ridge, walking with a halting gait, a small silhouette against
the night sky, glowing faintly white. He was moving away from the
road, across the fields toward Highgate's place and he stopped and
seemed to gaze at me. What would I do if he came sprinting down
the hill? I thought about diving into the Ineer to escape. We stood
there, watching each other for a few moments, before he turned and
lurched up the hill, moving beyond the horizon.

Each evening after dinner at the Five Bells I would wait at the top of the hill outside Nora's gate near midnight, watching Highgate's fields for the armless man. I found that he was a regular fixture, and I was able to observe him from the sanctuary of Nora's front garden without incident. He never came closer or varied from his course. But he knew I was watching. He would pause, and turn his long face toward me, the wind ruffling his shaggy head of hair, regarding me for a few moments before vanishing into the night.

Nora claimed to be unaware of such a man in Highgate's fields.

You could go ask Highgate himself, she said, setting a stack of toast on the table. He sells milk and cheese, so he's open for visitors.

Is this milk from his farm? I asked, pointing at the small jug on the table.

Oh, no, she said. Tourists buy most of it, I think? I know that he ships a bit to the mainland. I don't think any islanders use his products.

Why?

She shrugged.

Highgate and his woofers are a bit of an odd bunch, she said.

And nobody, I said, has ever mentioned seeing a guy walking through the fields at night?

Nora stood at the head of the table with her hands full of jam packets. She wouldn't look at me.

Go over to his farm, she said, and ask him yourself. That's all I can offer.

She blushed and scooted into the kitchen.

Chapter Four

I had been talking about the lighthouse enough to intrigue Fred, and so he arranged with Bill to take a day sail on *Ceres* out to Fastnet on a Sunday morning. When Bill brought his long white sailboat into the harbor the sun was brilliant and the skies clear, and as we walked down the cobblestone street to the quay it was hard not to cry out or hold your hands to the sky in response to such beauty. Fred packed a cooler full of bacon and tomato sandwiches, a tub of baked beans, crackers and cheese, and six bottles of white wine on ice, and we swung the cooler between us as we jauntily strode down the quay.

It is all shining, Fred declared in a loud voice, it is Adam and the maiden!

Fred had been making great progress with his research and was in an antic mood. He had determined that our voyage was to be an epic undertaking.

Bill wore a ball cap, the visor tucked low over his eyes. Like Fred, he wore cargo shorts and sandals even though the temperature couldn't have been more than sixty degrees. He stowed our cooler and the small bag of extra sweaters, hats, and a camera, and Fred started untying the lines. I stepped aboard and stood in the stern, holding the boom.

What do you need me to do? I asked.

Find yourself a good spot, Bill said. Enjoy the day.

I was hoping that Bill's wife would be along for the ride, and I asked him about her.

Nell isn't much for the boat, Bill said. Not these days. Gets a bit seasick.

Open one of those bottles, Fred said, clambering over the safety rails with coils of rope over his shoulder. The sauvignon blanc. There are some plastic cups in there.

It's ten in the morning, I said.

Fred grinned and shrugged. It was a disarming gesture that made me want to squeeze him with both arms and bite his earlobe.

Rules of the sea, he said.

As we motored out of the harbor Bill laid a map out on top of the hatch and showed me our route. Because the wind was strong from the north, we would beat upwind until we could turn and go downwind to Fastnet, and get a close look at the lighthouse.

A marvel of engineering, Bill said. The blocks are Cornish granite, locked together like a puzzle. The old Irish call it Carraig Aonair, the Lone Rock.

The upwind leg was the usual slapping, jerking affair, the boom hissing overhead and the sails cracking as they filled with each tack. Bill steered and worked the mainsheets while Fred struggled with the jib lines and winches. I huddled down on the stern benches, trying to stay clear of the lines. Fred had trouble getting the sheets coiled properly on the winches and Bill barked out directions that made little sense to me.

Three loops, he yelled. *Three* loops! There, now crank it. Crank it! Fred, you're going the wrong *direction* for god's sake. Now. That's it. Good!

Fred hurled himself around the boat cinching lines, pulling winch handles, going forward to free the jib from the safety lines. When we made the north side of Hare Island, we turned west and the beating eased into a comfortable long tack, Bill steering with his foot.

Hare Island, he said, or in Irish, Inishodriscol.

It was a low, flat island with sandy beaches and a few houses emerging from glades of stunted trees. Bill said that maybe a dozen people lived there, but he didn't know much else about it. The wind was strong and steady, and we ate sandwiches as the boat surged along in the green-black water. Bill explained that the Corrigans had been the dominant clan in this corner of Ireland since antiquity, and their descent from St. Kieran, the first saint of Ireland, gave them some kind of sacred right to rule.

It's the story of Ireland, Bill said, the same story over and over. That unflinching Irish obedience to the strong man.

Feudalism, Fred said. One of the reasons why I love this part of the world. The past is never really past.

We cruised on our starboard tack for a couple miles, passing north of three long islands, working our way west and out of Roaringwater Bay. We were now nearly abreast of the hulking black-green mass of Cape Clear. Fred was doing sketches of the islands in his notebook with a pencil stub, annotated with the nautical and geographical data that Bill pointed out to us. I never doubted Fred's single-minded zeal. His projects were often multiple and scattered, but he worked with such great intensity that he nearly always succeeded in his goals. The first time we met, at a small graduate student gathering in a pizza joint, Fred ranted about the postmodern genius of Martin Amis and Schopenhauer's veil of understanding. He wore a flannel shirt and came from a rural background, the star linebacker on his high school football team, and in certain moments, clouded in cheap pitchers of beer and the blueing fog of cigarette smoke, Fred seemed to me like the distillation of the working-class hero and the intellectual dreamer all compact. We were all drawn to Fred. He created the life he wanted for himself, carved out his own space, something most of us never do.

Those are the Calf Islands, Bill said. There's no one out there anymore. Just some cattle and a few summer homes.

Each island was perhaps a half mile across, pocked with small sandy spits of beach. In one cove a large three-masted sailboat lay at anchor. An American flag snapped from the stern, and on the wide, flat teak transom the name in gilt gold lettering: *Fortune*.

That's a hell of a ship there, Fred said.

Some nice swimming spots, I said.

Too *cold,* Bill said. Water is far too cold.

Fred slapped my knee, jostling his cup of wine.

Not for her. My wife here has a gift.

You're joking.

She can get in water, Fred said, that will kill most of us, paddle around all day. She could swim from here back to Baltimore. Or all the way out to Fastnet.

We are at least four miles, Bill said.

She's done it before, Fred said. She's done Alcatraz, Lake Michigan, swam all the way across Lake Champlain a bunch of times. She can go for hours.

Well, Bill said, just promise me you won't jump off this boat!

I was looking for Fastnet. Bumps and peaks seemed to rise up and disappear and the water deepened to a rich royal blue as we passed westward.

How do you do it? Bill said, I mean just keeping your head down in the water for that long. How do you hack the boredom?

I don't really know, I said. I don't get bored. You can just listen.

Listen to what? Bill asked.

The inner workings of your body, the actual sound of your muscles and tendons working. The process of breathing, your lungs. Your heartbeat.

Sort of like a form of meditation, Fred said. Or sensory deprivation.

Not deprivation, I said. More a matter of being able to allow your body to focus on one set of sensory inputs and your mind on others. It creates a kind of separation. Like two distinct beings.

Huh, Bill said. He squinted at me, one hand resting on the steering wheel.

Maybe it's just me, I said. I don't know. But you can listen to what is happening. You can hear if something is wrong.

My mother, a classic hypochondriac herself, told me that what defines hypochondriacs is how they are overly attuned or so sensitive to the feelings and sensations of their own bodies that they begin to interpret these sensations as signs of illness when really they are just the body going on about its business. Fred was the inversion of this idea; he never listened to his own body. He would walk around with pneumonia, broken ribs, a splinter the size of a toothpick in his palm without noticing a thing. He was not immune to illness, but its effects baffled him. When he got the flu he shuffled about muttering as if there was something going on he just couldn't grasp, like some kind of magic was being employed.

It's also surprisingly interesting down there, I said. You have things to look at. Fish, weeds, stuff on the bottom, jellyfish. Out here you have waves and currents and things to think about too. The weather. What's happening on the surface takes up a lot of attention.

Last time I was in the ocean, Bill said, was off Guadalcanal in 'forty-three. Don't plan on doing it again.

I pointed to a small grayish tick on the horizon.

Is that Fastnet?

Bill got a set of fat, heavy binoculars from below and handed them to me. I brought the horizon into focus and after I'd traced it to the south for a few seconds Fastnet leapt into view. The rock was heavily bunched and folded, like a clenched fist, the white lighthouse emerging like a protruding finger. Lowering the binoculars, I contemplated the long stretch of water between the western edge of Cape Clear and Fastnet. Open ocean, deep water. I felt my heart beginning to thump in my throat.

I'd like to swim out there, I said. I could go from the South Harbor of Clear. How far is that?

At least three miles each way, Bill said. But you can't. The seas rarely cooperate. It gets rough out there.

The swells were perhaps two to three feet on the outer edge of Roaringwater Bay. The sea undulated in gentle rolls toward Fastnet, wide troughs that would be easy to navigate. A swell every six to eight strokes in my normal breathing pattern.

It looks great, I said. The weather's nearly perfect right now.

Bill shook his head. He spread the map out on the cabin top and poked at it with his finger.

It's hard to explain, he said, but the weather, the currents, the ocean itself is just different out there. We are somewhat protected here in the bay, but out to Clear and beyond, the sea is wild. They get weather that doesn't make it to the mainland. They had to increase the tower height after the first beacon was getting swamped and all twisted. Made out of iron but just got all smashed up. This one they built in 1903, and it is solid. A hundred and fifty feet above waterline, the tallest in Ireland. But they still get the occasional rogue wave. In 'seventy-nine the sensors measured a wave more than a hundred and thirty feet, smashed the light clean out. Killed the keeper. A Force Twelve gale. That almost never happens.

Is it manned now? Fred asked.

Fully automated, Bill said, they took the last keeper off about ten years ago. Sheamais Corrigan was the last to man it. Kieran's uncle.

That would be a gig I wouldn't mind having, Fred said. Real solitude.

They did several months at a time, Bill said, between supply vessels. Sheamais served out there for twenty years. His brother before him did another dozen. Every keeper on Fastnet was a Corrigan. Baltimore is the physical home of the Corrigan clan, and Cape Clear is the spiritual home. But their attachment to Fastnet is even greater. They revere it with religious intensity.

You'd go nuts out there, I said.

Maybe, my husband said. Maybe not.

We made our turn to the southwest, Bill setting the spinnaker for the downwind leg, Fred holding the mainsail out wide, and the boat rolled before the steady push of wind, surfing the swells. I found a spot just forward of the mast to lie back against the slope of the cabin, my legs stretched out and the spinnaker billowing above me. Fastnet was now clearly visible on the horizon, still a few miles off, and it seemed we would make it there by early afternoon. I closed my eyes and dozed off, enjoying the slow roll of *Ceres* and the light crackle of the sails. I thought about swimming out from the Ineer at Clear, the long stretch of blue to Fastnet. If the weather was good, and I had seen days when the sea seemed as smooth as a farm pond, and I got a safety boat, I could do it. Since we'd arrived in Baltimore, I felt cut loose, like a dog let off the chain. Something drew me out there, to Cape Clear, and even farther out to Fastnet, and the spaces between Fred and me that normally drove me to distraction unspooled in every direction without end.

Fred was talking excitedly to Bill about something and I heard the pop of a cork. The sunlight was warm on my face and through my eyelashes the deck flickered and moved like an open palm guiding us through the blue sea. I was filled with contentment; glad to be in Baltimore, glad to have met Bill, glad to be married to Fred.

Dark matter, he was telling Bill, we don't even know what it is, except that it isn't there. There's more of it than what *is* there.

The wind carried the smells of the back of the boat over me, the bacon and tomato sandwiches, Bill's aftershave, the musty smell of the cabin, and the scent that was Fred. Only Fred.

Oh, what can you do with a man like that? The thought of this made me smile, and our trip to Fastnet seemed to me like a voyage of real import and consequence, a journey that marked us with significance, just as Fred had declared it would be. It was as if some other source moved us across the blue globe and guided our fortunes, something ancient and unknowable.

A few minutes later Bill was shouting something and Fred was stepping over me, struggling with the spinnaker lines. I sat up, Fastnet still due ahead, the size of my hand. The water was black around the rocks and the sky behind rolling up like a gray sheet while we still sailed in sunlight. The waves were peaking, forming delicate tops flecked with foam, and as the wind came around southwest the boat vibrated while it groaned and rolled. In a matter of minutes the wind turned completely around and increased in velocity. There was a bit of confusion as Fred and I tried to wrestle the collapsed spinnaker into the forward hatch, and we ended up dragging a good bit of it over the side. The boom banged back and forth as Bill slacked the sails.

Christ, he said, now we'll have to beat upwind. This might get rough.

Fred was peering at the LCD readouts on the navigation electronics above the cabin hatch.

Wind at fourteen knots, he said. Seventeen. Holy *shit* it is picking up.

We were nearly broadside to Fastnet now, the boat fighting the angle, heeling over sharply. I got on the rail and hung my legs over the high side as Bill instructed. You could feel the lead keel torquing with pressure and cutting through the forces that wanted to twist it in half. Fastnet was now covered by a thin layer of low clouds, and white spray exploded at the base of the rocks. We banged out a few tacks and seemed to be going backward.

This is not good, Bill said. We're not going to make it there.

On the rail I tried to use the binoculars as we slammed up and down, spray now surging up to the deck line and soaking my jeans. The water felt decidedly colder. Ocean water normally lightens in the shallows, but around Fastnet it seemed to get darker, as if the finger of rock was a thin spire, tunneling hundreds of feet straight down to the ocean floor. Birds clustered on the rusted base of the first lighthouse. The new lighthouse was built starting lower, at the waterline. This way the big waves would break on its gently curved base, transferring the energy up its full height and spreading out the relentless pounding. A narrow channel of stairs cut into the face of the rock wended up to a plateau. It was tough to keep the tight circle of the binoculars on anything, but as it lurched over parts of the exposed eastern side of the rock I kept seeing small things moving around the rocks, in and out of the water.

Are there seals out there? I yelled back to Bill.

He shook his head. No way.

A blast of fresh wind, coming directly from Fastnet, knocked the nose of the boat farther to the east. The boat heeled sharply and Bill cursed and shouted at Fred, who released the mainsail. The small crowd of birds on the rock took off in a group and headed to the mainland. There were gulls, terns, smaller birds, larger dark ones with giant wingspans. I'd never seen a group of different birds flock together like that. We were now nearly running away from Fastnet.

Twenty-four knots, Fred read from the nav.

That's it, Bill said. We've gotta turn it back.

We can't make it? Fred said.

Fred's T-shirt stuck to his body, his feet wedged against the opposite bench, his hands gripping the mainsail sheet.

Maybe, Bill said, this boat can take it, but it would be a long beat. Longer than I think any of us want to deal with. And the weather looks like it's turning. We'll run before this and make the North Bay of Clear in maybe an hour. Another half hour after that we'll be having Nell's scones and tea on the terrace. We can watch this thing play out from there.

I tried to keep the binoculars trained on Fastnet as it receded quickly but didn't see any more movement around the rocks. We were borne away downwind from Fastnet as if pulled by a string.

By the time we reached Cape Clear the skies over Fastnet were empty, the afternoon sun high and warm, and the wind had rotated back around to a fresh westerly. The golden seas calmed to a slight undulating swell that rolled out to Fastnet and into the Atlantic.

Chapter Five

I began spending half the week on Cape Clear that fall, swimming in the Ineer every day I was on the island. At Blananarragaun the black rocks were pocked with puffin nests, and coming in to touch the rocks before turning back across the harbor mouth I would set off small explosions of puffin flight, the birds popping out of their nooks and crevices, arching delicately into the air, and hitting the water so softly they seemed absorbed by it. They moved through the water like plump black and white bullets, and I could feel them zip around my legs.

Pointanbullig on the other hand was populated with razorbills, auks, and the occasional gray seal hauled out onto the rocks. Even when I drew to within a few yards, the seals were unperturbed by my approach, regarding me silently with apparent disinterest. But always at least one seal would shove off into the water after I made my turn, and I would catch them eyeing me from below or behind, shooting by suddenly or sometimes approaching head-on only to veer off, twisting in gentle corkscrews, their bodies flashing, disappearing into the sea.

Three miles to Fastnet and back would not be much of an issue, rather it was the conditions. But many days the sea seemed as calm and inviting as a warm quilt, the sun rippling across it. I thought about the lighthouse all the time. At all points on the island I found myself craning my neck or searching the horizon for a glimpse. It lorded over my sleep like some giant, silent sentinel. I suppose I was afraid, but the sensation somehow didn't take that shape. Fastnet drew me on, as if it was attached somewhere to part of me I didn't understand or couldn't locate.

I asked O'Boyle if he could arrange a boat to trail me to Fastnet and back.

You havin' me on?

No.

Ah, Elly, you *can't* be serious. It's too far. Too rough.

The wind rocked his caravan as we sat with a couple cans of Old Peculier and ate apple slices off of paper plates. I explained that this would take under three hours if everything went well, more if it didn't. The weather was still holding, but as we moved toward November it would only get worse, and in a few weeks the swim would likely be impossible.

I've done this distance before, I said. I've done longer, a lot longer.

What if you drown?

Not me, I said. Won't happen.

Posh. Anyone can drown. 'Specially out there.

Feel this, I said, and held out my arm.

O'Boyle touched my forearm carefully with his fingertips, running from my wrist to my elbow. His eyes crinkled into a smile. He took his other hand and held my wrist, examining my fingers and palm.

Huh.

Don't worry, I said. I can't be drowned.

I wrote it all down for O'Boyle on a sheet of paper: Friday, the Ineer, seven in the morning.

I'll do it without you if I have to.

Okay, okay, he said. Got a mate with just the rig. Dinny's got a good boat.

He taped the sheet to his caravan door with a used Band-Aid he found on the counter.

Don't tell anyone, I said. I don't want anyone to know.

I don't know why I said it. But the shock of saying it out loud made my skin flex and hum.

And you must make Dinny swear not to tell, I said. He comes to our pub. Make him swear. I don't want Fred to find out.

O'Boyle regarded me quizzically. Then he shrugged and ate the last of the apple and brushed his fingertips on his shirtfront.

Sure, sure, he said. No problem.

Fred shut down the pub and came out for a night with me at Nora's. I trooped him around the island in the early afternoon, showing him the old Napoleonic lighthouse, the birthplace of St. Kieran, the wind turbine, the Castle of Gold, and the Ogham stone. Fred was of course most impressed by the terrific vistas, rock and sea, and there is always plenty of that on Clear. We had dinner at the Five Bells, and I introduced Fred to Sheila and Ariel. I steered Fred away from O'Boyle, giving him a nod from across the room, which he returned with a wink as he wound a circular tune on his fiddle. We sat in a dim corner, munching our chops with leeks, roasted potatoes, and a mound of sweet peas glistening with butter. We had a few pints of Murphy's then ordered up some double hot whiskeys and clinked our glasses together and crouched over the table holding hands. Fred talked about his plans for buying a used car or truck, something he could take to pick up supplies in Cork, get to the university library, and generally give us more freedom.

Something practical, he said, like an old station wagon. Then we can get out of town if we like.

We felt like visitors, like honeymooners perhaps, just passing through, enjoying the brief, simple beauty of a quiet dinner in a foreign country, the sea crashing into the night.

After we left I talked Fred into taking a nighttime dip in the Ineer. We stripped down naked, and Fred spent a few minutes preening comically, doing a bit of an Irish dance and rubbing his bulbous belly.

Maybe *I'll* just have a baby, he said.

Fine by me. Go right ahead.

Gonna be a soccer player, he said, and hefted it in both hands.

Fred wanted to dive in from a high perch, so we walked out on the Giant's Causeway and clambered up the rock and crouched there like puffins, sharing swigs from his flask. The water was oily and undulating, a black field with a scattering of stars. We perched on the rock, Fred shivering, poking each other and giggling, our eyes silently warping and growing in the dark, until the bay was lit with our own happiness.

Fastnet cast its intermittent beam across us. Fred held my hand, tightly, and we stood up together, balancing. We were about twenty feet up and would need to clear a few feet of rocks below.

This is gonna be cold, Fred said. Real cold.

Yep. You won't be able to stay in long.

How deep?

At least twenty, but you are going to have to really stretch out if you want to dive.

Fred squeezed my ass and I squealed.

I almost fell you asshole.

We're gonna dive, right?

Of course.

That's what I love about you, Elly, he said. One of many things.

I gave his barreled torso a big squeeze.

We counted down and launched ourselves into the air, still holding hands at the peak of our flight. We didn't let go until we began to fall.

That night the wind howled across the island, rattling the windows in our room, where Fred laid me out on the bed and methodically licked the salt from my skin. He started at my toes, and I giggled and twisted at first. Then he parted my legs and I felt his whiskery cheeks along my inner thigh and I grabbed handfuls of the bedspread and writhed under him. The moonlight through the window illuminated one side of his face and body, silver and shining, and when he put his hands into my hair, still wet from the sea, I cried out in the hollow of his neck and jaw and arched into him.

In the morning we both ate huge breakfasts, and Nora seemed especially pleased that Fred was there. He kept up a steady stream of hyperbolic compliments on her cooking, her house, the island, until she flapped a dish towel at him and insisted he come back often.

We hugged in the yard by the gate, Fred searching my back with his hands. I inhaled his scent deeply, as if to keep him with me.

Stay as long as you like, he said. This place is amazing.

I'm gonna visit a goat farm today, I said.

Awesome, Fred said. I'm going to open up our pub, the pub we own. In Ireland. On the coast of Ireland. Sometimes life is so badass I can't hardly believe it.

I kissed him in the road and he jogged down the hill to catch the ferry and open up the Nightjar. I sat on the stone wall and drank my coffee. I realized that we'd rarely made love in Ireland, and it had been many weeks before last night. Watching Fred's retreating form, I realized how much I missed him. And yet I stayed.

The gate to Highgate's farm was whitewashed brick with a hand-painted sign: Cleire Goats—Milk, Ice-Cream, Cheeses. The door was answered quickly by a frowsy-looking young German man in a knit cap and a five-day beard. He turned and called out: *Someone to see you!* The large black German shepherd pushed his nose into my crotch and stopped me in the doorway to the main room. Another giant shepherd, brown with a ruff of black, lay curled in a sawed-off plastic barrel next to the door, eyeing me without concern. The door-mat was a slurry of mud, gorse, and grass stains, and the house had the general odor of a wet barnyard. The ceiling was low enough that I had to slouch under the lintel.

Highgate came out of the kitchen, chin up and smiling, trailing a finger along the couch covered in ratty afghan blankets. There were armchairs on either side of the couch, all facing the squat blackened stove, the floors covered in carpet textured with dog hair and the outside elements.

Hello, he said, nice to meet you.

His accent was off, not quite Irish, English, or Scottish. Highgate shook my hand, his hands white and fleshy, tapering down to points, his nails long and crusted. The black dog released me, stepping back and wagging his tail.

Highgate gestured for me to sit and took his place in one of the chairs. The black dog curled up on my feet, at least a hundred pounds of animal on my toes. Highgate smiled sweetly and raised his chin, testing the air. He was an old man, white bearded but his skin around his eyes was smooth and uncreased, eyes cloudy blue, barely cracked. This man is *blind*.

That is Ajax there, probably on your feet. The other one is Hector, who's officially retired.

He called back to the kitchen and in a few minutes Gus the German brought out two mismatched mugs of tea sweetened with goat's milk.

So you're the one who's been swimming in the Ineer, he said. A bit brisk in there now, isn't it? The cold must not bother you much.

The stove was barely warm, and a damp draft was circulating around my ankles. Highgate was barefoot, his feet gnarled and buckled with thick yellowed nails.

Never been in myself, he said. Sorry to say. But as you can imagine, it gets tricky for a man like me. I stay dry as often as I can. Is the tea all right?

Yes, wonderful.

And the Nightjar? Things going well for you there?

Yes. Mostly.

He chuckled and stroked his beard.

Tricky business, that. You just have to hang on till the summer.

That's what we've been told.

The gale season is long out here, Highgate said. It can be trying. But summer brings all kinds of fresh humanity to our shores.

I told Highgate that I was interested in goats. I didn't know what else to say. I didn't want to simply demand to know who was walking around his fields at night, watching me from the cliffs. He said he'd show me around the farm and introduce me to his helpers and goats.

First how about some lunch? We have plenty. Come meet the rest of the crew.

If a blind man cooks you dinner, you had better be prepared to have your food generously handled. I sat at the small Formica table in the kitchen with the woofers while Highgate prodded goat meat patties in a skillet with his fingers. He had washed his hands, but there was a layer of Cape Clear that could not be removed from the creases and nail edges. On the table was a pitcher of thick goat's milk, a bowl of crumbled goat cheese veined with blue streaks, a torn hunk of bread, and a plate of greens from the garden dressed with vinegar.

Highgate fumbled around on the counter, trying to locate some plates and glasses.

The trouble with being blind, he said, is other people. When I lived by myself, I knew where everything was. Someone else comes by, things get moved.

Besides Gus the German there was the slight, large-eyed Japanese girl named Akio; a young Frenchwoman, Magdalene, just back from hitchhiking through Africa, her hair tightly wound in a dozen braids colored with beads and feathers, each marking a place she'd been; and a clean-cut young man from Ohio named Patrick. The two other woofers, both American girls from Texas, had cleaning duty for the day and were mopping the upper rooms. They were all young, just out of college, save Magdalene, who was a hairdresser back in Marseille. They scrambled for the goat patties as Highgate ladled them out, spotted with beads of grease, and happily ate them with their hands like large cookies. Ground goat meat is not unlike very lean ground beef, and the cheese was pungent and crumbly, tasting of soil and salt.

Patrick poured me a tall glass of goat's milk, thick and sweet with a slight bluish cast to it. He was the only one who didn't bunk upstairs in the farmhouse; he told me that he had made himself a serviceable little home in an unused portion of the barn. I was amazed that someone who slept in a barn could appear so fastidious and clean. His blue polo shirt was crisp and his leather boat shoes had shining white soles. He was talking excitedly about the organic crops they had harvested and his plans for expansion, irrigation methods, and cultivation. He was rebuilding an old donkey engine tractor and spoke of the mechanics of the thing with sober expertise.

Next year, Patrick declared, we'll have two solid acres of vegetables, producing sixteen hundred pounds per acre, or more than forty pounds per person on the island.

He squirted a perfect disk of catsup onto his plate and sawed a piece of goat patty.

In three years, Patrick said, Clear could be completely self-sustaining. Subsistence farming is not only a possibility, it is the future.

The other woofers nodded sagely. Patrick's cheeks were flushed and rosy, his brown eyes flashing. He took out a small notebook. Highgate sipped his tea with a faraway smile on his lips.

In six years, he said, with an expansion of acreage of course to about one third of the island, we are exporting twenty thousand pounds a year. If we can just get the co-op onboard, put it to a referendum.

What about Kieran? Magdalene said. He'll never let it happen.

Kieran is the old world, Patrick said. The people here know what he is.

And what's that?

A feudal chief in an isolated outpost, Patrick said. A niche in the cupboard of modernity. His time is over.

This guy, I thought, talks like the twits I knew in graduate school.

Yeah, Gus said, tell that to the board. Or all the fucking Corrigans.

Magdalene poked a fork over her shoulder.

Don't forget all the new construction. All that crap.

What's the problem with the construction? I asked. Won't it bring business and money to the island?

Patrick turned to me with a stern look, a piece of goat cheese balanced on his fork.

At *what cost*? What is lost in this transaction? And who benefits?

Gus swung his arm over his head.

All this, he said, all this, lost.

Don't be so dramatic, Magdalene snorted.

He's right, Patrick said, still fixing his earnest gaze on me. If Kieran has his way the island traditions and culture, the traditions and culture created by *his people,* will be gone.

Why would he do that? I asked.

Kieran Corrigan, Patrick said, is motivated by things beyond understanding. He doesn't care about the world the rest of us live in.

Oh, come on, Magdalene said. She just got here, Patrick, leave her alone.

Highgate stood behind Patrick and placed his hands on the young man's shoulders.

Ambitious youth. How about we settle the western fence line first?

The woofers clattered to the sink with their dishes and bundled out the door.

When Highgate was finished cleaning up we went out back to see the goats. The farmhouse dated from the mid-eighteenth century, with a few later additions. When they bought the twenty-seven-acre farm, Highgate and his wife had arrived with one male and two female British Alpine milking goats. Within a decade their herd was up to forty goats with kids. They produced and sold nine different products, including yogurt, milk, meat, ice cream, and a variety of cheeses.

The goats were lurking by the concrete milking parlor, lined up in order of seniority. Highgate went down the line, holding their faces in his hands, feeling across their chests and groping the udders, telling me their names.

Angelica, Nai, Jenny, Penelope, Kate, Monica, Lucy, the last a castrated male named Ferrell.

Highgate didn't keep more than one uncastrated male around because two uncastrated males will fight violently, sometimes to the death, during mating season.

If the loser survives, Highgate said, he will get depressed, and will often wander off to die. But even a single uncastrated male can be dangerous. If he felt that I or one of the woofers was a threat to his place in the herd, he could attack.

I watched the seemingly docile group of goats nibbling on the scrub that poked through the gate. They were tall, waist high, with bony haunches and rough hair mottled with black and white patches.

Does that happen often?

No, Highgate said. And not with this one, Ferrell. But the fight instinct is in them. They can rear up to smash another goat with their horns. Some of the bigger males could deal me one right in the face, kill me dead. Not like I would see it coming.

We walked into a stacked-stone hut with a thatched roof so low you had to crouch to enter that now served as the goats' sleeping quarters. The air was pungent with the fetid wet wool and ammonia smell of goats. A layer of dry straw covered the dirt floor, and pieces of plywood created several small chambers. Highgate knelt down by one of these and handled a couple of bleating kids, checking their weight and health.

We'll be sending these fellas off soon, he said. Their time is almost up.

We walked down through the fields below the house, Highgate picking his way quite easily, his chin up, watch cap pulled over his eyes. Spread before us was the entirety of Roaringwater Bay, Baltimore and the mainland to our right and in the distance the long arm of Mizen Head stretching off to the left. As we neared the cliffs the sea roared below. Why would a blind man choose to live on an island dominated by such dangerous geography and persistent, deafening noise?

So, he said. That's about it. Anything else?

I asked him about the strange man I had seen walking the fences at night, leading the pack of goats, a man with no arms.

Highgate paused, sniffing the air. A fat tear rolled down his cheek, from the wind I supposed, an odd contrast to his constant grin.

So you've seen her then. Miranda must have taken an interest in you.

He turned and started to walk back up to the house. *Miranda?* I followed, waiting for him to say more. But he remained quiet, and when we reached the house he grinned and shook my hands and wished me good luck with my swim to Fastnet and told me to come back and visit soon. I said I would come back, and in the coming months I dropped by the farm often, having tea with Highgate and occasionally helping out in the fields.

It was hours later that I realized I had never told Highgate I was planning on swimming to Fastnet. I hadn't told anyone but O'Boyle.

The next day I called Fred back in Baltimore to check in and see if business had picked up. Just down the road from Nora's was the post office which had a pay phone in the back garden. Fred picked up with a rather morose: *Nightjar.*

Not much of a greeting, I said.

Yeah, well . . .

Everything okay?

I could hear music but no voices. It sounded like the pub was empty as usual.

Some guys came by, Fred said, from the island. Do you know who Kieran Corrigan is?

Yeah, he's an important guy around here. Was he there?

No, some other guys came by.

What'd they say?

Nothing really, they just wanted to take a look around. Did you say anything to him out there?

Who? Kieran? I've never seen the guy. Why?

You coming back?

I'll be home on the next ferry.

Chapter Six

I met Sebastian Wheelhouse at the Five Bells that afternoon as I was waiting for the last ferry. I could spot him right away as a twitcher. The bird-watchers started coming to the Cape in early October for the first seagoing birds of the season. Bruised and battered by their Atlantic crossing, the birds would alight at the first possibility, the westernmost tip of Cape Clear. Very often a bird would be alone, separated from its migrating companions by miles of vast sea and wind.

The bird-watchers themselves came in a variety of forms, arrayed in mostly muted colors, soft hues and delicate browns and greens. Some carried large and expensive cameras, hard-sided cases with telephoto lenses, tripods, sight glasses; yet others went nearly unencumbered save their rubber boots and mackintoshes, small binoculars and notebooks. Most of the Brits were what they call twitchers, birders who travel long distances to sight and log various species, ticking them off their lists. They were mostly male, and solitary. They seemed to me to be a part of that disappearing middle class of English gentlemen, men who carried themselves like something from an E. M. Forster novel, the upright, cheerful, and staid Britishness, always quick to stammer an apology, men who unabashedly wore houndstooth coats over rag wool sweaters, walking sticks and notebooks bound with twine clutched in their armpits. In the pub they placed their books on the bar and using nubs of charcoal or elegant silver pens filled their pages with artful and delicate drawings of the birds they had seen.

Sebastian Wheelhouse was unwrapped from his layers and enjoying a hot whiskey with nutmeg and drying his boots by the peat fire. I watched as he flipped through his bird book, studying the pages and occasionally running a finger over his sketches. His shoulders rolled slightly each time he turned a page, and his booted feet twisted before the fire. He was clearly deep in thought, his lips bunched together, and since he was the only remaining person in the bar, I figured he likely needed to catch the ferry.

Last ferry's leaving in a couple minutes, I said. If you need to catch it.

He seemed genuinely startled.

Oh, he said. Thank you. But I'm actually staying on the island for a few days.

He didn't move his body but craned his neck to look at me as I stood slightly behind him. He wore thin tortoiseshell glasses, and his hair was that low muddy color and streaked with bits of blond, like the chlorinated hair of a competitive swimmer, curling over his ears and forming a slight ruff at his collar. He had his forearms self-consciously covering his journal.

I glanced at my watch.

Well, have to get back to Baltimore.

Cheers.

His gaze didn't waver for a moment.

I nodded good-bye to Sheila and stepped out into the graying afternoon. The wind was light that day, and I knew the crossing would be nice and mild. A few birders lugging large bags were waiting on the quay, looking weary and windburned. I can honestly say that I thought nothing of this encounter, other than about his hair, and the way he bent his whole body over that sketchbook.

The Siopa Beag in Cape Clear's North Harbor sold coffee and tea and snacks, and in good weather they rolled out a few round tables next to the seawall. Bill Cutler was at one of the tables, holding down the *Irish Times* crossword puzzle with both arms in the breeze, his reading glasses on and touring cap pulled low. Nora's son, Finn, was there on his bike, working his figure eights around the parked cars on the quay, his flaming head bobbing. When Finn saw me coming he launched himself at the seawall and performed his high-wire act, his face in earnest concentration.

Bill lifted an arm high in greeting:

Elly!

The *Times* went flapping down the quay, Bill stumbling after, knocking the table over. Finn hopped his bike off the wall and raced after the paper, and leaning down like a Spanish gaucho in the reins he snatched the paper out of the air and came whizzing back to Bill, his face still serious and deliberate, glancing at me.

Thank you, Finn! Bill said. Elly, you have a moment?

Finn circled us as we talked.

Have you spoken with Fred lately?

Just today, I said.

Bill frowned and pursed his lips.

What?

There . . . there was a problem of some kind. At the bar.

Fred? With who?

Not sure, Bill said. Hang on a second.

He folded up his paper and took hold of my elbow and ushered me away from the Siopa Beag tables and the others who hung around waiting for the ferry.

The customers, Bill said, some local guys. Heard things were a bit testy. Just a rumor.

Bill held up his hands.

I don't know the whole story. I'm sure it's nothing. You gonna come see Nell and me sometime?

Sure, I said, but I don't even know where you live.

Ah, he said. Easy. Just take that little path to the right before you reach Nora's. We're the only ones up there. Around four Nell likes to have her tea on the terrace. Come any day.

*   *   *

Stephen-the-fucking-blow-in was on the ferry, and when I mentioned that Kieran's people had been to the Nightjar, he whistled and shook his head. He told me about the pair of prize mules that he owned; apparently they could not be contained in their fields and had developed a tendency to get into other people's gardens and cause a bit of damage. Stephen and his wife often visited their daughters, sometimes for a month at a time, arranging with someone to feed and look after the animals. Despite this, the mules would get free, and sometimes the minder would give up easy and the mules would wander for a week or more. Last time some of the islanders had appealed to Kieran to put a stop to it.

Kieran sent his son Conchur over, Stephen said, to let me know that next time they'll take care of it.

How?

Stephen shrugged.

Whatever they want.

Can he do that? I asked.

Well, there ain't exactly anyone here to stop him.

What about the police?

The guard? Who's gonna call 'em? It takes them at least a day to get out to the island, and when they did Kieran would buy his cousins a beer and they'd all have a fine time.

We were quiet awhile as the ferry threaded its way east, Stephen gazing at Sherkin, a mass of green gliding past on our starboard side. *Island justice.*

He sighed and rolled his head around a bit, then told me a story about a man from Galway, a bird-watcher, who came to the island one season. The fellow got drunk at the Five Bells and ripped out the plumbing in the bathroom. The ferry refused to take him off the island, and no one gave him shelter or food for three days. The man was howling in misery on the hillsides, sleeping in caves. Stephen shrugged. We came around the point of Baltimore, the beacon up on the cliff, entering the harbor.

Come see us, I said, at the Nightjar. I'd like you to meet Fred, my husband.

Stephen looked at me with a sad expression, gripping his bag.
Sure, Elly. Sometime, for sure.

The door to the Nightjar was propped open when I came up the
hill from the harbor. There was a kind of stillness in the air, and the
people on the docks and sidewalk seemed to glide past me with blank
stares. A couple of men stood outside the Jolie Brisée, the pub a few
doors down, watching me cross the street. When I came in the pub
was empty save a couple of English bird-watchers at a corner table
and Dinny perched at the bar nursing a pint. Fred was nowhere in
sight. I went around the bar and said hello to Dinny, who nodded at
me with a crooked grin. I found Fred in the kitchen huddled over
the stove, making an omelet. He came at me with an exaggerated
low-step and picked me up in a bear hug, kissing my neck.

Sweet, sweet E, he said.

I tried to look him in the eye. His face seemed especially ruddy
and his mouth loose. He smelled of whiskey.

Are you okay?

I'm good, I'm good. Want something to eat?

Been doing some drinking?

A bit, a bit.

How's business?

Fred shrugged and gestured to the front room.

Whaddya think? Not real great.

He slipped the omelet onto a plate and began chopping at it with
his fork as we walked back into the main room. He had stopped
shaving again, getting that furry-faced badger look that I didn't
really like. There were a couple open books on the bar and a stack
of scribbled notes. Every few weeks I would find new books about
particle physics or hieroglyphics. The next month it would be the history of Constantinople, Italian opera, Henry James, Chinese naviga-
tors of the fifteenth century. He was currently into Spinoza. I picked
up a used paperback copy of the treatise *On the Improvement of the
Understanding*.

He polished lenses, Fred said. For a living. Can you believe it?

Don't you say it.

What?

Don't tell me how that is such a great metaphor.

No, but listen, he said, his face a mask of due seriousness, this is interesting.

And I thought, *no, it isn't*. Only to you.

Whatever, I said.

I held out my arms.

So what happened?

Yesterday afternoon, Corrigan's guys come in, Fred said. You know the construction dudes? And a few other guys, ferry guys, in the jumpsuits? Anyway, they come in and sort of sniff around, just looking at stuff, and I say, can I help you gentlemen? all nice and shit. They just ignore me. I'm like, uh, can I get you a drink? Finally one says, don't bother. Not no thanks or even just no, he gives me *don't bother.*

Fred chewed thoughtfully, regarding the ceiling.

And there was this other fellow lurking outside. Huge motherfucker. Watching through the window. So, I say, whaddya guys want then? Then this one dude in a ferry jacket just sort of stares at me and then flicks a cigarette on the bar. So I say, hey asshole, what's your problem? And then a couple of the construction guys with the shaved heads, they get all bristly and step to the bar and start muttering shit in Irish. Then a big group of bird-watchers came in so they all just left.

You know Bill just told me, out on Clear, that he heard something bad happened.

Jesus, Fred said. News travels fast.

What do you think they were doing?

Fred shrugged and forked some omelet into his mouth.

Guess just checking the place out. Right Dinny?

Dinny touched the rim of his glass in reply, his eyes fixed on the bar. I thought about the builders on the island, working on Kieran Corrigan's holiday homes, the men on the ferry in orange jumpsuits. Why would they come in here? Would O'Boyle know something about this?

I glanced at a couple of the other books. *Electrical Conductors & Small Appliance Repair, The Wormhole Next Door, Time: A Traveler's Guide, Smelting for Beginners.* For a couple years Fred had been talking about what he called the Problem of Time Travel Wish Fullfillment. It was based on the idea that all of us have some imaginative episode in which we travel back in time and are able to become gods among men with our ability to dazzle the poor natives with our modern knowledge and technology. Except, he said, who really knows how to make gunpowder besides a Connecticut Yankee and Captain Kirk? Could you describe an internal combustion engine to the king's philosophers, and even if you could, how could you possibly attempt manufacture?

This again? I asked. What about the novel?

This *is* for the novel, he said. The protagonist has a sort of unhinged friend who is obsessed with this. I figured I should try the experiment myself so I can write about it. I'm thinking of starting with something like a clothes iron.

A clothes iron, I said. So you can amaze the medieval period with your ability to press tunics and get the wrinkles out of stockings?

Managing the steam action is key, he said. A clothes iron upside down is a hot plate. A cooking tool, a source of portable heat, a localized heat source. The possible applications are endless. Also, the construction is relatively simple, compared to a toaster or something.

Fred reached under the bar and pulled out a roll of dusty burlap. He set it on the bar and uncovered a small, rusty pickax.

Found this in the back storage room, he said. I gotta find some iron ore, first. To be true to the principle of the challenge, I can't use modern methods to find it, like maps or something. Just my own senses. But there's a lot of rock around here and I think my chances are good. Dinny's got a cousin with a used Peugeot that I might buy. Then I can get a library card at the university in Cork. You too.

He wrapped the pickax in burlap and put it back under the bar. Arranging himself on the stool, he returned his attention to his remaining scraps of omelet.

I walked back into the kitchen area and motioned for Fred to follow. His flip-flops slapped as he sauntered in carrying his plate. I closed the door behind him.

I'm gonna stick around more, I said, help you out here.

Don't worry about it, Fred said. There's bound to be some locals who don't like us, you know? We'll smooth it out.

What about *him*? I nodded toward the bar. He *is* a Corrigan, you know.

I know. But he's different. We've had a few chats. Like getting wine from a turnip, but we talk. He's on the outside, like he's been ostracized from the family or something.

Does he ever say anything about us, or the Nightjar?

Not really. But free beer does wonders.

I put my arms around his neck.

I should stay here more.

Fred made a long *blaaaat* noise with his mouth.

Are you kidding? This is the easiest job in the world. I love it. You should do what you want. That was our agreement.

Why would they care? I said.

Who?

The Corrigans. I mean about us.

Fred set his plate in the sink and started washing his hands.

Look, he said, I don't give a fuck who these Corrigans *were* or *think* they are now. It's just a pub. We aren't *doing* anything to anyone, and it's just going to take some time for us to be accepted. Gotta lay down the charm. This time next year we will be the most popular place in Baltimore.

It's our pub, I said.

That's right. The Nightjar. It's our new life.

He kissed me on both cheeks and my forehead and we held each other awhile. Out in the bar Dinny pushed his empty glass aside, slipped off his stool, and made for the door. The English bird-watchers in the corner were bent over their sketchbooks. Fred was trying to be calm and relaxed, but I could see he wasn't. In three days, if the weather held, I was going to swim out to Fastnet Rock, O'Boyle my safety boat. I don't know why I had decided to keep the swim to Fastnet a secret from Fred. There wasn't a good reason for it.

Fred reached into the fridge and retrieved his glass of whiskey. He raised it to me as for a toast.

And I'm gonna let some fucking local assholes come in the bar, *my bar*, and threaten me? No chance.

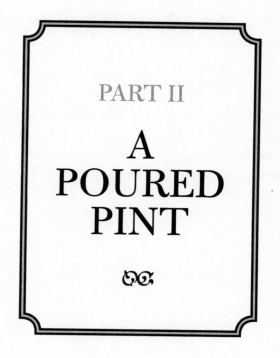

PART II

A POURED PINT

*When the beginnings of self-destruction enter the heart it seems
no bigger than a grain of sand.*

ଓଓ

*One could, with a touch, break the laws of the city and natural
world, expose the useless burdens of guilt and remorse, and make
some claim for man's wayward and cataclysmic nature. And for
a moment the natural world seems a dark burden of expensive
shoes, and garters that bind, tiresome parties and dull loves, commuting trains, coy advertisements, and hard liquor.*

The Journals of John Cheever

There isn't much to pouring a perfect pint. Anyone who practices a bit can get the appropriate timing down. You have to get the foam to settle right, a nice cap an inch or so, a gently swelling meniscus of cream just over the rim of the glass. The difference maker in this contest was the foam design, or what you can draw in the foam in the final seconds of pouring. The choices are limited as you have only a second or two to steer the flow of the beer into a design that will stay on the cap and not push it over the edge or cause it all to run together. A panel of distinguished bartenders from Murphy's pubs all over Ireland was gathered to judge the contest. No practice rounds, no do-overs. There would be only one shot.

We knew the prize pub was in County Cork on the southern coast, and so Fred had done a lot of research on the history and commerce of the area to stir up some ideas. He settled upon an Irish cross surrounded by a fish, to signify the famous medieval monks of southern Cork and the fishing industry.

Fred said that he learned to pour a beer from watching his father, Ham, who couldn't stand the sight of a sloppy pour. I'd seen him berate a poor cocktail waitress or bartender on a few occasions for spilt alcohol or even a dribble down the side of a glass. Ham always praised the bars of Britain, those men know how to pour a beer, he said. Can't make a mixed drink to save their fucking lives, but for a beer they never miss.

Murphy's provided the contestants with time at local Cork pubs to practice, but Fred had already put in plenty of time at a place we frequented in Burlington. There was the problem of differing levels of pressure, the mix of carbon dioxide in the tanks, the circumference and cleanliness of the hoses, temperature, the seal of the keg, the variations in the glass surface, such as contours and shape, microscopic fractures or bends, and atmospheric and barometric pressure. Fred sifted through these problems on his scraps of paper without any result other than to expose the maddening improbability of the task. But he was well prepared regardless.

The lights were dimmed, and a single spotlight at the tap illuminated each contestant as he stepped forward to pour. There was a smaller crowd of supporters this time, but the room was filled out with media, including a few television cameras. Sure enough, all the other contestants went for the obvious choices: a three-leafed clover, the three bands of the Irish flag. A sunburst or shining sun. A few even tried the Murphy's seal, with disastrous results.

I couldn't see the pint as Fred poured, but when he flicked the tap back to shut it off and raised his hands up in triumph, fixing me with that broad grin, I knew he had done it.

When I first met Fred, his father hadn't yet acknowledged him as his son. It's hard to believe, but Ham insisted that he was not Fred's father. Fred's parents separated when he was a baby and he never had any real contact with his dad, other than a few letters to his mother, which she would never share with Fred. His mother died from lymphatic cancer when he was eighteen.

There was a picture at the heart of the matter, a little black-and-white photo taken in 1971, a young Ham standing in a white T-shirt on a sidewalk somewhere holding a baby in one arm like a football. He is looking directly at the camera, a kind of stunned, openmouthed look. The baby is tiny, swaddled in white hospital blankets, just the tuft of black hair emerging from the top.

How could he deny it? I said. You have a photo.

Fred shook his head, his eyes wet and shining.

He says that it was a doll he was holding. It's not me.
What?
A doll, Fred said. My father said the baby isn't real.

Fred said he fell in love with me the first time he saw me. We were standing outside the English Department, the first week of school, a loose group of new graduate students waiting to go inside for class. It was a raw September morning, the ground damp, and we were small-talking and trying to be coolly intellectual, smoking cigarettes and gently probing for potential friends among the shrewish and haggard gathering. Graduate students, on the whole, are a remarkably unattractive group, and we were a particularly sad case of toadstools.

Right there, he said to his buddy Seth, nodding at me. *That* is the girl I want.

This is the story that Fred told me, and I believe him as it sounds precisely like something he would do. He was fond of bold predictions, and this was one rare case where he was right.

I hadn't even noticed Fred that day, but that was mostly because I had the tunnel vision of the extremely self-conscious individual, seeing the world through the wrong end of a telescope, each word and gesture a macro decision that involved all my mental faculties. But that same week, when we had our first class together, American Romanticism, I certainly noticed him. From the first question thrown to the class it was clear not only that Fred had already read all of the assigned material but that he had actually pondered the vagaries of Romanticism and worked out an ordered explanation and definition. By our second class it was clear that Fred could also be an intellectual bully who steamrollered those who stood up to his onslaught. He would flare up, lean forward, and jabbing one finger into the table he would use words like *clearly* and *obviously* to make it seem like what he was saying was gospel and anyone who opposed this was an idiot. Still, his declarations were cloaked in an easygoing friendliness that made him hard not to like, as long as you weren't the one fixed in his sights at that moment.

In retrospect it was quite silly, the whole act, as we were merely half-assed graduate students at a second-rate university, having debates of minimal import. Yet Fred made it seem important and somehow elevated the entire program. He had a way of doing that, making the mundane and ordinary shine with a kind of holy light. Even when I was behind the curtain and learned about his damaging sense of nobility and belief in the importance of candor at all cost, even then, sitting at a small table in a diner, Fred's jiggling knees making our coffee cups rattle, Fred gesticulating at the rest of us with a fork speared with pancakes, I would find myself feeling as if I was participating in something of real import, that this conversation, this moment, and these people *meant* something.

A few weeks later I was nervously small-talking my way through a somnambulant dinner party when Fred burst through the doors wearing his black watch cap and scarf. He plunked down a liter of Jack Daniel's on the table and loudly demanded to know who among the gathered crowd was a sophist. We laughed, nervously, but there was a palpable sound of relief as we rose from our chairs and gathered around him, as if he were bearing literal gifts. Within a few minutes the music rose from the background into something vital, the talk became animated and even volatile. I watched Fred interrogate a poor invertebrate zoologist by the kitchen range top about his research project involving spiral-shelled mollusks that he collected and killed by baking in a kiln. Then we were smoking a joint with a jazz flautist. Fred was blunt about his disdain for the instrument but somehow couched his insults in such a way that the flautist laughed with us until he shot beer out his nose. Then a group of us took a cigarette break on the front steps, sitting under a single bare yellow bulb listening to the pattering of moths. Fred was making notes on a folded-up piece of paper.

That was some good shit from the mollusk guy, he said. He's like some kind of invertebrate Nazi. He's got a shellfish holocaust going on there. Priceless stuff.

Fred was taking it all in, saving it up for something, always adding to his pile of esoteric flotsam, while the rest of us nodded and smiled and drank our cocktails with due attention. Things *mattered* when you were around Fred.

He tucked his pen and paper into his blazer pocket and turned to me. The others had stumbled back inside, where a circle of people danced around a coffee table to a Stone Roses song.

Are you a writer? he asked.

No, I said. I mean, I'd like to be.

Me too, he said. Definitely.

I hadn't thought seriously about being a writer, but suddenly it seemed like a real possibility. The idea shivered through me like a sheet of ice. I loved to read, I loved stories.

But, Fred said, you are clearly an athlete. Tell me. I want to know all about it.

I murmured a few things about swimming and he snapped his fingers.

Perfect, he said, you must go to the beach with us. Fall break. Cape Hatteras. I need someone to get in the water with me.

He jerked his thumb at the apartment door.

These fools are afraid. They think the water's too cold. You have a problem with cold water?

No, I said. I don't.

He stared at me for a moment, a faraway smile on his lips. I shrugged nervously.

I believe you, he said. I can see it.

I told him that there was no way I could afford it or spare the time, but Fred was relentless. It was the off-season, a bunch of people going, it would be cheap. We would road-trip, I could ride in Fred's old Saab. By the end of the night he had me committed to the trip and we kissed awkwardly in the darkness of the backyard. He was shy about it, coming at me like a small bird, and my fascination with him began to deepen into something else.

* * *

Fred showed me the picture a few weeks later when we were at a little Greek place that the grad students used to frequent because the beer and gyros were cheap. The university graduate jazz program played in small trios and quartets there in the evenings, led by a serious, bearded professor who played a decent alto sax. I ended up at one end of a long table, sitting next to Fred, who was holding court. He gestured with a cigarette in one hand, in his other a fat, dripping double-stacked hamburger called the Maximilian, a pitcher of Budweiser before his plate as he extolled the virtues of his favorite Pre-Raphaelite painter (Millais) and denounced his least favorite (Rossetti). He was thick in that generally masculine way, powerful without being particularly fit, swarthy, and his jigging knees vibrated against mine. He made me feel *small*. He stuck a fiver in the band's jar and asked them to play "Someone to Watch Over Me," and the bearded professor bent over his horn and hooted a low, meandering version that nearly made me climb into Fred's lap and fall asleep. It was a wonderful night.

When we were the only ones left, Fred began talking about his father. If Fred drank enough he got remarkably emotional, and at that time this seemed like a revelation to me. I kept his glass filled with beer so he would continue. He had the photo in his wallet, sealed in plastic. It was creased and worn, but you could clearly see a young man holding a baby. Fred said that the man in the photo was his father, and that the baby was him, but that his father wouldn't admit it.

We sat silently for a few minutes, watching the saxophonist warble through a variation of "A Love Supreme" with moderate success. I thought of my own father, in my parents' house in Virginia, stretched out in his recliner, watching the History Channel. His murky, labored breathing, the linty smell of socks and peanuts, his hairy ears. His wide-set, calm eyes, the way they flitted over you when you addressed him. He had always been there, a stable, looming figure throughout my childhood and early adulthood.

I opened my mouth.

*   *   *

When I was a freshman in high school, my sister, Beatrice, was in the junior class homecoming court and rode sitting on the backseat of a convertible Corvette around the football field at halftime, a bouquet of purple pansies in her lap. I took her picture, a Polaroid instant, while I was standing along the chain-link fence that separated the stands from the field, the stadium lights behind her shrouding her in white light. Her dress was a deep green, her hair a more subtle version of my flaming red, and her smile twelve-toothed and electric.

After school Beatrice taught me how to smoke cigarettes by letting the smoke drift out of your mouth while you sucked it through your nose, which she called French inhaling. She claimed she did this so that I would not embarrass her socially, but even then I was aware that she was protective and somewhat proud of me.

Toward the end of that year there was an incident in the junior class locker-bank bathroom. Someone saw part of this happen, or Beatrice told someone, but not me. By the time the story filtered down to me, the origins were lost.

There were three boys hanging about the locker bank. Beatrice had left her fourth-period chemistry class, a hall pass in hand, her hair tied up in a thick, high ponytail, her two crisp polo shirts, pink and white, with the collars up. I imagine her chewing a stick of spearmint gum, thinking vaguely about the periodic table and the coming weekend. These three boys followed her into the bathroom, locking the door behind them.

Fred didn't say anything, just took me by the hand and led me out of there and across the silent court square, the lamplight flickering and the sound of the train yard booming in the distance. I guess I was a bit drunk. We drove to the old Victorian house where he had a tiny room and lay on his bed, and Fred held me, stroking my hair and arms, until I fell asleep.

Fred lived in a house full of Phish heads with a serious pot-growing operation in the attic. His books were stacked hip deep and he slept on a blow-up mattress. He had four boxes of notebooks and journals stacked on the floor and his desk was covered with scraps of paper, bits of napkins, or gum wrappers that he carried in his pockets. They formed piles, settling like snowdrifts against his computer monitor. Every few weeks he'd sift through the piles of paper doing a sort of triage. The scraps with the most potential made it into the second round, which was his desk drawer, packed so tight he had to jam it closed. From these notes he would select pieces to enter into his word processor files, of which there were legion. While we were in graduate school Fred wrote at least three full novels and large chunks of several others. He wrote one about a dwarf in a small town in Wyoming who practices for his death by burying himself in a field with scuba gear, another about a gang of bootleggers in Depression-era Virginia, and another about an American Egyptologist working at the British Museum in London. They were getting progressively larger. He had them stacked up along one wall like a series of paper steps. The last one was over eight hundred pages.

What I learned in those two years in graduate school was that the world is full of many, many good books, most of which sit on the shelves undisturbed for their entire existence, and yet to become part of this vast silent council required a tendency of mind that I simply did not possess. This was not devastating news to me. It was actually quite a relief. I ended up doing a thesis on the journals and stories of John Cheever, more of an appreciation than any kind of actual scholarly work.

Fred and I began dating quickly after that night when he showed me the picture, but we didn't become serious until the trip to Cape Hatteras. Fred had organized a group of graduate students to take on a crumbling, unpainted four-bedroom beach house on high stilts perched in a set of rolling dunes. We got it for extra cheap because Fred somehow sold the owner on the idea that we were a group of writers there to do some important work. In reality we drank Bloody Marys and beer all day, smoked a generous pile of cheap weed, and spread out a dozen hits of Ecstasy through the week. Sure, there was some writing going on, most of it by Fred and his frantic scribbling whenever he was struck by something, mostly while hammered out of his gourd, but on the whole it was a trip devoted to that desperate sort of debauchery practiced by young adults without responsibility or real career prospects other than something we loosely categorized as "the life of the mind."

From the minute we arrived it was clear that Fred and I were now an official couple. We had our own room, the best room in the house, with a sliding door opening to the beach, and in the morning we slept in and listened to the sound of the waves.

We arrived late at night, and it didn't take long for Fred to try to rally a group to swim. The wind was strong and the water temperature near sixty-five so most refused, but after slamming another cocktail a few of us were bounding down the steps to the sand, Fred leading the way, shedding his clothes as he ran toward the water. I was wearing my suit and Fred kept his shorts on in deference to me, I think, and I followed him out into the breakers, high-stepping through white water and then diving under the head-high waves. Fred broke the surface and bellowed like an elephant seal. It was a starry night and the water oily black and shimmering, and I stroked out to where he stood.

Look, he said.

Back on the shore the handful of others had halted about knee deep and were now retreating to the house. I knew it would happen. I was impressed that Fred followed through with it, but I would come to never underestimate Fred.

Blackguards! he yelled. This inconstancy of thine doth seem like the second fall of man!

His teeth were chattering already and he gripped his torso with his arms. I wanted to wrap myself around him, to warm him up, but I didn't want him to think that I was somehow unaffected, or stronger than he. Fred didn't know about my skin condition at the time and so he didn't understand that sixty-five degrees was warm for me. I didn't want to tell him.

We should get out, I said. It's freakin' cold.

Yeah, he said. I think I could use another drink.

We walked out of the water, the beach house glimmering like a fallen spaceship, the faint sound of music and laughing. I felt my skin swelling as the air hit our wet bodies, the blood rushing about, warming.

Just a second, Fred said.

He turned me so I was facing the sea and the waning moon. Then he stepped back, watching me. He fell to his knees on the sand and held up his hands in a gesture of supplication or defeat.

Christ, Elly, he said. You are a *vision*.

He actually fell to his knees!

You are like some kind of goddess, he said. A goddess from the sea.

The flush of modesty that comes from near nudity was unfamiliar to me. I had little embarrassment or regard for my near-naked or even naked body, inured by the many years of competitive swimming, my childhood perpetually in a suit, the year-round meets. The feeling of Lycra or nearly any other wet fabric next to my skin had become a source of familiarity and comfort. But there was always the disconcerting objective sense of my body that lurked just behind this confidence. People often talk about a swimmer's body as if this is always a desirable thing. On occasion you will see a beautiful body on a competitive swimmer, usually at the Olympics, with the classic V-shaped torso, tiny waist, elegantly sculpted limbs. These are people who would be desirable and attractive no matter what they did and whatever sport they chose. The true swimmer's body, on the other hand, a body that is molded *only* by the act of swimming, is a different thing altogether. Most competitive swimmers develop a hunched back, the source of power for their stroke, a concave chest, as except for the butterfly the pectorals aren't required, bulbous shoulders, thinning arms and delicate wrists, no ass to speak of, and stick legs that taper away to nothing. I inherited my grandmother's generous chest and ass, no help to me as a swimmer but they helped balance out my oversize proportions. By the time I was sixteen I avoided full mirrors and full-body photos.

The eyes of other people, as they looked at my body, became flat and shining like blind coins. They were just characters in a painting. The portrait done in oils of the French dandy with the ostrich feathers in his hat and the brass buttons on a red tunic, the one whose eyes follow you across the room, isn't really watching you. That's what it felt like to me. But even a blank stare casts a thin cone of energy, and you feel it. I could never shake it entirely.

This was different. This was the first time that the eyes of another person made me feel a part of some essential connection. I wanted his eyes on me.

That week I fell into the regular rhythm of a midday swim, doing an hour in the muddy chop, swimming against the current parallel to the beach, sometimes slipping into a riptide and fighting it for a bit of a challenge. The first day people lined up to watch, but after that it was largely ignored.

But Fred thought it was fantastic, and he always accompanied me to the water and waited for me on the sand in a beach chair. When I got out he held open a towel and made a great show of rubbing me down vigorously, sitting me in the chair and covering me with towels while he massaged my shoulders, arms, and legs, like I had just finished swimming the English Channel. He made up a special hot whiskey drink with nutmeg and cumin in a thermos and watched me sip it with earnest attention. When he was satisfied that I had recovered, he put his arm around me and guided me back to the porch of the house, where some goggle-eyed lunatic poet was grilling oysters basted with herbed butter and white wine while other young writers and scholars shuffled about grinning, sunburned and high, making proclamations about the sea, the sand, the sky. Fred would make some grand announcement concerning my epic swim, then we'd do giant bong hits and settle into deck chairs with beers and margaritas and face the coming evening.

That week we discovered the common threads that would bind us together. We were always the last to go to bed, the ones that people were always coming out of their rooms to tell to turn the music down and shut the fuck up. We spent a lot of time on the beach, in and out of the water. Fred wore himself out trying to spend time in the water with me. He would be grinning, neck deep in the ocean, teeth clacking and his hands going white. I would take him up to our room and nurse him back to warmth with my hands, my mouth. What Fred and I had in common was that we never wanted to do anything halfway.

Our most powerful experiences in bed came when we read novels to each other late at night until we both dropped off to sleep. I read him *Pride and Prejudice,* Fred loved my hackneyed English accents; and he read me Charles Baxter's *The Feast of Love,* which brought us both to tears nearly every night. I like to think this is when we fell in love.

One morning we lay in bed twined together. Fred had moved the bed and arranged the curtains and screen door so that I could wake up looking out at the ocean. The sea was blue-gray and formal, the lines of surf advancing with military precision. The inshore breeze was strong, creating big shore break, and the waves' pounding crunch reached us a second after we saw them hit the sand. The curtains billowed into the room, striping us with rising sunlight, and the sweet briny smell of the ocean. I took his arm and gripped it, holding his fingers up to my lips.

I could hold you like this forever, he told me.

This is nice.

Don't ever let me go, he said.

I won't.

Then he jumped out of bed and ran into the kitchen in his boxers and made everyone gingerbread pancakes and pitchers of mimosas, a cigarillo clenched in his teeth, his eyes shining with delight.

Oh, I was gone, gone, gone. He was all I wanted in this world.

By the time we were married I would begin to miss Fred almost the instant he would leave my sight. The closing door, the car driving away, and this dull ache, like a panic, would settle in my chest, a sensation that felt something like being in a descending elevator. I went about my life, in the world, a mask of complacency or even happiness on my face, my body like a shield, but my joints ached like old stone with every step, every turn of the handle, every chattering conversation. He was like a source of heat or energy that I had grown used to, and when it was gone the world seemed cold. Fred had such passion for me, for everything. I fed on it and became addicted to it in all its fucked-up glory.

There was some solace in the suspension of water, and my desire to swim was magnified until it was nearly all I thought of. I could somehow crowd the panic of Fred's absence back down to a manageable burning knot when I was immersed and churning through a body of water.

When Fred traveled for business I had to exercise a lot of restraint. I had to hold myself to two swims a day or else even I would feel like some kind of freak. After my late swims, pulling myself out of the lake in the darkness, driving up the hill in my suit, the truck seats slippery with lake water, I would strip down and build a large fire, the wood stacked far too high, and when it was raging hot I would pour myself a drink and stand in front of it like a campfire, trying to breathe normally. I never told him about this of course. Instead I just tried to manufacture reasons and ways to be with him.

When he returned from a trip he seemed to sense this and would spend the first couple hours holding me, without saying anything. Then he would talk about children.

They will never know this, he said. I'll stop traveling. I'll work from home. They will never feel what it's like to have a parent leave.

But not yet, I'd say. I'm not ready.

I know, he said. I can wait. 'Cause when you are it's gonna be awesome.

On the final evening of the Cape Hatteras trip we all took the last of the Ecstasy during a thunderstorm. The rain was light and warm, so we huddled on the beach and watched the terrific flash and stroke of lightning at sea. Fred brought the stereo onto the porch covered with a towel and cranked up Moby's *Play* album. When we started rolling hard, everyone else began to freak out and ran inside, but Fred and I shucked off our clothes and sprinted along the shoreline, Fred chasing me through the surf, the flashes of lightning suddenly illuminating us in various poses and contortions. He caught up to me and tackled me in thigh-deep water, a set of waves knocking us down. We stood in the water with the rain, the lightning, the distant thunder coming down around us, Fred's face and body slick with sweat, clutching each other, kissing deeply, the taste of salt all over. His penis was large and urgent between my legs, and he reached down under my ass and picked me up, walking into the water. He carried me out like he knew exactly what I wanted. Out past the breakers he found the sandbar, and Fred planted his feet and moving with the ragged swells I took him inside me in the storming ocean.

Chapter Seven

The BBC shipping report was clear that Friday morning. I ate a double breakfast of fried eggs and sausages washed down with a carafe of Nora's bitter coffee. I thought of my husband snoring through a hangover in a pile of blankets back on the mainland, his jug of filtered water and aspirin on the nightstand. The wind whistled thinly through the muslin curtains and my skin began to hum. I missed Fred. In my room I snapped on my orange tank suit, then my jeans and sweater. In the kitchen I mixed up a protein shake in a squirt bottle and a thermos of chicken soup for O'Boyle to feed to me in the water. Nora watched me curiously as she rucked the dishes and made tea for her husband who was reading the paper, the parlor fire crackling with fresh peat.

Out for a trek again, I said to her.

Ah, Nora said, well enjoy it then.

Dinny's boat was tied up at the quay, the motor running, he and O'Boyle sitting on the steps drinking tea out of large clamshells. Dinny's boat was a short fishing trawler of the kind you see rotting in boatyards and harbors all around Ireland, chipped red and white paint, a short cabin to shelter in for sudden blows, a flat transom good for hauling up nets and traps.

What say we call it off, O'Boyle said. Instead go back to my caravan and have a few cans?

No way, I said. We have good weather.

The day was chilled and gray, but the seas running only a foot in the harbor, and the reports called for a calm, slightly overcast day, winds mostly westerly, which meant I would be fighting a headwind on the way out but would be pushed in on the way back. O'Boyle poured some tea in a shell and held it out to me.

In honor of your voyage, he said. A shell for the maiden of the sea.

I drank a bit, it was gritty and sour, but tasty. I finished it off then drank from my water jug, loading up on fluids. When I disrobed O'Boyle turned away and shuffled the nautical charts, but Dinny sat on the wooden stool that served as the captain's chair and watched me, smoking a hand-rolled cigarette, his face composed and serious. He tapped the ash on the deck, the white stubs of his fingers like grubs. His watch cap was cockeyed, and you could see the mottled remains of his ear, now just a swirl of scar tissue. He didn't miss a bit of my preparations, and I suppose it is possible that Dinny hadn't seen a real woman this close to naked before.

I put on latex gloves and slathered myself with lanolin, getting it extra thick in my underarms and neck area, where the chafing was worst, with a healthy dose between my legs. In the open ocean the sea lice would try to burrow into your warm parts, and heavy lubricants kept them from attaching. I slipped on a Hothead insulator cap and then a latex cap over that. Most people who drown on long ocean swims, such as the English Channel, die of hypothermia because their brain temperature drops. They feel fine; their minds are telling them they are okay, there isn't much pain, and so they stay in the water until their bodies shut down and they go under. I knew that my arms and legs would go numb as the blood retreated into my chest, but if I kept my head warm I would be less likely to suffer such dangerous delusions. It would take a lot longer for me to become hypothermic than most people, but that didn't mean it couldn't happen. There is a reason why far more people have reached the summit of Everest than have swum the English Channel. A dying mind is a strong magician, especially in the water. When I swam I paid attention.

I hit my wristwatch chrono and dove into the harbor. O'Boyle and Dinny would lead the way, staying a bit off to my left so that I could see them in my normal left-side breathing pattern and so that I wouldn't spend the whole swim eating diesel fumes.

I stroked out while Dinny drew the boat up ahead of me in position. At the harbor mouth I stopped for a moment and fixed Fastnet in my sight line. The sky over the lighthouse hung low with cirrus clouds, swirling like a river, heavy with rain. The swells were perhaps up to two feet, and I could feel the gentle tug of the northern current. The water was cold enough that I would need to keep moving, so I motioned the boat on and started stroking, going into a five-stroke breathing pattern, stretching it out and rolling my shoulders.

As I swam away from the island, the water moved from soft jade to forest green. A quarter mile out of the harbor the visibility was shot, the water murky black speckled with particle matter, krill, and the occasional drifting wrack or other seaweed, solitary circular jellyfish doing their slow convulsions. I did the first mile in twenty minutes, which was a bit quick but I felt strong. I hit a few heavy patches of floating weed, and at one point I had to climb up and crawl over the stuff, my body out of the water, shuffling along on my elbows and knees. On the boat O'Boyle was sitting in a folding chair drinking a can of beer. Dinny had a transistor radio tuned in to a mainland pop station, and the baleful anthems of Robbie Williams floated across the water, alternating with the crackling of the sea and the rushing sound of my own body.

When I reached the mile-and-a-half mark, I knew something was wrong. A warmth in the pit of my stomach, intestinal churning, and at first I thought I may have to endure the humiliation of an open-ocean defecation with O'Boyle and Dinny circling nearby. I wasn't fatigued, but my arms felt wooden and disconnected, I started losing my stroke count and my breathing became lopsided. I looked at my hands, and they were still fleshy and pink. Flaming red meant the body was struggling to fight the cold, and white meant numbness and real danger. The lighthouse didn't look any closer, but that was a common optical illusion for open-water swimming. The weather was good, the water conditions decent, I knew I wouldn't get many chances. There was a gentle tug that pulled through the center of me, a subtle current that kept my arms moving, my eyes on Fastnet. I just had to keep going.

I passed into the second mile and over the deepest part of my swim and my underwater visual perspective flattened out, making it nearly impossible to judge distances. Occasional specks moved and darted in a way that suggested they were alive, but I had no way of knowing how close they were. My hands entered in front of my face like desperate white fish springing into the darkness. Despite this I knew the floor of ocean was dropping away, the spaces opening up, I felt it in my skin, in my heart. It even seemed like I could *see* that depth. It was a glorious feeling. I felt absurd, like a spider crawling across the back of an elephant.

The boat was still up ahead, though a bit too far away and fading to the left, the diesel engine chugging softly. O'Boyle and Dinny had their backs to me, looking over the other side, leaning over the gunwale, pointing at something in water. The boat continued on, now heading southerly, away from Fastnet. I couldn't fathom what they could be looking at in the water, but to see them in that crappy little boat, bobbing on the sea, slowly tailing off to the south as the wheel spun freely, suddenly struck me as extremely poignant and sad. I clutched my knees and let myself float, head back, rising and falling with the swells.

After some time I opened my eyes and discovered I was closer to the lighthouse; the surf was pounding on the rocks and etched stone blocks of Fastnet, maybe a half mile off. I figured I would just go on without O'Boyle and Dinny, get to the lighthouse and back on my own. The nausea was gone, and rather than fatigued I felt explosive and strong, and I powered up and over the swells. I felt like I was flying out of the water, my body rising, the fierce winds whisking under my belly and legs.

The clouds roiled in formations over Fastnet, the beacon shining like an opening eye. The lighthouse, now the height of my forearm in front of me, seemed to move; the light wasn't rotating anymore, rather the sea and all of its contents, including me, were rotating around *it,* as if the lighthouse was some kind of pivot around which the world turned. I spun around, but the boat was nowhere in sight. I checked my watch and found that another hour had gone by, which was impossible. A sudden feeling of vertigo struck me, like I was standing at the edge of a great height, and when I looked down into the water I saw streams of light erupting from the bottom of the sea, like long strands of golden seaweed, thousands of feet down, pulsing with energy, winding their way up around my feet. I hung facedown in the water like a limp marionette, watching. It was the most beautiful thing I'd ever seen.

Then I began to gag, and when I lifted my head I vomited a heavy gush of fluid, which spread around me on the water like a golden moat. I was treading in a sparkling stew of light and shadow, wavering forms wending their way around my legs like ribbons of fluorescent life. This was when I became afraid.

Then the boat was there, bobbing like a toy just off to my right, two silhouettes on the rail, watching me, one holding a long pole. I felt a tug under my arms, and I was being pulled through the water to the side of the boat. Dinny's twisted face gazing down at me, the mottled thrust of scars skittering across his visage like some kind of segmented cave dwelling insect, his eyes swimming disks of black.

Christ, he said. Completely buggered I'd say.

Then O'Boyle had his arms around me, a rough blanket, and I was sitting on the floor of the boat, cross-legged, looking at my hands in my lap. They were fleshy and pink. I pinched my palm, still warm and full of feeling. O'Boyle was apologizing, the sound of tears in his voice.

It isn't your fault, I said. I just got sick.

I *told* you it was dangerous, O'Boyle said. Listen to me next time, eh? Will ya?

The engines throttled to life as Dinny steered for Clear. Empty beer cans rolled across the deck and tumbled over my legs. I was angry. I shouldn't have had so much trouble. That had never happened to me before.

I'm okay, I said. Just take me back.

By the time we got back to the harbor I felt steady enough to get up the hill to Nora's. O'Boyle insisted that Dinny would go get his

Renault from the North Harbor and would run me up there, but I wanted to walk. The world still seemed wispy and bright, the edges of things streaking as I moved through space, but I took this to be the effect of seasickness and the pressure of my goggles.

That was quite a scare, O'Boyle said. Really thought you mighta had it.

Yeah, I said. Thanks for fishing me out.

I remember that look on his face, how strange and tortured it was. O'Boyle was many things, but he was an honest man at heart. Deception didn't come naturally to him.

Just before I reached Nora's gate, I saw a glinting flash of light farther up the road, near the wind turbines. It was a man balancing a large camera lens on a monopod, pointing in my direction. Behind me glowered Fastnet, and I figured he was likely getting shots of the lighthouse in the oddly lit afternoon. After a moment he turned away, shouldering his camera and disappearing behind a hedge.

I took a long hot shower at Nora's, then caught the afternoon ferry back to Baltimore. At the Nightjar I found Fred holding court with a small crowd of young people at the bar. It was the woofers, Gus the German, Akio, Magdalene, Patrick, and two young women, wearing jeans and rag wool scarves, with headbands and healthy straight teeth. They sipped colorful drinks through tiny straws. *American girls.*

Fred followed me into the kitchen. I asked him what they were doing here.

The woofers?

I didn't know that Fred even knew about the woofers.

They've been coming here for a while, he said. Cool people.

Those two American girls woofers?

Stacy and Sara? Yeah. They're nice. You'd like 'em.

I went up to the apartment, intending to lie down and sleep, but spent most of the time staring at the pulsing ceiling and the wavering bars of light through the window. The muffled sounds from the bar

sounded like a subterranean language, and I began to sort and trans-
late the sounds that rose through the floor like spirits of the dead.

When I came downstairs a couple hours later Fred was showing
the woofers how to shotgun beers. There was a small crowd of emp-
ties on the bar. Fred was punching holes in the sides of the cans with
his keys and handing them out, the jukebox jamming old tunes from
Supertramp and the Smiths, part of his nostalgic set. The Japanese
girl stared at the punctured can, beer spilling on the floor, clearly
baffled by not only the method but the purpose. Patrick waved to me
and when I walked over he introduced me to Stacy and Sara. I stood
close so I loomed over them while we exchanged greetings.

I just have to keep moving, Fred said that night in bed.

Sometime after nightfall the dizziness abated and things generally dimmed, a great heaviness settling on me as I lay in bed. I read
Cheever's journals until Fred stumbled in later, reeking of cigarettes
and lager.

As long as I'm moving, he said, I'm all right. It's when I stop, relax
for a moment. It creeps up on me.

What?

The feeling. I don't know. It's like, some kind of malaise. I feel
like the world is continuing on without me and I'm just here, standing still.

And drinking helps this?

Yeah. And smoking. Something to get me out of my head, to stop
thinking.

Is it your book? I said.

Yes, he said. And . . . not. I mean maybe that is just part of it.
Sometimes the book seems like a physical manifestation of this thing,
whatever it is.

Fred turned on his side, putting his broad back to me. His voice
cracked and wavered.

I feel like, he said, I feel like I'm groping around in the dark.

He sighed and went quiet. The wind howled outside the window, the faint clicking of sailboat stays. I could smell the cigarette smoke in Fred's hair. I closed my eyes and tried to think of Roaringwater Bay, and the ocean. Even the golden light in the water by Fastnet, that terror bubbling up in my throat. But I kept coming back to the woofers in the pub, Stacy and Sara, their plastic smiles and smooth skin.

My mother had the habit of digging her thumb and first finger in the square of my back, grinding her knuckle between my shoulder blades.

Straighten up, she said. For god's sake, Elly, stand up straight.

I have caught myself as I passed a mirror in the hall of a house or the reflection in a storefront window, wearing an off-the-shoulder dress, with my head forward and my shoulder blades jutting out like fins. I have always tried to make myself smaller. In childhood pictures with my girlfriends, I'm always in the back, hunkering down.

You know what that sounds like to me? I said.

What?

You really think you are doing this to stop your overproductive mind? Maybe that creeping feeling is something else.

He raised his head and shifted toward me.

Like what?

The shit you *should* be doing.

We lay there for a while, both of us motionless, as if we were afraid to move.

Well, he said, what should I be doing?

You could start, I said, by drinking less. And by just paying attention.

To what?

Do you have any idea of what I'm doing? What I'm thinking?

Yes, he said. I do.

Chapter Eight

Later that week Bill picked us up in *Ceres* to sail to Clear and have tea with Nell. Bill was constantly on the move, in and out of the harbor, around the islands, and so it struck me as odd that his wife was so stationary, spending all of her time out on Clear. By this time Fred was comfortable sailing with Bill, though I could see his face tighten up when he was handed the wheel. The wind was always brisk, and the sails had to be reefed and worked with a strong hand. A J/105 is a ten-thousand-pound boat, thirty-five feet long with a seven-foot lead keel, and is not easy to knock down, as Bill said, but occasionally a gust would heel the boat over to a point where I was hanging on to the shrouds, my feet dangling in space, Bill whooping as Fred worked frantically to release the mainsail. They wanted to scare me, watching me expectantly as they brought the boat to near capsize. They should have known better. I wasn't afraid of going in the water.

We brought the boat around the Ineer and got her settled in. Bill's place was the southernmost house on the island, set behind Nora's on the high mesa above Pointanbullig. A long cement-block-style building with bright green shutters, a flagstone patio in back and steps leading up to the bluff. Nell was waiting for us outside in the front, smiling and holding her hands together like a young girl. She was a small woman, a little hunched with age and frail of bone, wearing a polyester sheath dress, stippled with faint flowers, a fat string of fake pearls. Her white hair tossed in wisps around her face. She immediately latched on to my arm and took me inside to allow me to "freshen up" while Bill took Fred out back to the patio. A black box stove stood in the middle of the main room, which was neatly decorated with Bill's military mementos, framed photos of him in uniform, standing on a beach somewhere in Southeast Asia, a set of Japanese-style swords, commendations, plaques, unit photos of hard-chinned young men in battle gear. A large bolt-action rifle on a rack was placed over the door, the parts oiled and gleaming.

Nell had a wooden tray set with teacups, saucers, plates, a tiered stack of cakes and cookies, juices, fruit, and a large teapot covered with a crocheted cozy that had USMC emblazoned across the front.

If you'll carry the tray, Nell said, we'll go up to the patio and bring the gentlemen tea.

She struggled up the steps to the high bluff, leaning on the hand-rail and planting each foot with diligence. I was struck by how old she seemed, and it dawned on me that either Bill was a remarkably preserved old man or he had married an older woman.

On the upper patio Fred and Bill stood facing the sea. The view was tremendous: a short grassy hill leading to sheer cliffs hundreds of feet high, jagged spires and jutting formations of black rock spread-ing into the booming surf. To the west was the green bowl of the Ineer, and beyond the hump of the Ballyieragh highlands, the finger of Fastnet. To the south nothing but miles of shimmering sea all the way to North America.

I stood beside Fred and squeezed his hand.

Jesus, he said. This is something you don't see every day.

If you spend any time out here, Bill said, you'll see pods of whales, right, Nell?

Nell was under Bill's arm, squinting at the sea, nodding.

And down on the rocks here, Bill said, loads of seals, puffins, and every kind of bird you can imagine. Nell's seen a killer whale pull himself up here on the rocks going after a seal pup. Got the pup in its teeth and flopped back in the water like a giant trout.

We settled into the chairs, and Nell made a fuss over serving us all. Bill told a story about a lawyer from California who bought a farm on the eastern edge of the island a few years back. He bought it unseen, never having been to the island. Then he bought an expensive bull and had it shipped over from the mainland, perhaps with an eye on starting a new herd. But before he arrived the bull got loose and tore up several farms. A few days later it was found at the bottom of the eastern cliffs, near Douglass's Cove. The lawyer tried to make a thing of it in Cork, but it was soon clear nothing would be done. He sold the place, never having set foot on the island.

Island justice, I said.

Corrigan justice, Bill said.

We drank the tea, watching the horizon, the endless sheets of clouds, the patterned peaks of the ocean that seemed almost motionless.

This is Nell's favorite spot, Bill said. And the real reason we bought this house.

I can see why, Fred said. It is amazing. I could stay up here all day.

Nell just had to have it, Bill said. There was no stopping her.

Nell grinned and shrugged her shoulders, pleased. There were blue veins mapping her pale temples, and her hands shook.

Oh, you should see the sunsets, she said. The way the light falls over Fastnet. Sometimes the rocks glow, golden, like it's on fire.

We watched the gentle play of sunshine and water around the lone rock, the slender finger of stone. The more you watched it the more it did seem like the sea somehow revolved around the rock with purpose, like it was moved by some kind of energy from below. The sight of it filled me with contentment.

I could look at it all day, I said.

Oh, Bill said, Nell will be up here all times of the day and night. I've come out and found her in a January gale, wrapped in blankets, the wind howling around her.

I never get tired of it, Nell said.

It was November before I got a clear look at Kieran Corrigan. On the ferry he remained enclosed in the pilothouse, his sons, nephews, and cousins collecting the fares and off-loading the goods. I suppose

I could have gotten a decent look at him if I had tried, but I didn't really want to attract his attention.

I was waiting for the evening ferry back to Baltimore on a bitterly cold Friday, streaming with rain, looking forward to the comfort of the Nightjar, depending upon Fred's state of sobriety. A generous batch of English birders were holed up in Baltimore waiting for the rain to break, and Fred said they had run through a keg of Murphy's and were keeping the jukebox wailing. I stood under the short awning of the Siopa Beag. A few cars idled on the pier, but otherwise the harbor was empty, save one man who was standing on the edge of the outer concrete quay, looking to the mainland, hands tucked in his gray slicker, hood covering his head. I could see his profile, the wide heavy mouth of the Corrigans, large square glasses with thick lenses, dotted with rainwater. He looked like my high school algebra teacher.

In the alley behind the Nightjar there was a ten-year-old tan-colored Peugeot 205 hatchback, its wheel wells rimmed with rust and the rear window spidered with cracks.

Six hundred pounds, Fred said. A lotta miles but still a good deal. We have transportation.

On Monday when the pub was closed we drove up the N71 to Cork to pick up supplies and go to the library. The backseats were ripped up as if an extended knife fight had occurred there, but Fred just laid them flat for more cargo space. It was just the two of us, he argued, and the point was really to be able to pick up our own supplies for the bar. It would cut down on our costs, and as no money was coming in anything helped. The car reeked of cigarettes and fried fish, and the windows had to be cranked down with a set of pliers. Still, it felt good to be up and moving across the landscape, a thin spray of rain, the shining narrow road.

Fred played tapes he found in the glove box, *The Best of Sam Cooke,* as we drove into the city. Cork's working-class roots, even in a working-class country like Ireland, are glaringly evident everywhere you look. Some areas have a pasted-on veneer of urban sophistication, but driving along the river that cuts through the center of the city, you can see the old bones not yet buried. Despite the new pedestrian shopping mall and gabled edifices of gastropubs, the eye is drawn to the long rows of empty warehouses and the rusty towers of manufacture gone cold.

The other day, Fred said as we searched for parking, when it was blowing real hard? I think it was Tuesday? Anyway, the boats were all knocking around in the harbor, stuff flying around, and this big gust knocks the door open. Slam! The power dimmed for a second, and out the doorway there was lightning forking into Roaringwater Bay. It was intense. Anyway, just me and Dinny there and as I go over to close the door I swear he muttered something about High-gate. The goat guy. I mean, I heard him say that name. But when I asked Dinny what he said he wouldn't repeat it. Just clammed up.

The Corrigans don't like him, I said.

They got a problem with goats?

Not sure. I think it goes deeper than that.

But what he said wasn't like that. It was almost more like a recita-tion? Like a prayer?

That's bizarre.

Fred dove the nose of the car into a parking spot under the loom-ing gray edifice of a church, cranked the wheel and nestled us up to the curb, the Peugeot shuddering with effort.

I know, he said. It's a strange little world here. Library time.

We got ourselves settled with library cards at the university, and Fred went to work on his smelting research, nautical charts, and Spinoza. I wandered the literature section of the stacks for a bit and picked up a copy of Iris Murdoch's *The Sea, the Sea* and a collected Yeats for Fred. Then I did some basic searches on Cape Clear on the computer index and found a couple local histories, *Cape Clear Island: Its People and Landscape, Naomh Ciarán: Pilgrim Islander, Fastnet Rock: An Charraig Aonair,* all by Éamon Lankford. *The Natural History of Cape Clear Island,* by J. T. R. Sharrock, had extensive lists of bird sightings on the island broken down by sea-son and species. It was the kind of book I figured Sebastian Wheelhouse and his twitchers had in their satchels. Then there were a few like *Aistí ó Chléire,* by Donnchadh Ó Drisceoil, written all in Irish. Most of my searches on the history of the area directed me to one or more of the "Annals" contained in *The Chronicle of Ireland,* a remarkably succinct record of events from AD 432 to 911. Most years got only one or two sentences, often about who was slaughtered where.

According to the Annals of Innisfallen, St. Kieran of Saighir, patron of the diocese of Ossory, was born on the island in AD 325. He was consecrated a bishop in Rome and returned in AD 402 to his native district to preach, and the Scholiast of Aengus records that the islanders of Cape Clear were the first to believe in the Cross, thirty years before St. Patrick came to Ireland. Kieran is referred to as *primarius sanctorum Hiberniae,* the first of the Irish saints. The church he built, Cill Chiaráin, lies under the ruins of a succession of later churches in Clear's North Harbor, now just a weathered outline of stone with lichen-covered tombstones slanted and scattered like broken teeth, the decipherable names nearly all Corrigan.

The miracles attributed to St. Kieran include an incident when a young island girl was raped. She became pregnant and came to Kieran in desperation as she did not want to have the baby. St. Kieran prayed for a few days, then went to visit the girl in the hut she lived in with her mother. He instructed her to lie on the dirt floor and then made the sign of the cross over her belly. When the girl arose from the floor, the baby was gone.

It was St. Kieran who predicted that his clan, the Corrigans, would be chieftains of their race forever.

By the thirteenth century the Corrigans were already famous for buccaneering and terrorizing the coastal towns of Western Ireland and even England. The southwest tip of Ireland was perfect for this kind of work; the countless channels and small cays ringed by treacherous slabs of rock that, because of the intense geological pressure of the grinding European plate, rose out of the water, part of a vast fold of Old Red Sandstone and Carboniferous strata, shale on limestone, the folds at ninety to one hundred forty degrees, developing long, sharp lines, rows of basaltic and igneous like black knives, some hundreds of feet high, others just a few feet under the surface of the water. The Corrigans were able to strike coastal towns and merchant shipping, then retreat into their maze of rock, where no one dared to follow. A good third of the eight hundred or so people living in Baltimore still bear the surname, and Corrigans occupied most of the preeminent positions on town councils and local boards, the guard, and had fingers of influence that stretched up through West Cork and into the national government.

We came back in the afternoon with the car full of paper products, canned goods, and two large sacks of organic animal supplement that Fred picked up for Patrick. Back at the Nightjar, Fred made soup while I mopped the floors and wiped down the windows. We turned up the jukebox, Bryan Ferry and Roxy Music, and as the lights in the harbor winked out one by one through the window, we danced across the empty floor.

Fred held up his glass of whiskey.

To our new life, he said.

To our new life.

We both drank deeply.

It's a beautiful thing.

Yes, it is.

The first week of November brought Sebastian Wheelhouse back to the island. I found him standing before the graveyard in the North Harbor in his gray mackintosh, studying the plaque about St. Kieran and his journey. He had a giant cylindrical lens case with a collapsible monopod strapped to it hanging over his back. I walked past, half hoping he would turn and see me, but he remained facing the plaque, and I trudged up the hill to Nora's. Finn Cotter creaked up the hill on his bike, overtaking me as I walked, his white legs churning, mop of red hair swaying. When he reached the top he turned and came zooming down, standing on the petals, his face a grimace of seriousness, the wind snapping his clothes like sails.

Fred was spending his mornings either out in the harbor tinkering with Bill's boat or working on his smelting project, coming in after noon to eat something and open up the pub. He drank his way through the evening, and after closing he sequestered himself in his office space and tapped away at his massive files, probing the Internet until the early morning hours, occasionally sorting through the pile of scraps on his desk. Sometimes when I returned to Baltimore I didn't see him for a whole day and night, and we began communicating with cryptic notes left for each other on the main bar. His almost invariably said "on the boat" or "Cork" or "research" while mine merely said "Clear." Standing in our rooms above the pub, the evidence of Fred everywhere, the smell of him on the sheets in the bed, I felt the insistent longing for his presence, the rising panic that made me pace the hall and the kitchen of the pub, drinking large glasses of juice, staring out the window over the harbor. I found that when I boarded the ferry for Clear such feelings subsided to a point I began to forget about them, and upon returning again to the Nightjar, I would be surprised by the dread of such momentary and subtle isolation. I began staying most of the week out at Nora's, coming back only to get fresh clothes.

There were several groups of bird-watchers on the island, but in the Five Bells that evening Sebastian sat apart from the others, elbows on the bar, scratching away at his little bound notebook. When I went to the bar and greeted Ariel and asked for a hot whiskey with lemon he glanced over and smiled.

How are the birds? I asked.

Haven't seen much yet, he said. Though I haven't exactly been looking.

Why's that?

Can't say. Perhaps I'm not really a birder at all, just a chap who likes to take long walks. The glasses and camera just a cover.

What are you looking at then?

He shrugged. Ariel brought my drink, and I raised it to him.

Just the thing, I said, for the chill.

It was the kind of stupid thing that blow-ins or tourists said, trying to sound casual.

Sebastian nodded, and I told Ariel I'd have the pork chops and went over to my table by the fire. He settled back into his sketchbook. It reminded me of Fred nattering away into his Moleskine notebooks or on the backs of receipts with a chewed pen. Since we'd been in Baltimore he'd taken to using the computer more. He wanted to arrange, rather than compose, he said. He already had loads of material for the novel, now he just needed to get it sorted out. I never once asked to see what he was writing. I think I was afraid of what I would find.

When I went back to the bar with my plates, Sebastian turned and offered to buy me a drink.

Like a bit of the hot whiskey, yeah?

Ariel sliced a lemon and made pinwheels with cloves stabbed through the sections, a shot of Jameson and a packet of sugar, topped with hot water, stirred with a cinnamon stick. We clinked glasses.

For the chill.

We drank.

So you know what I'm *not* doing here, Sebastian said, what about you?

Quite similar, I said. Except I'm mostly swimming rather than walking.

He cocked an artful eyebrow. I could smell the sweet cloud of whiskey and sugar on his breath.

You takin' the piss?

I'm not, I said.

Where? How?

He signaled to Ariel for another round.

These drinks are futile, I said. This single measured shot business you have in the UK is bullshit. The free-pour system, like in the US, that's the method.

This was something Fred had said once in a pub in Cork. Christ, I thought, suddenly I'm incapable of original small talk?

Right you are, Sebastian said. But there's a remedy.

He turned and called out to Ariel, raising his hand like a student in class. He was wearing a pin-striped oxford shirt under his mack. Birding in a dress shirt?

Make it a treble for the lady, he said, cheers.

I became aware, just for a moment, of the other people in the room. We clinked glasses again, mine spilling over the top. It was delicious. Sebastian was leaving on an early ferry to head back to Cambridge. He said he'd return, soon enough. He came to the island all the time.

So say that again, he said. Where you have been swimming.

The ocean, I said.

Sebastian stared at the bottles behind the bar, his mouth slightly slack.

You are havin' me on. That water's too fucking cold and rough.

Nope.

I'll be buggered.

He turned on his stool to face me fully. His top lip formed a single arch, without the normal dip and curve under the nose, the bottom lip thin like a turtle's. His eyes were clear and bright, the pupils flexing and expanding, his glasses speckled with dust. I looked right at him, and it seemed like he was vibrating. Or maybe it was me. There was a singular focus of attention that I had forgotten. Either way, I realized then that I had been thinking about his hands on my body.

Yep, I said. It's true.

Back in Baltimore there was a note from my mother to call. My sister Beatrice was pregnant again.

She seems deliriously happy, my mother said. But of course your father and I are concerned.

She didn't say anything about the father and I didn't ask.

She's still in Delaware, my mother said. Anyway we're hoping she'll come back here, to have the baby and all.

I told her to tell my sister that I was happy for her and that if she needed something to let us know. I'd fly back in a second.

Oh, my mother said, you know Beatrice. She won't ask for anything, then she'll let us know how we let her down. Again. Be careful, okay? Take care of yourself.

When I told Fred he whooped and picked me up in a bear hug, carrying me across the bar and out onto the sidewalk into the bright November sunlight, boat motors humming in the harbor. We kissed there on the street, Fred swinging me from side to side.

That's fantastic, Elly, he said. Oh, wow. That's gotta be wonderful, right?

I hung on to him and kissed him, hard.

It's a good thing, he said, right?

The next night I crouched at the bottom of the steps and spat in my goggles. The waves of the Ineer washed up over my hips then sucked away, pouring over the mossy stone. A few lights on the northern hillside, the Waist and the pub, Bill's place up behind me, but these small embers were dwarfed by the full grace of the moon, so bright I could see my shadow on the water. In the center of the Ineer the water was nearly flat, the moon rippling streams of light down into the water like a giant searchlight. The shaft of light illuminated the bottom of the bay, creating a golden bowl of water.

I dove in and swam to the middle of the bay, then porpoised down, equalizing pressure once, twice, three times, to the bottom and held on to a piece of jutting rock. At the open end of the bowl, a deep black slot, the darkness of the open ocean. A few small forms flitted about, coming into the light and disappearing. The smash and bubble subsided in my ears and was replaced with the deep thrum and crackle, and I looked up to the surface, allowing myself to slowly rise, pulled by the chest, the air in my lungs, my head back and arms trailing like a puppet with cut strings.

I thought about Fred, sitting on a stool behind the bar, a glass of bourbon in front of him, the ice nearly melted. Was he thinking of me? Was he watching the harbor, the shapes of the islands to the west, hoping that I might come up the road and through the doors? I had a sudden longing for the feel of his body on mine, his arms around me, and as I ascended through the water my loneliness felt like a place of habitation, a comfortable room that I could enter and stay. It was as if I was inside my own loneliness. It wasn't the panic of absence, rather the contentment of safety, like I could rest in this place without worry.

On the surface the howl of the wind and the immensity of night sky was like poking my head through the skin of a world of giants. The faint orange stripe of Fastnet swept across the hills creating quick images of windswept grasses, twisted gorse, and crumbling fence lines. There was a flash of white, a shape in the grass, and as the Fastnet light came around again I could see a figure standing at the edge of the field, looking down into the harbor. Miranda. Watching me swim.

I floated on my back, rising and falling with the push of the sea, looking up into the fullness of the moon.

Chapter Nine

I spent a week at the pub, trying to relieve Fred, but he insisted on staying behind the bar and serving customers. He had Crock-Pots of French onion soup going in the back and fresh rolls, and he moved among the tables like a dervish when we had a crowd. He'd announce the ferry departures in a booming vaguely Irish-accented voice and had developed the knack for carrying three pint glasses cradled in each hand. A group of English birders came in and after a couple rounds gave him "one for yourself." Fred dramatically poured himself a whiskey neat then capped off a Murphy's pint and slid the beer down the bar to Dinny.

And one for Dinny!

Dinny neatly caught the beer in his mottled hands, gratefully lining it up with a couple other full ones. He and Fred raised a glass and silently toasted.

The Murphy's is still free, he told me when I gave him a look. They fronted sixty kegs. Besides, Dinny deserves it.

He was almost belligerently trying to stay true to his word about me not working in the pub. I told him to forget about it, that I didn't mind pouring a few beers, but he was adamant. I made some sandwiches and generally cleaned up. The regular pub patrons of Baltimore consisted mostly of men covered in brine and bottom mud, farmers bringing in manure and the green sheen of grassy fields, people who had recently been handling livestock and fishnets, bird-watchers back from their long slogs on the Cape, and the occasional tourist trucking in all manner of shite from all points, everyone wading through puddles and bogs in the gale season, which meant the floors always needed mopping. Fred was developing a tendency to let such things go.

We made a deal, he said. This was my idea, my plan.

It was *our* plan, I said.

Despite Fred's relentless efforts we had little repeat business and mostly subsisted on whoever strolled in on their first visit to Baltimore. Fred may have been pushing it, his type of overbearing interaction failing with the sullen-faced locals who shuffled around the harbor. When we walked around town, it felt like we were totally alone. It wasn't like we were ignored or shunned, but there was this curt indifference, a willingness to pass by without a nod or look. It wore on Fred especially.

Fred sat on the barstool in his T-shirt and flip-flops, sipping a Murphy's and milling through a pile of rocks in a tin bucket, tapping them thoughtfully with a small hammer, scratching them with his fingernail, making notes in a spiral notebook. He'd been collecting samples from hillsides outside of town. The end of the bar farthest from the door was turning into a kind of satellite office, covered with books, papers, rock shards. I didn't say anything about it. The few customers gave the arrangement some strange looks, but nobody seemed to mind. This was a part of Ireland where it wasn't unusual to see a blind, mangy dog sprawled on the floor, a wet pile of boots and slickers on the bar, or an old man sleeping in the corner with a piece of buttered toast in his fingers.

Okay, I said. What can I do?

I just want you to swim, to enjoy yourself. I want you to be happy.

I shrugged and began wiping down the tables. I wanted *us* to be happy. I wanted to say *I just want to be with you.*

The next morning I came downstairs with my bag to catch the morning ferry and found Patrick sitting at the bar, inspecting one of Fred's rocks in his delicate hands. He was wearing a blue blazer and boat shoes, like he was heading to a yacht club social.

Hey, Elly.

He stood up, straightening his coat, giving me his awkward smile. He pointed at my bag.

You're headed to Clear.

I am. What's going on?

Fred offered to help us out with a delivery. I'm picking up. Wanna ride over together?

Fred came out of the back room cradling a small pallet and a couple bundles of peat sticks wrapped in plastic. Patrick opened the front door and retrieved a dolly and helped Fred ease the packages down.

Just a couple more boxes, he said. Make sure you have everything.

Fred reached down and worked a couple small boxes out of the plastic wrap and handed them to Patrick.

Don't forget these. I'm sure the old blind man needs his moisturizer and chocolate sprinkles.

Fred wiped his hands and gestured with his thumb at Patrick.

This dude's buying some gifts for some lady friends.

Patrick flushed and tucked the boxes back into the plastic.

We thought the sprinkles would help with ice cream sales, he said.

Whose idea was that? Fred said. And the bottles of facial moisturizer?

Patrick sighed and put up his hands.

What do you want me to say?

Fred punched him in the arm.

I'm just messing with you, bro! Loosen up.

When Fred ducked back into the kitchen Patrick pulled a wad of bills out of his blazer pocket, held it up to me, then went over to the cash register, punched the register open and dropped the money inside.

He said he wasn't going to take payment, Patrick said. We don't work that way.

We helped Patrick trundle the dolly down to the quay where the ferry sat idling, a few passengers already aboard. The harbor was

busy with craft, and the air was thick with diesel and gut bait. A couple Corrigans, conspicuous in their safety jackets, stood at the end of
the pier. They watched Patrick and Fred struggle with the pallet of
canned goods, stowing the parcels on the slippery boat deck. Patrick
did not hide his displeasure.

Anybody else, he said, they'd be helping out.

He looked at the pilothouse and held out his arms. The man
inside gazed at us calmly, bringing a cigarette to his lips.

Bastards, Patrick said.

It's not a big deal, Fred said. We got it.

While Patrick tied down his packages, I asked Fred when he
started buying stuff for Highgate.

They got fucked by the Corrigans again, Fred said. They needed
some basic supplies. I figured I'd help 'em out. The rate we get with
our Murphy's supplier is way cheaper and faster now with the car.

Fred hitched up his shorts and gazed out toward the islands.

You know, he said, they're running that farm on nothing. I'm
amazed that old man is still chugging along.

Yeah, I said. I know. I'm sure Highgate appreciates it.

Yeah, Fred said. Well, have a good time.

He kissed me on the forehead and gamboled up the hill to the
Nightjar, the wind whipping his T-shirt.

On the ferry Patrick and I huddled under the lee of the cabin. I
asked him about what Fred had said about the Corrigans.

It's complicated, he said. And then again it's not.

He told me that with the creation of the European Union came a
raft of new regulations for food production. Highgate figured no one
would concern themselves with such a small, remote operation, and
for years no one did.

Last week, Patrick said, we get a surprise visit from an EU
inspector, out of Cork. Says it was a normal random sweep of local
businesses. Didn't check a single other business on the island, or in
Baltimore. Somebody reported us.

Patrick told me that the inspector found the farm in violation of
several statutes. The equipment and work necessary to be in compli-

ance would cost at least twenty thousand dollars. This was of course impossible.

We're shrinking the operation, Patrick said, down to seven milkers.

They could produce only a few products: milk, ice cream, and kid meat that would be shipped and processed on the mainland. Patrick nodded toward the two Corrigans who slouched against the side of the pilothouse.

We all know who reported us, he said. Probably Eamon there, the one with the black hair and bad teeth. Kieran's little brother. He does a lot of the dirty work.

The Corrigans saw Patrick pointing at them, and one grinned a gap-toothed smile and gave us a wink. He nudged the man next to him and they both stared at us with their hands thrust in their pockets.

They can't control Highgate, Patrick said. They're afraid of him.

Eamon Corrigan muttered something, and the two men laughed together for a moment. Then Eamon turned to me and with a fore-finger pulled down his bottom eyelid, then spat overboard.

These people, Patrick said, they think they own this world.

What do they want from Highgate? I said.

Patrick gazed out at the passing hulk of Sherkin Island for a few moments.

Why does the raven kill the lamb? There is no answer for it. It is in their nature.

Highgate unlatched the feed barn and the line of bleating goats trooped inside.

Why'd he do it? I said. Why does Kieran even care?

Well, Highgate said, waving his arm around at the fields and buildings, all of this. Prime real estate, great views of the bay and the mainland. The other reasons are more difficult. Kieran was born here of course, lived the first eighteen years of his life here. But he was gone for more than two decades. He was kicked off the island by his own family.

What for?

He was trying to seize control of the ferry service.

Highgate told me that the present Kieran Corrigan, whom I had seen on the quay surveying the gray waters, was somehow banished from Cape Clear in the late 1960s, and had only come back recently. When Kieran returned he purchased large tracts of land from a couple old Cadogan and Cotter families, the other most ubiquitous names on the islands of Roaringwater Bay, and set about getting himself elected to the planning commission, the co-op council, and the ferry board. His brothers and nephews ran the ferry, and his son Conchur took over the lucrative salvaging business that operated around Fastnet and throughout the southern coast of Ireland. Kieran began his construction on the Waist a few months later, determined to transform the face of his ancestral homeland. He was now in possession of the title The Corrigan, the acknowledged chieftain of his clan.

Highgate worked his way around the feeding trough, feeling the face and throat of each goat in succession, saying little things to them, and they licked his fingers and made grunting noises of contentment.

That's when I showed up, Highgate said. And we had some good years, hacking out a bit of a livin'. Though I had plenty of trouble myself during that time.

Thirty years ago Highgate's children, two sons, left for the mainland for school and never returned, as did his wife. She was working in Schull as a teacher, commuting to the island on weekends. In the winter of 1972 the family was going to gather out on Clear for a Christmas Day dinner. The day before Highgate received word from his wife that they wouldn't be coming. And he needn't bother coming to the mainland, either.

It was the island, he said. She didn't . . . she didn't take to it like me. It was a struggle. I understand. It's not a life for everyone.

Do you still see her?

I'm afraid not, he said. I'm blind you know.

I'm sorry. You know what I mean. Are you in contact?

No, he said. I haven't spoken to her since that day.

Highgate's sons came to the island a few times a year to visit, but

that winter the stress of the destruction of his marriage caused Highgate's blood pressure to skyrocket.

Common thing in blind people and their dogs, he said. The stress
of the owner gets transmitted to the dog. Poor Hannibal, he just took
it all in. He was dead within a month.

Highgate came to the end of the line, little Lucy, the runt of the
pack, and he held her nose and said, there, that's just fine, isn't it?

The little goat murmured and nosed in his pockets. We went out
into the muddy yard, Highgate with his hat pulled low over his eyes,
smiling, reaching out for the gate, and when he found it he carefully
unknotted the frayed bit of twine. The clouds over Roaringwater
Bay were alive with light, pinks and purple on a blue field.

Isn't it something, Highgate said. You never get tired of it.

He had never seen the view himself. Highgate had been blind
since he was a child. The first eye went to polio, and the second he
took himself with a fork when he was three years old, sitting at his
mother's table, eating peas. He said he remembers colors, and some
vague shapes, but that is all.

We stood there for a few more moments, enjoying the elements
in our separate ways.

I've seen her again, I said. Miranda.

Oh yes?

From the Ineer. She watches me from on the top of the hill.

I'll bet she finds your swimming curious.

The goats began to file out of the feeding barn, tossing their heads.
Highgate's hands trailed down their backs as they passed. Ajax, sitting at his heel, sniffed them all in turn as well. Highgate exhaled
deeply.

I suppose we ought to see if we can make a formal introduction.

Highgate led me down toward the cliffs to another fence line
tucked out of sight from the house and barn. There was the faint-
est track in the grass, the thin, punched marks of goat hooves. After
the fence the ground dipped into a small hollow in the field that was
thick with heather and shrubs. The grass was dense and hip high, the
gorse climbing like trees and we were enveloped in a maze of growth.

Ajax trotted behind us, tail tucked between his legs, his head low.
The wind diminished considerably as we neared the small grove. I
heard the ticking sounds of water, and I could detect certain smells,
goat feces, foxglove, and ragwort. The plants were unlike anything
I'd seen on the island, with waxy leaves a yard across, corpulent blossoms thick with amber tendrils, long heavy flowering bulbs in lurid
colors. Highgate seemed to pick his way by scent, nose up into the air,
the faint smile on his face. Ajax whined and turned, heading back to
the house.

The dogs don't like Miranda much, Highgate said. They have a
kind of understanding.

We reached a small clearing, and Highgate stopped about ten
yards away from a large clump of gorse rimmed with tall weeds,
a stunted tree spreading its rough canopy over the nest. He put his
fingers in his mouth and produced a series of low whistles, barely
discernible. Then it was quiet, only the faint roar of the sea in the
background. We waited there for a few minutes, Highgate sniffing
the wind, smiling, until finally he shook his head.

Not ready to meet you proper it seems, he said. Or she's about
somewhere.

He turned and led me out of the grove, coming up a sharp little
hill, and then we were suddenly in his field again, Roaringwater Bay
to the north all whitecaps and deep blue.

Miranda keeps her own counsel, Highgate said. She decides her
own hours and visitors. She often likes to hang about the windmill
up on Knockcaranteen. Let's take a walk.

Highgate skirted the gate at the end of the lane, stepping over
the fence and continuing through the ditch to the road, never breaking stride. The hills of Knockcaranteen stretched out before us, a
series of humped rises heavy with rust-colored bramble and gorse.
The wind turbine at the top stood out against the sky like a white
scarecrow, arms spinning silently.

Miranda was born six years ago, Highgate told me. In March,
which is unusual for a goat.

She was born without fully developed front legs, and for the first few days she pushed herself around in circles in the straw and dirt while Highgate tried to make a decision. Normally such an abnormality would call for euthanasia, but there was something about the way Miranda persisted in her attempts at locomotion, her unflagging desire to be part of the world, that moved Highgate. In a week she could drive herself along in straight lines on her belly and chest. The other goats, including Miranda's mother, avoided this strange mewling creature that butted up against their legs.

I couldn't do it, Highgate said. The vitality in her, her life force is strong.

Most goats are born in sets of twins, and Miranda's twin, a black and white named Juno, was her only companion in those early days. Miranda was unable to go out into the fields with the other goats, so she spent most of her time alone in the barn.

One afternoon a pair of ravens caught Juno alone and pinned her in the grass and ate her eyes. Juno lived for another few days, crouched in the barn with Miranda, bleating piteously. After her sister died, Miranda seemed determined to get out into the fields with the other goats, and Highgate had a hard time keeping her in the barn. She started to push herself up against the feeding trough and other objects, and one day Highgate came in to find her standing on her hind legs, leaning on a wall, eyeing him defiantly. In another month she was standing on her own, and by that summer she could walk upright with an awkward, bobbing gait, her two devastated forelegs dangling uselessly. The other goats were quickly cowed by Miranda, and she became the alpha goat, leading them in and out of the barn and feeding area. But they remained skittish of her, and most days Miranda wandered by herself in the fields.

Soon she was able to climb stairs and step neatly over fences and could not be contained. Highgate gave up trying to breed or milk her and let her roam as she pleased. Miranda took to wandering around the island at night, though she was rarely seen by anyone. She stopped coming back to the barn at all, and weeks would go by before Highgate saw her again, lurking around the wind turbine or striding across the cliffs overlooking Roaringwater Bay.

We followed a narrow switchback path of spongy grass up the slope, the gorse waist high and impenetrable. You could hear the slow whoosh-thump as a kind of deep background to the howling wind, and by the time we reached the clearing, the steady rush and heave of air over the blades was like a giant heartbeat and I found it hard not to flinch with each rotation. The white steel column of the turbine, made of bolted I-beams covered with steel plates, was surprisingly clean and free from the rust and chipping that everything else metal on the island suffered from. The concrete blockhouse power station stood just off to the right of the column, the same stark white as the turbine, a few head-high windows covered with heavy iron bars.

The turbine hadn't been connected to the island's power supply for years, Highgate told me. Kieran put together the project in 1993 but nothing ever came of it. They sealed it up soon after, bars on the windows and a metal plate bolted over the door. There was power being generated, lots of it, but it had nowhere to go. It was all just churning and writhing in the blockhouse. It felt as if the hillside was throbbing under my feet.

The co-op wouldn't agree to Kieran's deal, Highgate said. He set it up so that the island would buy power directly from him, all the profits going into his pockets. There was enough power to supply the island and even push power back into the mainland grid. The island could sell the power all over Ireland. There was a considerable profit to be made, enough to put money in the hands of every islander. It could have been a way out, a kind of salvation for the dying economy of the island. The one limitless resource they had was wind. But Kieran wouldn't share it, and quite a few of the old island families, the ones who knew Kieran's people from generations back, they lined up with Kieran. They felt it was his right, after all, to profit from the project that he'd single-handedly arranged and financed. Highgate and a few others, mostly blow-ins, fought back, earning an injunction from the Cork County Council, so Kieran merely pulled the plug on the whole thing. He dug up the spiderweb network of power lines they'd laid throughout the island, cut the connection to the mainland cable, and sealed up the blockhouse.

Highgate turned from the turbine and surveyed the slope of land down to his farm.

I'd better go, he said.

He put a hand on my shoulder and raised his chin. His watch cap was pulled down almost to the tip of his nose.

You be careful, Eleanor. You probably shouldn't hang about here for long.

He gestured at the turbine.

There are forces that will not be contained. Not forever.

He smiled, two wet tear tracks on his ruddy face.

You are welcome at my place, he said, anytime. If you ever have trouble.

Thanks, I said. I appreciate it. Sometimes it is . . . lonely.

That's the way of things, he said. Islanders are desperately suspicious folk. There are reasons, of course. But it is good that Miranda has taken an interest in you. She doesn't show herself to just anybody. Few on this island know that she exists.

He squeezed my shoulder, a strong grip, and a warmth spread through my chest.

Miranda is very special to me, Highgate said. Like my own child.

The waves in the bay advanced in slanted rows of knotted white, pushing desperately into the island.

Do me a favor, he said. Keep Miranda a secret. I don't know what would happen if I lost her. I don't know what I would do.

Sure, of course.

She will look out for you, Highgate said. You'll see.

We turned and started back down the slope to the road, Highgate leading the way.

I had taken to dropping in on Nell in the afternoons to have tea on the terrace. She was always home, and if I came at four she had the kettle on and cookies on a tray with two plates and cloth napkins, ready to go. It became clear that neither of us were particularly interested in the conventions of small talk, so we ended up spending a lot of time on the wind-blasted cliff, staring across the sea. The open ocean is always the same, and yet always different. If you look carefully, you will notice the slight variations in color, wind, smell, and waves. It was all about patience and focus. I mentioned this to Nell, and she nodded knowingly, her face pink from the wind.

When I asked her about Highgate, or the Corrigans, or nearly anything else, the answer was always the same.

That's something for Bill, she said. He's the one who is out and about.

She would gesture to the open sea.

This is my world, right here.

After a few visits, hours spent blasted by the ocean, the golden sea unfurling before us, I could tell that I was changing, that the vista was altering my perspective of everything else. I became more aware of the distances all around us. The spaces above me, the vast skies and the headlong rushing sensation of a planet spinning through space. And the spaces below, the depths of the ocean, a kingdom of darkness and cold. Standing on the seawall of the Ineer, walking the fields below the wind turbine, or in the Nightjar with Fred, or watching the hatchet-faced man take his picture of the ferry passing Douglass's Cove, I began to feel the eternity of space. Everything is so much farther away than it seems. There is more space in even our own bodies than actual matter. We are not close to anything.

Nell had been gazing at the sea for more than twenty years, and whatever world she inhabited before she moved to that house on the cliff was certainly a long way from the world she inhabited now.

When Bill barged in the peace would be shattered. Bill was a force of nature in a way similar to Fred, with one essential difference. He wanted Nell, the prettiest girl in town, and he got her. He wanted to become a marine, a war hero, and he did. He wanted to retire to an island, so he moved to Clear. He wanted to become a writer, so he wrote novels, poems, and essays. He simply sat down and churned out everything he thought of and sent it everywhere possible. Bill published pieces in nearly every small newspaper, community newsletter, and local hash sheet in County Cork, as well as military journals, obscure literary journals, artists' collectives, sailing magazines, tourist pamphlets. He wrote like he lived, with an aggressive, grandstanding style. But he became what he wanted.

By December, Fred was going almost exclusively to bourbon, which was fine as no one else at the Nightjar was drinking it. He also seemed to have developed an adversarial relationship with the local patrons, what few there were, and a positive animosity toward the other pub owners in Baltimore. Our only business came from Bill, Dinny, the woofers, and the occasional groups of tourists who wandered in. We were losing money, and the coming months would only be worse.

Can't figure out what these people want, Fred said. We've got all the usual shit, fireplace, beer, cozy little tables. Maybe we need an old dog.

He dug around in the ice bin with his glass. He poured himself a four-count Maker's Mark and kicked a couple pieces of stray ice under the bar. It was two in the afternoon and the cleaning service was coming in later and it was sorely needed. The Nightjar wasn't more dirty than most pubs, but there was a growing look of disarray, especially as Fred's projects migrated downstairs. His end of the bar was presently covered with nautical charts and lengths of rope that he used to practice his knots. The pale winter light filtered through the grimy windows. Neko Case bellowed a rockabilly tune from the jukebox.

Maybe we should change up the music, I said. Or at least turn it down.

No way, Fred said. We play good music here.

We gotta do something.

Agreed. We'll brainstorm during the holidays, come back fresh.

I spent the next couple weeks at the Nightjar trying to get the place sorted. As the bar traffic diminished we cut back on the keg orders and food offerings. If you wanted something to eat at the Nightjar that winter, what you got would depend on what was in the fridge and what Fred felt like cooking. Though Fred claimed he had it under control, I went through the ordering logs to make sure we would have everything we needed come January, prepping the bar to shut down for the holidays. We had a flight out of Cork to Washington, DC, to stay with my parents for a week, then to see Fred's father up in Atlantic City.

On our next trip into Cork I picked up some nautical histories of the waters off southwestern Ireland and Baltimore. Essentially the stretch of North Atlantic surrounding Fastnet Lighthouse was arguably one of the most dangerous seas in the world, a whirling maw of currents and weather that sank thousand-ton tankers, destroyed frigates and yachts, that drove seasoned skippers into rocks or a thousand miles off course. The history books were full of tales of smashed ships, floating wreckage, distress signals in the night, hulls ripped wide open and the drowned sucked into the void without a sound. In 1979 a Force 10 gale ripped through the area, killing fifteen men participating in a yachting race and destroying dozens of boats. On Christmas Eve in 1972 there was a storm that measured Force 12, a remarkable occurrence, which meant hurricane-force winds and waves greater than fifty feet. A Cape Clear ferry was lost trying to reach the mainland. What was most notable about this storm was the suddenness of the rising winds and seas, taking a couple hours to reach its peak fury. It was the same day that Highgate was effectively banished to the island by his family.

As I read these horrid accounts, I strangely felt all the more confident of my ability to make the swim to Fastnet. I just knew that it wouldn't happen to me. It couldn't. It was as if these other people had engaged in some kind of tragic wager with the sea, putting up their lives in a foolish bet, and lost. But for me it wasn't like that. It wasn't about odds, or my natural ability. The ocean was not my adversary. The sea would never destroy me.

The pile on Fred's desk grew each day like a fresh volcano flow, a river of paper, pamphlets, canceled checks, statements, mounds of paper clips, stapled pages crosshatched with Fred's heavy script, hardbound journals, wads of tissue, sticky mugs rimmed with collars of coffee tar, pens and markers, takeaway containers, a few tumblers with the resin of whiskey, cantilevered stacks of books feathered with Post-it notes, and a dense thatch of paper scraps covering the whole thing.

Do not trust your instincts. It is instinct that makes us want to lope through the night and burn down the barn. It is instinct that makes us act cruel to strangers at the breakfast table. Your instinct is wrong and because we know this we are human.

There are several species of animals, and loads of insects, that routinely eat their own offspring. Innocence has no rights in this world. We are all capable. Eat what you need.

Fred assured me that all was well. The mess on his desk, he contested, was mostly his novel. Or the first part of a three-novel triptych as he called it. He had over three hundred thousand words in first draft, another two hundred thousand in notes and scraps, and then there was all the stuff he had yet to transcribe. Fred blew his nose into a paper towel and tossed it behind his computer monitor. I was worried about our finances.

We're gonna be okay, he said. Hey, Bill said he'd give my manuscript to his publisher.

How are we gonna be okay? I asked. We haven't taken in any money.

It was after midnight and the wind rattled the windowpanes. Fred used a kitchen knife to open a box of books he'd ordered. He sifted through them, muttering, stacking them on a corner of his desk. I knew that since we had no mortgage on the place, including no rent on our apartment, and the taxes and insurance were already paid up for three years by Murphy's, we simply needed to pull in enough to cover expenses and our own living costs. We had almost no savings except what we made on the sale of the Vermont house, and I knew that must have been gone by now. The trickle of money coming in couldn't possibly offset our expenses, especially several thousand dollars for holiday travel.

We can skip the holidays, I said. My parents will understand.

Fred held up a finger, head down in a book.

Let me worry about it, he said.

No, I'm worried, too.

He slapped the book closed and stacked it with the others.

Okay, he said, Ham sent me a check for it.

Ham is paying for our trip.

It's not a big deal. We just have to hold on till summer. Then we will rake it in. That's how everyone operates here.

Fred stood and hitched up his shorts. It was fucking fifty degrees out and my husband was wearing flip-flops. He was dressed like he was on vacation. His eyes were large and swimming, and I stepped into his bearish embrace.

Hang in there, little buddy, he said. Just hang in there. All under control.

He fell on the bed, put his feet up, and covered his face with the top book on the pile. DeLillo's *White Noise*.

Fred was one of those readers that the writer dreams of: deeply serious, willing, and indefatigable. When he read an author he read every book in the oeuvre, regardless of reputation or worth. He consumed books, reading at all hours, through the night and into the morning, and Fred read *fast*. He could read a three-hundred-page novel in an afternoon. His retention, however, as he was quick to note, wasn't quite so admirable. This problem plagued him in nearly all things.

My sense of myself as a reader and writer in graduate school was shaped by Dr. Mark Facknitz. It was Facknitz who helped me understand that I am no writer; rather I am a reader, and that is where my talents lie. He was a surly man, with a vast intellect and a broad red face and the habit of massaging his temples as he spoke, particularly when some simpleton graduate student tried to contest some notion about Hegel or Keats. Facknitz taught a fiction-writing class, and after reading my first attempt at a story, he rubbed his massive brow as we sat in his office and told me to read John Cheever. I went to the downtown bookstore that day and found solid hardback editions of his collected stories and journals. I still do not know what it was that Facknitz saw in my writing that suggested Cheever, more likely he was actually identifying my urges as a reader, and the next three years were so heavily imbued with Cheever that I cannot honestly separate him out from my waking life.

What I'm doing here is an act of admittance, something Fred would have approved of. Cheever's value to me is not merely as a storyteller but also as a model of the difficulties of navigating morality in an immoral world. Everyone has their moments of glad grace, the sudden clarity of vision, when all the world seems like crystal and wine, music from the hall, a man with a cigar on the balcony, the moon and the rain at the depot with a small child holding a basket of flowers. Those times when you are gifted to be alive in this terrible and unrelenting world of desire. His voice is the narrator of my life, and even now when I read his lines or just think of the gentle cadence of his syntax, my heart is rent with astonishing gratitude. As long as his work exists I have no need of a biographer.

Fred understood my compulsion for Cheever, and had a decent amount of respect for him, but Fred preferred the snarky postmodernism of Martin Amis, the catalogs of grit and filth, the juxtapositions of science and shit, math and murder, the endless puzzle of fragmented narratives. To me it too often seems like a lock to pick. Or an exercise in self-flagellation.

I called my parents to talk about plans for the holidays. My mother sounded stricken and tearful.

Oh, Elly. We think Beatrice lost the baby.

Oh god, no! What happened?

She hasn't told us anything. She just all of a sudden stopped talking about it. She's drinking, smoking again. It's not there.

What?

She . . . she was showing, you know? A nice round . . .

My mother blew her nose. In the background I could hear my father watching football.

Now it's gone, she said. It's gone.

Chapter Ten

In the first week of December the temperature was hovering around forty-five in the Ineer, and I had taken to wearing my 3/2 mm full-body wet suit, and even then I could only do about an hour before I lost sensation in my face. I was doing laps across the mouth of the bay, and after about a mile my eyes began to swell, filling my goggles, my fingers and toes sending faint prickling warnings like distant satellites. I told O'Boyle that I was going to reattempt the Fastnet swim in the spring, as soon as the gale season died down enough, and I wanted to get as much time in as possible before the Christmas holiday.

On my last day I staggered up the steps, slipped into the notch behind the Illaunfaha or Giant's Causeway, and stripped off my gear and laid it on the rocks to dry. The sun was out, so I spread myself on the rocks as well, my skin flushed beet red, letting my swimsuit dry on my body.

I was thinking about Virginia, the trip home, when I heard a scuffling of rock and realized someone was climbing over the causeway to my hidden spot. Occasionally a tourist or bird-watcher came across me while I was entering or leaving the water, and I often got bemused looks or even staring uncomprehension. We usually exchanged polite greetings and then continued on our way. A shadow raised itself above me, a man, and I tried to smile warmly, my face still mostly numb.

Hello, Elly, he said.

I sat up, trying to focus on his face. He had a bag slung around one shoulder, one hand on the rock, a knee bent.

It's me, he said. Sebastian.

Oh, Christ!

I sat up, bringing my knees to my chest, and wrapped my arms around my shins.

Sorry, he said. I didn't mean to . . . sorry.

But he didn't move, still standing there on the rock, looking down at me. I suddenly felt twelve again, an awkward crane stooping on the pool deck, my nipples burning in my suit.

It's okay, I said, grabbing a towel and my sweatshirt, I'm just drying off. While the sun is out.

Yes, he said, hell of a day.

Sebastian rearranged his position on the rock. I put on my sweatshirt and tied the towel around my waist.

I saw you swimming, he said, from over on Ballyieragh.

He patted his bag.

Have a pretty good lens so I could tell it was you. Though I don't know who else it would be. At first I figured you for a seal. I was going over to the Five Bells for some lunch and I saw you come out, so I figured I'd walk over.

Oh yeah?

I slipped my jeans on and fumbled with my shoes. I stood and tied my hair back while facing the water. The ocean was brisk and white-capped, the breeze westerly, insistent.

So, he said after a few endless moments, I guess I was checking to see if you needed a bite. A bit of lunch, anyway. Care to?

He stammered slightly. I watched him, his eyes round and alive.

I could eat a horse, I said. Starving.

Me too, he said. Right, off we go then?

Ariel brought us each a crowded plate containing a pair of whole roasted potatoes, a baseball-size clump of sautéed leeks with bacon, and a mound of spicy coleslaw. Two pints of Murphy's. My wet suit was hanging over a few chairs, steaming by the peat fire. I went after the potatoes with my hands, breaking them open, and plying them with butter and sour cream. While they cooled I picked at the cole-slaw, trying to resist gorging myself.

Just the thing, Sebastian said, after a long swim in the cold chop?

I could tell by his collar that he had been sweating that morning, and there were brambles and gorse thorns scattered across his sleeves. He couldn't have been older than thirty-five, yet he carried himself with the calm assurance of a much older man.

I was dragging myself, he said, across the Ballyieragh most of the morning.

See anything good?

Not yet, he said, a few petrels, Manx shearwater, some other things I couldn't get a fix on. But I'm headed to the Bill this afternoon, and that is nearly always a guarantee to catch something coming west across the ocean.

We talked about life in Baltimore, the Nightjar, and about winning the contest. Sebastian seemed to regard this bit of my history with a bemused tolerance, as if he didn't really believe me. I started asking him about his background and how he came to be here, and he told me that he had been coming regularly to the Cape for about six years. He managed to get here several times a year, for a few weeks each time. He was evasive on the question about work, saying something about how he read biology at Cambridge, and apparently for a time specialized in single-celled organisms and invertebrate species. He talked about teaching at Cambridge, going through the rudimentary elements of cell division and reproduction with glassy-eyed undergraduates, but it was all years ago.

What about now? I said. What are you doing now?

Not much of anything, he said with a sheepish grin.

Unemployed?

Something like that.

I found myself watching his hands, playing with his notebook and pen, flipping through the pages, tucking it away in his bag only to take it out again a moment later. He had long, slender fingers, smooth and umblemished, the hands of a young boy, and he kept giving me an inquisitive glance, as if he was checking to see if I desired his notice. He had a generous cone of attention, like a wand of light, and it never faltered. Being in it was like being carefully studied, though not in a way I was used to.

Isn't it a bit late in the bird season? I say.

He was cutting his potatoes in chunks, using that curious overhand fork maneuver you see so many Europeans employ. He swatted at his throat for a moment and looked away. Was he nervous?

Yes, he said. That's true.

Decided to take one last shot at it, I said. Just in case?

Sebastian fixed me with his eyes, blue like the Ineer in early fall, a hint of steel, gray, cold, but full of depth. He smiled.

Yes, that's right. Thought I'd get one more look. Just in case.

I left my gear at the the Five Bells and after lunch we trundled along the western edge of the Ineer, up to the East Bog, across the bleak windswept highlands of Ballyieragh.

The Bill of Clear, Sebastian said, is the best spot in the world for migrating birds.

Once we reached the plateau of Ballyieragh the wind howled from the west, flattening our jackets against our bodies. We leaned into it, trudging along, occasionally exchanging smiles as it was too loud to say anything. At the West Bog we took the small raised footpath that led through the spongy ground, ahead the line of cliffs and the North Atlantic beyond, a dim pounding beneath the roar of wind. The Fastnet Lighthouse came into view, a hazy smudge, the beckoning finger. Sea spray came in occasional gusts, vaulting over the cliffs and tumbling over us.

The western point of Cape Clear is like a deeply serrated knife edge, with peaks of basaltic rock jutting into the ocean, coming to a sharp point where the most resilient veins of rock resisted the everlasting beating of the sea. As we came to the cliff edge the difference in the water from the Ineer or Roaringwater Bay was shocking; this was the North Atlantic in full winter mode, and looking out to the lighthouse I was amazed that just a short time ago I had swum out there and nearly made it back.

Sebastian tapped my arm and pointed to the north. A long, flat ship of black iron with a squared prow was chugging into Roaring-water Bay towing the shattered remains of a large wooden sailing yacht. The sailboat was demasted and had a gaping hole punched in the hull near the stern, just at the waterline, and it was clearly taking on water. It bobbed like a fishing cork as it was dragged landward. The black ship had a pair of heavy cranes and other lifting tackle on the forward deck, a small pilothouse midship with a single battered smokestack belching raw exhaust. A few men shuffled through a pile of materials, what looked like sails, duffel bags, boxes.

Salvage ship, Sebastian said. That sailboat must have come up on some rocks. The locals scavenge everything the sea gives up.

A single figure stood on the bow of the wrecked sailboat with a hand on the towing lines. Even at this distance we could tell he was an enormous man, bareheaded and wearing brown coveralls. He turned his head toward the island and seemed to immediately find us on the cliff top, as if he already knew we were there. Sebastian raised a hand, but his greeting was not returned.

Sebastian paused on the trail and pointed to a little brown smudge like a patch of lichen on a flat rock embedded in the hill. It was a small bird, huddled in the lee of the rock.

Nightjar, Sebastian shouted in my ear. You can tell it's a male because of the white spots on the wings. Nocturnal, so they huddle up most of the day. They won't move until you step on them. The old Irish call them goatsuckers. Used to believe they sucked milk from goats.

The wind was changing directions quickly and buffeting us from all sides. We walked leaning into the hill, one hand clutching the ground, Sebastian's binocular case dragging through the grass, until we came to where the land formed a dramatic tight V with the actual point only a few feet wide. Below us the ground sloped away another hundred feet till the cliffs, a sheer drop of another two hundred feet to the sea. We sat on a jutting rock and Sebastian took out his binoculars to scan the horizon.

There, he said, pointing, and he handed me the binoculars.

I tried to keep them pointed in the same direction. All I could see was exposed and magnified sky, a rich shade of blue.

Like a bobbing comma, Sebastian said, coming straight at us. A large seagoing bird, I think, perhaps a black-browed albatross. A large, dark thing.

I can't see it, I said, and handed him the binoculars.

Just wait a bit. It's coming right at us. It's only going to get bigger.

The wind tore through our clothes, the rocks below boiling with white surf. On the narrow rock our shoulders and thighs were touching, and I was acutely conscious of that warmth.

Watch, keep looking. There!

He pointed into the blue at a bobbing wisp, a line of black flexing, high above the water, a thousand feet or more.

Awfully high, Sebastian said, frowning. For an albatross this close to land. Might be something else.

He raised the binoculars to his eyes and focused.

Odd, he said after a moment. Take a look at this.

I took the binoculars and the bird popped into view, a large, wide-winged black thing, heavy flexing shoulders, long ponderous strokes. A thick bill like a wedge, the color of a lemon.

A raven, Sebastian said. Never seen that before. No telling where that chap is coming from. Something must have compelled him to come this far across the ocean.

It was getting late and I had to catch the ferry. I stood up and needed to put my hand on his shoulder to steady myself in the wind. He looked a bit surprised, but pleased. He stood up and took my hand, and we laughed a little as we swayed and lurched.

Shall we go then?

I'll go, I said, you can stay.

You sure? I'd say be careful on the walk back, but I guess if you fell in the water it wouldn't matter much, would it?

Not really, I said. You'll be around?

Sure, Elly. I'll be here. Right at this spot.

I left Sebastian there, scanning the horizon.

Chapter Eleven

My parents married late, and my older sister Beatrice was born when my mother was well into her thirties, and so they had recently begun the mild eccentricities of the aged. Since I left home my mother had taken to arranging ever-widening fans of newspaper around the kitchen door where all visitors entered, imploring everyone repeatedly in remonstrative tones to remove their shoes. My father disappeared for hours in the basement, most of the time in the bathroom. The holidays at my parents' house were a testament to the ability of my mother to contrive ways to tint the celebration with the veneer of joy, while underneath the constant reminder of disappointment echoed like a dirge.

The year Fred and I returned from Ireland for Christmas, Beatrice brought to dinner a man who had the improbable job of restoring flintlock muskets.

He's got this sweet farm on the Eastern Shore, Beatrice said, her mouth full of cheese dip. It's got a barn full of bullet holes from the Civil War.

The gunsmith was working alongside Beatrice on the bowl of corn chips and dip, chewing, his thin ponytail slung across one shoulder. He had a half dozen leather thongs around his neck bearing various amulets, most of which appeared to be made of lead. Nobody had brought up the topic of the baby.

Fred had retreated into the den with my dad to watch football.

Through the door I could see him in the armchair that was covered with an old print sheet, a glass of bourbon balancing on the arm. My father was crammed in his worn corduroy recliner, the footrest under his calves, enormous feet in slippers dangling. Mother worried over the stove, boiling water for tea. On the table she had laid out three boxes of Entenmann's pastries: coffee cake, raspberry strudel, and something called the Cinnamon Wedge, all covered with thick laces of crusty white icing. Also on the table was the crock of cheese dip that Beatrice had brought, which consisted of ground beef and Velveeta, and the plate of tomato caprese that Fred had arranged, alternating fans of red and yellow tomatoes topped with disks of creamy mozzarella, chopped basil, olive oil. I told him that no one would eat it. Beatrice stared at me with a puzzled look, chewing. She was waiting for my response.

Wow, was all I could think to say. That must be interesting.

It is, Beatrice said, and there's lots of money in it. You wouldn't believe it.

The gunsmith nodded. His fingers were tattooed with Gothic letters, but he moved so deftly between chip bowl, dip, and mouth that I couldn't read them.

The Christmas Eve gathering took on the same general configuration each year; after rising early to Mother's gentle bed shaking, we made a trip to the store for whatever odd purchases she had missed or created the need for, had lunch of cold cuts and white bread, then the steady diet of Entenmann's pastries and whatever unholy dish Beatrice came to town with, Dad and Fred in the den diligently watching sports, putting away nearly a fifth of whiskey between them before dinner. The turkey was always served at four thirty, dry as a bone, cut into shreds with an electric knife by Dad while the meat was still hot, such was the old man's zeal to dismember the bird, the buzzing knife rattling against bone and cartilage. My mother watched each year with trepidation, a towel at the ready to stanch bleeding or make a tourniquet as her husband lurched into it, his eyes filmed over like a feeding alligator, a faint smile on his lips. But he seemed to take genuine, honest pleasure in the ceremony, which for my dad was a rare thing, and so everyone left him to it.

Beatrice was still living in Ocean City, Maryland, working at an Italian restaurant that catered to tourists. In the winter she went on unemployment. She was thirty-two years old, divorced, and wore belly shirts to show her pierced navel surrounded by a Polynesian scrawl. Beatrice was tall like me and had the lean look of a habitual drug user. She kept her hair dyed black and had stopped using most hygiene products. Our father paid for her car insurance, when she had a car, and for her phone bill, in an attempt to get her to call. During dinner she took numerous bathroom breaks as well as getting up to step out onto the porch and smoke, the gunsmith tailing behind her, gripping his hand-tooled leather tobacco pouch.

Later in the kitchen my mother and I were discussing how unfit my sister was for motherhood, her complete lack of any sense of responsibility and how this marked her for a problematic and difficult career as a breeder. I had a few glasses of wine, and I think I was trying to gain some insight into my sister's life by talking to my mother. Which was a mistake.

Maybe some people just shouldn't have children, I said. My mother was spooning butter and sour cream into a giant bowl of mashed potatoes, mixing it with her hands.

I wish you wouldn't go, she said. Why can't you stay here?

Her eyeliner was caked under her eyes, and my mother suddenly looked clownish and absurd.

You could help your sister, you know, she said.

I can't do anything for Beatrice, I said. *You* are her mother, *you* do something.

She paused, and looking at me my mother said: You know Eleanor, some women are mothers, and some women have children. I was no mother. I was just a woman who had children.

Mom, I said, that's a terrible thing to say. Particularly to your daughter.

She shook her head, tried to wipe her eyes with her sleeve, and left a streak of potatoes across her cheek.

I'm afraid, she said, that you will likely have to confront this your-self at some point.

I can't take much more of this, I whispered to Fred.

We were sleeping in my old room, in the separate twin beds that Beatrice and I had slept in as children. The mattresses were special-order, an extra six inches in length, like all of the beds in the house.

Hmmm.

Fred was solidly drunk. He would snore, I knew, and I would spend half the night getting him to turn over.

And what's with the gunsmith?

Take it easy, Fred mumbled.

What?

You are awfully lucky, Elly.

Something pawed on the window screen, and I craned my neck to look. Branches, the holly tree that towered over the side of the house. No real snow this year. For Christmas, Fred had given me a flannel bathrobe and a Tiffany charm bracelet with two charms. The first was a heart shape that said: "If Found, Return to Tiffany & Co., New York City." The other was a fish.

To mark our introduction to the island, he said. Each new adven-ture we'll add another charm.

Thinking of it, I wanted to roll onto him and give him a squeeze. I stuck my hand out.

Hey.

He reached out and clasped my hand.

We fly to Ireland on Tuesday, Fred said. We'll be in Baltimore again on Wednesday. Try and enjoy the time you have.

I think Beatrice is on something, I said.

And this is a surprise?

I can't believe it, I said, but I'm actually ready to go back.

I'm glad, Fred said. Me too. But first Atlantic City and Ham. You up for it?

Sure, I said. Always.

We held hands for a few moments, our arms stretched across the darkness.

Fred?

Yes.

I'm scared.

Of what?

A baby.

No need to be scared, he said. They're tiny little things. Not particularly aggressive. You can overpower them.

You know what I mean.

The old house wheezed and cracked with the press of winter. It was the only home I'd ever known.

Yes, Fred said. I do. But I'm not scared. Not with you.

The airport security screeners located a small penknife in Fred's bag and pulled him aside. We had a flight up to Newark to spend New Year's with Ham in Atlantic City. This knife had made the trip to and from Europe undetected, and lain forgotten in an obscure pocket for many years. The penknife was inlaid with mother-of-pearl and capped with gold, engraved along one side: "HJB—1930." Fred's grandfather, the original Ham, would have been eighteen years old at the time, Fred explained, still in Virginia, working at a sawmill before he began his forays out west. It seemed a precious and expensive thing to procure during the Depression, but Fred said that his grandfather was known to run a little whiskey in those days.

The penknife would have to remain behind, and the security agents gave Fred the option of mailing it to himself. They provided him with a standard business envelope, which Fred addressed to our hotel in Atlantic City.

It was the day before New Year's Eve. Ham wanted to take Fred up in his new plane. I made him promise not to get in a plane piloted by his father, under any circumstances.

We arrived at the address with a frozen turkey in the trunk of the

rental car and a gallon of Canadian Club. It was a slate-gray afternoon, with a fine mist of rain, and the boardwalk looked particularly
decrepit. Ham was meeting us in an Italian restaurant on a side street
where black prostitutes gathered to seek out the lonely tourists who
wandered out of the casinos. We found him perched in a giant booth
near the door, with a window overlooking the parking lot. He was
doing the *New York Times* crossword puzzle and drinking scotch.
He seemed genuinely happy to see us, and after we shook hands he
waved over the waitress, who took our drink order. Ham was looking better than when we saw him last; he had healthy color in his
face and was wearing a well-tailored suit. His leather valise sat on the
table. He reached over and stroked my arm.

Elly, how's the water over there?

It's great, Ham, thanks.

Good. Great to see you. You look great.

So do you, Ham.

The restaurant was full of pairs of people, black woman/white
man, all slurping piles of spaghetti carbonara with carafes of pinkish
Chianti. At regular intervals these pairs would wipe their mouths on
their napkins and exit through a back door in the alley, returning a
few minutes later and exiting out the front. Ham ordered for us, and
a grizzled old troll trundled out vast plates of pillowy cream-colored
ravioli the size of doughnuts, accented with artful splashes of mari-
nara. Ham took out a crumpled pack of Camels and shook out a bent
cigarette.

So what do you do here? I asked.

I have dinner. Do the crossword.

No, I mean for employment.

I'm a gaming consultant.

Ham popped a match on the table and lit his cigarette, leaning
back and stretching an arm across the top of the vinyl booth. Some
kind of little kingdom you have here, I thought. Congratulations.

Which casino? Fred asked.

The Golden Castle, Ham said.

Never heard of it, I said.

That's because you aren't a serious gamer.

Don't you mean gambler?

Gamblers flip coins and hope for luck, Ham said. Gamers are people who play to win. I'll show you what I mean. C'mon, eat up. Let's get out of here and go back to my place.

The ravioli were excellent, and Fred and I ate a couple each while Ham polished off the crap wine. We were never given a bill, and Ham left no tip.

On the boardwalk the sky was the color of cement and a steady sleet pounded the boards. Ham's place was only a few blocks away, in a building with a series of unmarked solid steel doors on a stretch of wall decorated with a vaguely Mardi Gras–esque mural. Next door was Caesars, then Bally's, then the rest of the strip. The upper stories were blank, windowless, with more lurid paintings of carnival behavior. Ham seemed to choose a door at random. Inside was a cavernous warehouse area, naked neon bulbs and packing materials piled in the back.

Jesus, Fred said. What kind of place is this?

Ham grinned and beckoned with a finger, his shoes clacking across the concrete floor. He took us to the back of the room and into a freight elevator, the walls covered with heavy packing quilts.

This is a bit of a perk, Ham said. Watch this.

The elevator had no buttons or doors. Ham stuck a key in an unmarked slot and the car lurched upward, moving remarkably fast, the wall of brick a blur in front of us, cut occasionally by an opening, blinks of light and glimpses at various interiors as we flashed by the floors: a small stage with couches around it, tables with men playing cards, someone's bedroom, a woman holding a glass pitcher full of water, a room full of glowing computer screens. Ham's place was on the top floor, a vast loft space painted in muted colors, the kitchen great slabs of obsidian marble, gleaming stainless-steel appliances, polished hardwood floors and a wall of twelve-foot windows overlooking the Atlantic City strip.

Ham fixed us cocktails and the sleet stopped so we went out onto the veranda and up a small set of stairs to the roof. A covered and heated patio with a teak wet bar and deck furniture overlooked a long, rectangular pool, the water glowing deep red.

Twenty-five meters long, Ham said. Regulation distance, right Elly? Climate-controlled. And salt water too.

The ocean pounded itself into the sand below us and there was the faint sound of laughter and shouting from the boardwalk, the lights of the casinos washing out the night sky. I bent down and felt the water. Perhaps sixty-eight, seventy degrees. I put my finger to my tongue and tasted the salt. It wasn't the briny, gritty taste of the ocean, more of a clean, sharp sensation, but delicious nonetheless.

Watch this, Ham said, and turned a small dial on the control panel. The pool lights faded to white then to emerald, then sky blue, then a hazy yellow.

This is incredible, I said.

I thought you'd like it, Ham said. I thought of you, actually, when I had it made.

He led us to a small table with cushioned chairs.

Wait here, he said, I need to get something.

This place is insane, Fred said as soon as his father went down the stairs.

How is it possible? What's this consultant thing he's talking about?

I don't know, Fred said. I don't know what he's doing.

Ham came up a minute later with his valise and a bottle of scotch.

Bring your suit, Elly? Dive in if you want.

I shrugged. I didn't want to give him the satisfaction.

Ham took out a yellow legal pad and slid it in front of Fred. On the pad was a list of names and dollar amounts. Fred's name was there at the top of the list. The amount next to his name was extremely large.

What's this? Fred said. I don't understand.

This is what I calculate that you owe me, Ham said.

What?

We just stared at him for a few moments, until he cracked up.

Kidding! This is a rough draft of my will. I'm gonna have it drawn up soon. I know a guy in Hoboken who can do any legal document in twenty-four hours that'll hold up in any court in the world.

How . . . Fred stammered. Where did this money come from?

Ham shuffled around in the valise and pulled out a folder.

All I need, is a signature on this here and it'll be all set.

You want me to sign . . . what?

Ham sighed and ran a hand through his hair. His fingernails were battered and chipped, gunked with dark material in the creases like a mechanic.

This whole thing is going to collapse, Ham said. This world will eat itself. I'm not just talking about Atlantic City. The whole thing. You guys have the right idea, going out to that island.

Our pub isn't on an island, Fred said, it's in Baltimore, on the coast.

Yeah, Ham said, waving his hand, but you know the island I'm talking about. Look, I've been thinking about what to leave behind. Something that will poke out of the ashes of this disaster, something to go into the next world.

What are you *talking* about? Fred said.

Probably be a lot like where you are now, Ham said. That sort of life. But anyway this document merely says that on the delivery of an heir this money will be rightfully yours. I don't even have to be dead! It's a win-win as we say in the business.

An heir? I said.

Dad, Fred said, that's kinda . . . fucked up.

Be that as it may, he said, here it is.

We're not signing that, I said.

You don't need to sign it, Elly, only my son here. You are merely an accessory to the fact.

Thanks, I said.

But with that money you could build a pool just like this, even better. Anywhere you want. Even on your island.

Ham stashed the document back in the folder and handed it to me. There was the smell of something burning, like plastic or rubber. Small plumes of smoke were drifting over the tops of the casinos.

You just think about it, have a lawyer look it over, whatever.

Really, if you don't . . . do anything, nothing will happen. It is only a reward system. No penalty.

I don't know, Fred said. This is kinda unorthodox.

Ham poured us fresh glasses of scotch.

You bring the turkey?

Yeah. In the trunk.

Good, he said. Leave it out to thaw. Bring it over tomorrow, say, noon. You'll want to pick up some tarragon, thyme, sage, salted butter, lemons. Stuffing, I prefer corn bread. And the usual sides. I detest that sweet potato—marshmallow shit, so none of that. I'll supply the wine.

What's that smoke? I said. What's burning?

Rome, Ham said.

The next morning the envelope Fred mailed to himself arrived. It was empty, with a small tear in one corner.

Motherfuckers! Fred screamed. He tore the envelope into shreds and threw it out the window.

At the airport Fred insisted on going into the smoking lounge.

It's like a circle of hell in there, he said, look at it. Got to check it out.

I read *The New York Times* while Fred entered the lounge, sans cigarettes, disappearing into the fog. At one point I looked up and he was crouching on the floor chatting with a seated man. When he came out we walked to the gate, Fred sniffing his clothes. He said the lounge was mostly full of young soldiers, deploying overseas.

They didn't seem scared, he said. Not at all. They were like kids before a football game.

Probably a good thing, I said. Better than being afraid.

I suppose.

We had a four-hour layover in JFK, our plane leaving at eight in the evening, so we decided upon a strategy of heavy cocktails and light appetizers in order to facilitate the holy grail of international flight: to sleep through the whole damn thing. It never worked, of course, but it could be great fun as it gave your drinking the added element of unarguable purpose. We started with dry martinis, Bombay Sapphire, shaken, up, one olive.

After a few drinks a small band of soldiers rambled in with their rucksacks and took a table. They were laughing, punching each other in the arm. Rawboned, knobby heads, thin wrists poking out of their rolled-up sleeves, freckled and razor-chinned, they looked freshly skinned. I saw Fred eyeing them, and I asked if those were the guys he'd seen in the smoking lounge, but he said no. He called the bartender and told him he wanted to buy the soldiers a round of beers.

Whatever they're having, Fred said.

The bartender took a tray of drafts over to the table, and when they looked at her curiously she pointed to Fred, who held up his martini and nodded. Their eyes narrowed for a moment, taking both of us in, calculating, then they softened and a few nodded in return. Then one soldier picked up the beer and mimicked Fred's nod, and they all laughed. They all picked up the beers and nodded and blinked at each other in turn, slapping the table and looking over at Fred, shaking their heads. Fred stared for a moment before he turned back to the bar, his face wooden.

What pricks, I said. What assholes.

Yeah, Fred said. It was a dumb thing to do.

What?

It's so cliché, he said. Buying the soldiers a round.

But it was sincere, I said. It was a nice gesture.

Yeah. Still.

We rolled up to the gate just as boarding started. Fred was lumbering and drunk, his face all twisted up, and throughout the flight he punched through magazine articles and stared at the ceiling and scribbled in his journal, swearing under his breath, and neither of us got any sleep. But the great thing about Fred was that by the time we touched down in Cork six hours later he wrestled our luggage into the cab with a frowsy, sleepy grin, giving me a squeeze on the hip, and we cuddled sleepily as the cab headed west to Skibbereen.

Can't wait to get back to the Nightjar, he said. Missed the place.

I fell asleep on his shoulder as we passed through Cork and into the countryside, the windows a wash of green.

Chapter Twelve

It was halfway through March and the winds from the west brought the high seas crashing into the Baltimore cliffs, sending sheets of water skyward for a hundred feet. Waves of salty mist pushed over the town in intermittent bursts, squeezing through windowpanes and under doors like exhaled breath. Everything was coated in a rime of salt and icy mold, and the ferry was relegated to once a week, depending on the weather. Fred read the paper sitting at the bar, wearing a T-shirt and flip-flops. The draft was relentless, but he never felt it. He had let his beard go lately and was developing what he called the full box hedge, but with his shaggy hair it made him seem more like a giant hedgehog drinking a pint of beer. It was nearly noon, and we both knew that nobody was coming.

Why don't we just shut down, I said. We could get out of here.

He didn't look up from the paper.

Where would we go?

Through the window I could see a few solitary men, Corrigans, stalking the ferry pier wearing bright orange survival suits. When we returned from America we'd found a note slipped under the door. It was something in Irish, just a single sentence, written in a precise hand. I wanted to have it translated but Fred chucked it in the fireplace.

That morning the water in Baltimore Bay was a white churning froth and the BBC reported dozens of pilot whales were smashed on the rocks just west of town. I knew that Sebastian would likely be back on the island, perched on the Bill of Clear, watching the coming waves of migratory birds. The Ineer a choppy green bath, the cool feel of those slick stones, that quiet submersion. Fastnet, the glowing path. The pub felt suddenly tight and close.

I think I want to go back out, swim a bit.

Go ahead.

You don't mind?

Nah.

Wanna come?

I'll stick around here.

Fred raised his head and looked around the empty room.

Maybe somebody'll show up.

We could use some paying customers, I said.

Fred mumbled and shook the paper.

As opposed to all of our friends who come in for free drinks.

He looked up at me.

Ah, come on. Like who?

The woofers for one.

Please, Fred said, don't even start.

Start? I'm not the one handing out free drinks to anyone that rolls in here and hangs out with you for a bit.

How would you know? You're always on the island, running around with the goat herder and who knows who else.

What are you talking about?

C'mon, Elly, it's a small world here. People see you on the island, they see what you are doing. Everybody knows.

The room was tightening, smaller, and a faint *ping,* a pinprick of sound, started ringing in my ears.

Knows what?

I tried to take on a defiant look, to dare him to say it. I knew that he wouldn't, even if he had heard something. I thought of Sebastian and me in the Five Bells, laughing over our hot whiskeys, his delicate fingers fanning open his journal, the pencil drawings of jackdaws, house martins, shrikes, yellowhammers. His steady, attentive gaze.

Fred filled a tumbler with ice and poured himself a glass of bourbon. He took a long sip. His T-shirt was torn around the back of the collar, and he had yellow pit stains under his arms. His shorts hung below his belly, perched on his hips.

Look, he said. Let's not do this.

Do what?

Okay, he said, I'm gonna say it. You ready?

I was not, I was not ready for what he was about to say. I was terrified.

You saw that number Ham showed us. The contract. What do you want to do?

I can't, I said. Not now.

Not talk about it? Or . . . it?

Not now, I said. I couldn't possibly . . . We'll talk about it later.

I slung my bag over my shoulder and left. The ferry was mercifully waiting at the berth, and a few minutes later I was on my way to Clear.

The ferry had just passed around the southern edge of Sherkin and was heading through the series of rocky straits that separated the islands, the area known as Gascanane Sound, when I saw a pair of large animals perched on a small rock plateau. The island was about thirty feet square, rising out of the sea at an angle, the broad side facing the eastern end of Cape Clear and Douglass's Cove. As we drew closer I could tell the animals were large and impressive-looking donkeys. They were humped together, their heads down between their trembling forelegs, their wet manes draped over their faces. They were Stephen-the-fucking-blow-in's donkeys.

Waves of sea spray whipped through them and they shifted their back hooves, trying to keep their footing on the slippery rock. They had been suffering for some time and clearly wouldn't last much longer.

Hey! I said aloud to no one in particular. Then I stood up, pointing. *Hey!*

There were a half dozen islanders clustered behind the pilothouse, the pilot obscured by the fogged window. The other passengers looked at me, then at the donkeys. Then everyone looked away. The pilot flicked his cigarette out the window. Standing in the bow in a peacoat and wool cap was the hulking form of Conchur Corrigan, watching me. The bow of the boat rose and fell, and Conchur seemed to rise above the island, then drop beneath it with each passing swell. He smiled, a tight, bristly grin out of one side of his face, almost like he was proud of me. Like it was some kind of test, and I had passed.

Patrick explained to me that there is a kind of prejudice in Ireland about goats. To be a goat farmer is to signal the confines of one's fortunes. They are the perfect animals for Ireland, Patrick said, with their resiliency, milk and meat production, the simple care, and their ability to subsist on nearly nothing. The most common goat in Ireland, the basic British Alpine, can also be easily trained to stay in moderately confined areas, and they quickly establish their own pack authority, with all of the animals lining up in order. They obediently move into enclosures, indoor feeding areas, or out to pasture. Disease is limited and rare, and even a crippled or deformed animal, born with a clubfoot, for example, will drag itself around the yard and produce milk and kids without complaint.

That spring I helped Highgate and the woofers with the kidding and dehorning. One of his best milkers, a gray speckled goat named Jenny, was coming down with mastitis, or milk fever, a teat and udder infection caused by bacteria. Highgate had me touch her udder, which was strangely warm. In the advanced stages the udder will actually get hot to the touch, then harden like a rock, eventually dropping off. *Mastitis* in Irish means "lump in the ground" because eventually the goat will lie down and be unable to get up.

Does this hurt them? I asked.

Gus and Magdalene held a young male on the barn floor while Patrick plied the cruel-looking dehorning tool, long-handled with heavy teeth that literally bite the horn buds out of the goat's skull.

Highgate stood by with the blood-stop paste in a small can, his fingers dipped in ready to apply to the wound.

It's hard to say, but we know it isn't like our type of pain. The advantage of animals is that they have no imagination.

How is that an advantage? I asked.

Without imagination, what is fear? What is pain without fear?

I'll bet it still hurts, Magdalene said. I hate this.

But if we don't do it, Highgate said, they will hurt each other. Next we have to do Rachel, which is going to be tricky.

Rachel was a strong candidate for a champion milker, and so Highgate wanted to make sure he took care of her. Her horns had been cut once already, but one of them wasn't scooped out deep enough and began to grow again, a twisted, knotted spiral across her forehead that was growing back into her skull. It would have to be fully removed, and to do that they had to put her out. Highgate held a soaked rag over her nose until she collapsed. Then we slid her onto a large piece of cardboard and carried her into the kitchen, laying her on the floor. We need hot water, Highgate explained, and keeping her temperature up is vital, so it is better just to do it in here. I couldn't watch, so I stepped outside and stood in the back pen, gazing at the waves of Roaringwater Bay. It was heavy out there, dark, and the swells six feet or more. Back to the east the lights of Baltimore winked. I tried to count the lights in the harbor, to see if I could determine which was the Nightjar, but I never could be sure.

Gus stepped out the door, a streak of blood on his cheek. He smoked a cigarette and we stood looking at the sea.

How long are you staying? I asked.

'Nother few months. Then I go.

How about the rest?

They leave next few months. 'Cept Patrick. He says he stays, *ja*? For at least another year. Till he finishes.

Finishes what?

Gus scratched at his beard and shook his head.

Shit, I dunno. Save the farm. Stop Kieran.

Stop him? From doing what?

Gus pointed down the hill toward the Waist.

The guesthouses, new pub? He's acquiring land. People are selling.

Are you talking about tourism?

I don't really, I just feed the goats, you know?

Sure.

I like goats, Gus said. I like this farm.

Okay.

Hey, you seen Miranda, *ja*?

Yeah, a couple times.

She watches you?

Gus smiled in the wind.

You are lucky then, he said. She never shows herself to me. Just to Highgate. Some of the others claim they've seen her, but they're full of shit. But Highgate and Miranda, it's like they have a way of talking. They communicate.

How?

Gus shrugged and stubbed his cigarette on the bottom of his boot, then stuck it in his pocket.

Must be something about you. The swimming, *ja*? She's never around, but she protects the other goats. Never lost a kid since she came. No ravens, nothing.

We heard a shout from inside, and something knocking, like a hammer on wood. Gus pushed inside, and I followed him.

In the kitchen Rachel was writhing on the floor, her hooves pounding the cupboards, the air filled with a shrill, high whistling sound. There were small green clumps, like mushed seaweed, and streaks of blood all over the floor. Highgate was holding her head, one hand in her mouth, searching for something. Rachel thrashed, her eyes wild, Patrick trying to corral her kicking legs. Highgate cursed and removed his hand, then clamped both hands over her muzzle, holding her mouth shut. He bent down and put his mouth over her nose. Blood came foaming out of the gory hole where her horns had been. Akio started screaming, and Patrick whipped his head around and told her to shut up. Then Rachel's sides were heaving and Highgate sat back on his haunches, blood smearing his face and hands. Gus knelt and felt her pulse.

She's breathing.

Rachel's eyes settled closed, and her breathing became regular.

Mon Dieu, Magdalene said. What the fuck was that?

Highgate slathered some paste on her wound, then taped a large piece of cotton over it, winding the tape around her head.

She choked on her cud, Highgate said. She wasn't breathing and we had to clear the passageway. I think she's okay.

He lifted his head and sniffed the air.

You got the teakettle on, Akio?

Akio was sobbing, but she went to the range and turned off the heat.

All right, Highgate said, let's wash up and have a bit of tea. She's going to just sleep it off here for a bit.

We sat in the main room, Magadalene and Akio still dazed, and slurped our tea. Patrick loaded the stove, his forearms scratched and pink from scrubbing. He used a rag to wipe mud and goat hair off his boat shoes. His khakis were streaked with blood and his face was swollen, his eyes a bit glassy. Patrick had never flinched, I thought, but he was not impervious. The dogs piled in their beds, looking a bit embarrassed. After a few minutes there was a clatter of hooves and a groan and Rachel came bounding out of the kitchen, bucking like a wild bull.

The door, Patrick!

Patrick was already in motion, vaulting the couch, and Rachel went straight for it. He got the door open and she launched herself out without breaking stride, giving a few more kicks, then trotting over to the pen where she waited to be let in.

The next afternoon I was walking across the cushiony turf of the East Bog of Ballyieragh when I came over a rise and saw Ariel among a small stand of trees that lay in a shallow ditch. She was tying little clumps of bones into the trees with strips of cloth; in the lower branches hung skulls of small animals, and underneath the trees on the damp earth there were more stacks of broken bones, children's toys and dolls, all torn asunder or broken significantly, scattered in circular patterns. Ariel saw me approaching and smiled warmly, her parka hood tight around her face, her gloveless hands reddened with cold. I wanted to turn away from this scene but there was nowhere to go, so I walked under the tree and pretended to admire her work.

I know it isn't pretty, she said.

No, I said, it's nice.

All the bits are ruined over here, she said. On the other side they'll be beautiful again.

I raised my hand and steadied a swaying fragment of a picture book, torn in half with a hole in the middle and a loop of wire passing through. The wind was only slight here, buffered in the natural depression, barely shifting through the trees, and toys clinked together lightly like wind chimes.

I don't understand, I said.

It's for the children of the sea, Ariel said. The ones who passed through.

She was beaming, her wide face open and glowing.

You've seen them, out in the water, on your swims. You've been close to them.

Who?

Lost at sea, Ariel said. All thems that are lost.

That afternoon on the long finger of Blananarragaun I scrambled down the black rock, crabbing myself through the boulders to where the swells dashed their full height. The water was thick with feeding pilchards, the air full of terns and auks. A few puffins gazed from their rock niches out to the western sun. Above me the cliffs thundered with echo and shadow. I slipped in and let the current push me quickly seaward. I felt a thousand motes of light on the water, the gentle churn of creatures about my body, the ebb and pull of tides. The sea throbbed with life around me as I drifted from land.

That spring Fred and I adopted a regular schedule whereby I would spend four days on the island midweek and then return on Thursday for the weekend. As the bird-watchers clustered in the harbor looking for passage to the islands, and other tourists came in to holiday on the beaches of Sherkin, Hare, or Long Island, or to take walking tours of Clear, the Nightjar began to do more business. Fred banged around the kitchen and started making up large batches of soups on Friday mornings, and I delivered food, cleaned tables, and ran the dishwasher when the pub filled up in the afternoons. He started selling Highgate's cheese, using it on our toasted sandwiches. Its salty, earthy taste was unmistakable, but I'm not sure if our patrons enjoyed it. We still did a smaller trade than the rest of the pubs, but it didn't take much to break even. I don't think Fred or I ever thought of this enterprise as a way to make money, but we needed a cushion for when the gale season came around again. Fred still made the occasional trip into Cork in the Peugeot for pub supplies and materials for Highgate's farm.

I told O'Boyle that I wanted to do the Fastnet swim again, soon.

He was drinking a deep bowl of mutton stew in the Five Bells, whiskered and hungover. He put down his bowl and stared at me.

Why'd you want to do that? he asked. Wasn't it bad enough last time for ya?

I was sick, I said. I can make it if we have good weather. I need the boat out just in case.

The builders mumbled at the bar, nose deep in stout, a few chattering birders, the groaning whine of floorboards and stools, the hiss of a pan in the kitchen. O'Boyle sat perfectly still, watching me. He was thinking, hard.

Can I ask ya not to do it?
No, I said. You can't.

I flung myself into the ocean and hacked away for hours at a time in a red heat, my underarms, neck, and groin chafed to bloody rags, the muscles of my back and arms shredded and knotted with cramps. I wanted to be prepared. I would drag myself out of the water and shudder with exhaustion, and in those moments I forgot that my marriage was coming apart, the layers peeling away like pieces of a broken satellite reentering the earth's atmosphere. It was only a matter of time before we exploded into a fiery flower of carbon and cinders.

Chapter Thirteen

I was relieved to see Dinny's boat alongside the quay in the Ineer, the engine thumping a slim trail of smoke, O'Boyle standing on the foredeck in his sandals, hands in his pockets gazing out to sea. It was overcast, the sky slate gray, but the sea was light, an undulating field shimmering in the glare. Fastnet was clear and unshrouded by fog or spray. I tossed my bag into the boat and stripped down to my suit.

Where's Dinny?

Ah, he wouldn't come.

Why?

Just wouldn't, is all.

O'Boyle stepped around the pilothouse and hopped down on the deck. He fiddled with the throttle. I took some latex gloves and began applying lubrication.

I'd really rather we didn't do this, he said.

Look at the water, I said. It's perfect. I'll be done in three hours.

Still, he said.

I snapped the gloves off and worked my cap onto my head. There was no breeze, the air temperature in the sixties, water temp mid-fifties. I walked down the steps and sat to spit in my goggles.

It's not safe, he said.

I can do this swim, I said. I've done longer distances. I'm in shape, the conditions are perfect. Just relax.

O'Boyle riffled in an old rucksack and produced a battered thermos.

Care for some tea?

No, thanks, I said. I'm keeping it simple this time. Just water and toast.

He continued to hold the thermos out to me with a wide-eyed look. I shook my head. He tossed it in the sack with resignation and sat on the stool with slumped shoulders. I stood on the bottom step, the water lapping around my waist, and began to stretch my arms and shoulders. O'Boyle rose off his stool and turning to me seemed about to say something when he froze in a crouch, one hand raised toward Fastnet. He closed his eyes and tilted his head to the side slowly.

O'Boyle?

He moved his lips, mumbling something, a frown of concentration on his face.

Noises, he muttered, sounds, sweet airs . . .

He shook his head and straightened up, looking around as if he was lost.

You all right?

Yeah, he said. I'm just . . . just a little knackered you know.

He rummaged around under the wheelhouse and came up with a can of Old Peculier. He snapped the top and took a deep drink, then took a cassette tape out of his pocket and snapped it into the player he had lashed to the center console. Robbie Williams.

Is that the only tape you have? I said. Kind of annoying.

O'Boyle gave me his long, rubbery smile.

Got your kit aboard? he said. Then let's go.

He put the boat in gear and pulled out into the middle of the Ineer. I cinched my goggles down and stood and stretched for a moment before diving in. I felt strong, and the water was smooth and comfortable.

The glare reduced visibility under the water, but I quickly locked into a nice five-stroke breathing pattern, focusing on the long reach, rolling my shoulders, my fingers stretching out before my eyes just under the glassy film of the water. Then the angle, fingers together for the catch, elbow out and pull through, a five-beat kick and a snap of the wrist to the release and my hand out and swinging low over the water, elbow high. I wanted to go fast, not only to make sure I beat any weather coming in but also to show O'Boyle that there was nothing to worry about. I did a quick sighting every fifty strokes, keeping the finger of Fastnet dead ahead. It was easy without much in terms of swells; every time I looked up, the lighthouse was there. O'Boyle puttered along up to my left, perched on his stool and drinking beer, one hand steadying the wheel. I felt calm, fast, and completely assured, and I cleared the first mile in twenty-five minutes.

The roar and slush of the water, the cavernous inhalations of my breathing, the plunk and drum of bubbles, all of those things faded into a kind of white noise and I was left with the machinations of muscle, sinew, tendon, organs, the electric pulses of my mind going about its subtle tracings of thought. All these normally background sounds came to the fore, and by focusing on them individually I could hear the fracture of tissue, the slow grind of a ball in a socket, the drip of pooling lactic acid in my arms, the push and ebb of blood to my heart, the pleasant whir of my mind calculating and displaying a memory. It was easy to while away the time immersed in this pleasant suspension, and when I raised my head above water the rush of the external came back like a daytime phantasm in which swaths of time and space had passed through my fingers. The stone column of Fastnet, its yellow eye gently spinning, rose up before me.

The sky had darkened, a scattering of clouds, but as the seas kept to a gentle roll and pitch I wasn't worried. Underwater the stray filtered beam of sunlight created twisting tunnels into the deep, my hands stretching out into their dusty light. Another hundred strokes and the swells began to rise up, heading nearly due east, right into me. My sight line was still decent, and O'Boyle chugging away, the sound of Robbie Williams singing a dramatic ballad drifting over the water, but the increased swells made it tougher going. My hands started slapping the coming waves and as I crested the peaks my upper body started to rise out of the water, then crash down the slope. I stopped and treaded water for a moment, trying to get some read on the sky, what it was planning to do. The cloud cover was lowered, bending down into the horizon, and there were strong curving streaks of black above Fastnet, which was not a good sign. O'Boyle was idling the boat up to my left, standing at the wheel and watching me over his shoulder. He made a beckoning gesture, to come to the boat, then pointed to the clouds, but I shook my head and pointed at Fastnet. I had maybe a half mile to the lighthouse and in fifteen minutes I'd be on my way back. My shoulders ached slightly, but other than that I felt great. I cleared my goggles and put my head down, intending to churn it out to the lighthouse then cruise back as the weather stacked up behind me and pushed me in. I began to raise up to sight every thirty strokes to make sure I wasn't pushed off course, and soon I could see the crashing spray on the rocks. The water was now black and took on the oily consistency that comes before rain.

I couldn't help but think of the first time out and the way strings of light wound themselves from the depths, how the water seemed charged with gold. But the second time it was all blackness, no movement, nothing. I knew from the charts that around the lighthouse the depths get near a thousand feet.

But I began to feel something. I thought it was my own heart at first, a regular resonant thrum and echo that I felt through my chest and up into my head. But it was coming from below me. Then it was as if I could see this sensation radiating from the ocean bottom, thick halos like smoke rings, ascending in concentric circles. They seemed to grow as they ascended, and multiply, until they were everywhere. I thought I was suffering from sea blackness, a form of simple hallucination not unlike when you close your eyes and stare at the black of your eyelids and all sorts of shapes begin to appear.

I stopped and got my bearings, just a hundred yards from Fastnet, the weather growing worse, the swells setting up and topped with hard winds that pushed spray in raining sheets in my face. As I was treading water I saw the rings bursting on the surface, all around me. They were rings of bubbles, air or gas from somewhere down in the deep. The air was suddenly thick with the warm, sweet smell of blood and must. For the second time in my life I felt real fear in the water.

I lit out for Fastnet at top speed, suddenly desiring land, to get out of that water. I felt like I was being buffeted by underwater forces and I figured I was feeling the currents off the rocks. When I was a few yards away, at the base of an egg-shaped boulder the size of a house, I let a wave carry me onto it, and when my body slapped on the rock, I gripped it spread-eagle with my arms and legs, clutching handfuls of barnacles, and when the wave retreated I hauled myself up before the next swell could tear me away. As I climbed I saw my arm was a mask of blood, my suit tearing and snagging, and I knew that I was cut badly all over.

I looked up, the tower of the lighthouse rising above me, and that was when I saw her, clinging to the side of the lighthouse. She was at least a hundred feet up, hair whipping in the wind, naked, a white form on the gray rock. A small child. She was looking right at me. She seemed to nod, then plying her limbs like a lizard she began to climb up the tower, circling it to the left, moving faster and coming around the other side, moving with impossible speed, like film sped up. The sky was now completely black, as if the entire day had gone, and I turned and hurled myself back into the water.

I had the vague bulk of Cape Clear on the horizon and I made for it with everything I had. I was screaming as I breathed, sprinting even though I knew that I had more than three miles to go and needed to conserve my energy. Underwater currents tore at my legs and I struggled to stay on line with the island. There were sounds in the water I hadn't heard before, long groans and whines, and I couldn't tell if they were from me or something else. Suddenly the sea seemed to bulge, and I had the sensation of being lifted up in the water, as if something very large was rising underneath me. Then the water dropped and I was sucked down at least ten feet and pulled forward in an invisible wake. As I struggled to the surface I saw shapeless patches of white moving at terrific speed, a flash, and then the swell of water subsided as the white patches disappeared into the murk. *Where was O'Boyle?* On the surface, straight ahead I could see Cape Clear, still a couple miles off, lights on the hillside, the harbor mouth.

Then I saw the fin, triangular and black, at least six feet high, surging through the water at a terrific speed, moving past me. Then two more, like dark sails, the tops of the fins slightly curved, and a broad back of black skin with a mottled white patch broke the surface. I was treading water and my face opened up and I screamed, staring hard at Cape Clear, desperately hoping, for the first time in my life, that someone would save me.

There was a crash and a surge of water, and I cowered as a shadow rose up. Something knocked me in the head, a loop of heavy rope, an iron craft with tall black sides topped with stooping cranes and tackle. I grabbed the rope and was yanked from the water and over the side of the ship like a gaffed tuna, landing in the arms of an enormous man. He was so large it didn't seem real, but I clutched his neck. He cradled me for a moment, then I was set down on something soft and other men were there, hovering over me. I saw the man who caught me stand up and look at his arms, slick and shining with blood. *Conchur.* Broad floodlights were pointed at us from the pilothouse, casting the deck and the other men gathered around talking in Irish in a harsh black-and-white negative image. They seemed confused and tried to avert their eyes. My suit was torn to ribbons and I curled into a ball and someone threw a blanket over me. I convulsed hard a few times, then vomited a sheet of green water and bile. The men cursed, and I was picked up again and carried somewhere into the interior of the ship. I hid my face in my hands, wishing to be as small as possible, wanting to be dwarfed by the arms of the man who held me.

Conchur Corrigan's salvage craft was long and wide and flat-bottomed, with all manner of cranes, cables, winches rigged like webbing along its length. Essentially a low iron box, it seemed like a boat that should not be able to move, much less float. The men aboard looked like the survivors of a mining disaster; the bleak pallor of their skin contrasted with the blackened smudge on their faces and hands, their stained canvas jackets.

Conchur sat beside me while we steamed back to Baltimore in the streaming rain. He was an outsize man in every sense of the word; his head looked like someone had hewn a set of eyes, nose, and mouth into a block of speckled pine, his chin squared, lantern-jawed. He was nearly seven feet tall, and broad in the shoulders. The men clustered around chattering in Irish, and Conchur grunted a few syllables in reply. They were all inspecting me carefully. Where was O'Boyle? Did the boat swamp? Was he safe?

My teeth were chattering hard, despite the blanket, and I wasn't sure if I was going into shock.

Conchur finally addressed me in English:

What the fuck were you doin' out there?

Swimming, I said.

He looked at his compatriots and they all shrugged and raised their eyebrows.

Where?

To Fastnet. And back.

That set off a string of Irish.

Conchur leaned in close. The one item about him that was off: his eyes were small, deep-set, vaguely pinkish, like the eyes of a pig.

Don't do that. Swim. Out here.

He put a large hand on my shoulder, his thumb at the base of my throat and forefinger curled over my spine. He could have wrung my neck like a chicken.

You should stay in Baltimore, he said. Or even better, back where you came from.

He wasn't hurting me, but I started to cry, ducking my head and sobbing into the blanket. Conchur gave me a pat, then took his hand off my neck. More rattling Irish with his comrades.

Did you see them killers out there? he said.

What?

Them killers. Killer whales. Sea wolves.

I think so, I said.

Almost had ya, they did.

Where's the little girl?

Conchur squinted at me.

She was on the lighthouse, I said. A little girl.

Conchur turned and said something in Irish to the men, and that set off a new round of curses. I was shaking and crying, my flesh swelling as it warmed. I couldn't shut my eyes.

There's nobody out there, he said. Just you.

Conchur dropped me on the quay in Baltimore and before I turned around they were already backing the salvage ship off, the smoke-stack belching gouts of black smoke, heading out into Roaringwater Bay. Conchur stood at the rail, and when I looked at him he shook his head and raised one giant hand and waggled a finger at me. *Bad girl.*

The sky behind him, over Roaringwater and out into the Atlantic, was broken with blue, the winds calm and the seas mild. The storm had come and gone in less than an hour.

When I staggered into the pub, wrapped in a blanket, Fred was setting up a round of drinks for a small crowd of people. Standing at the bar I saw the shaggy form of Gus the German, Akio, and Magdalene. Patrick stood off to the side with the American girls Stacy and Sara. He was describing something and building shapes on the bar with his fingers. Fred saw me and started to smile, then his eyes widened and he rushed around the bar.

Jesus fuckin' Christ, Elly!

I'm sorry, I said. Please don't be mad.

I burrowed into his shoulder, and he held me, feeling my back and arms for injury. The bar fell quiet, the Smiths' "Cemetry Gates" playing on the jukebox, and I could sense everyone's eyes upon me. I felt a sudden exhaustion, like a spirit leaving my body.

I just need to lie down, I said.

Upstairs Fred hustled me down the hall into our rooms.

Let's get you in a hot shower.

I peeled the remnants of my suit off of me, the blood caked and half-dried all over my body. There was no way to hide it.

Elly? What the fuck happened?

I hit some rocks, I said.

After a shower I lay on the bed and we examined all of the cuts and Fred dabbed the bleeding spots with wads of toilet paper and taped cotton balls on the largest scratches. He was trying to be tender but his hands were clumsy and he swiped at the cuts, leaving swaths of blood. His face was loose, and he shifted from side to side. He wasn't drunk as I thought. I knew this look. He was *high;* my husband had been smoking pot with the woofers. I looked down at my body, the rising swell of my breasts, crosshatched with cuts, the poke of my hips, the soft pad of my stomach and pelvis, the looseness of my thighs. I pulled the sheet over me and started to cry again.

Oh, honey, Fred said. Please, I'm sorry.

You better go back downstairs, I said.

You sure?

Yeah, I'll be fine.

Okay, he said. Come down and tell me all about it.

He bent over and kissed me on the forehead. Laughter from the pub downstairs and the insistent wind tugging at the windows. I pulled the covers up to my chin and stared at the ceiling, blinking away tears.

They implored me to tell them what happened, so I played down any real danger because I thought that Fred was going to be upset about me doing the swim without him. The woofers were dutifully impressed, some I think even incredulous that I would attempt such a thing. The American girls eyed each other over their beers. Akio was touching my arm and saying, *no no no, don't do that.* I didn't mention the girl on the Fastnet Lighthouse or the killer whales.

Patrick was shaking his head with a serious frown. Standing among the crusty woofers and my husband, Patrick looked like an accountant who'd wandered off the golf course. He was clearly sober.

You don't want any part of Conchur Corrigan, he said.

Why? I asked. What are they doing out there?

Salvage operations, Patrick said, essentially scavenging ship-wrecks, garbage, anything that becomes lost or damaged at sea. The old salvage laws still apply around here. You leave a wreck unmanned and it becomes fair game, and few places in the world have as many shipwrecks as this area. You don't want to mess with that area around Fastnet.

Ja, Gus said. He's right.

And Fastnet sinks ships, Patrick said. Been doing it for a thou-sand years. Those rocks are littered with wrecks, Spanish galleons, tankers, military ships. A hell of a lot of personal craft, sailboats.

There's a fucking U-boat down there, Gus said, just a quarter mile west. Ships down there, stacked up deep.

And the thing is, Patrick said, nobody else can get to them. The Corrigans have laid claim to the whole area. His crew takes what they want, and nobody else gets any. Like their own personal junkyard.

The other woofers were nodding in agreement, sipping their drinks.

They saved me, I said. Conchur Corrigan, his boat, they saved me out there.

Fred put his arm around my shoulders and gave me a squeeze. It was quiet for a few moments. Rain beat on the front windows, and I looked at the hot cup of tea in my hand, the swirls of milk, and felt like I was about to cry.

Don't you think, Patrick said, it's funny how they just happened to be *right* there?

Fred slapped his hand on the bar.

Another round of shotguns, he bellowed, for Conchur and his band of pirates!

I'm sorry, I said, I gotta go to bed.

I'll come up later to tuck you in, Fred said.

Sure. Good night, everybody. Have fun.

*   *   *

I slept through the night and well into the next day, awakened by the sounds of truck horns in the harbor. My body was dotted with the tiny bandages Fred had put together, blotched with dried blood. A few of the cuts stung badly, and peeling back the tape I could see the yellow crust of infection, likely caused by some kind of toxic barnacle on Fastnet. I replayed in my mind the vision of the girl on the lighthouse, her lizard speed and staring, blank eyes. Her body had been smooth and almost asexual. Perhaps it was some trick of the weather and my vision. After a few hours of swimming your eyes will often swell, filling your goggles, and this often affects your eyesight. Conchur and the other men on the boat must have thought I had lost my mind, bug-eyed and babbling about a girl climbing the side of a lighthouse. And where was O'Boyle?

I dragged myself out of bed and surprised Fred on the computer in his office. He had his headphones on like he normally does, and when he sensed my presence he quickly alt-tabbed away from whatever he was looking at. I didn't see the screen clearly, but it was obviously some images, fleshy oblong shapes, human forms.

You okay?

Yes, I said. I don't know what happened. It wasn't that long of a swim.

Elly, you swam to the fucking lighthouse.

Just a few miles. You know it isn't that far.

And you didn't have a boat, someone with you?

Yeah. It was that guy O'Boyle I told you about.

The busker? Well, what happened to him?

Not sure. The weather got weird, got rough pretty quick. He might have lost me.

Lost you? How . . . how could you lose a swimmer in the open ocean?

I don't know, I said, but I don't think it's his fault. I was fine until about halfway, when I reached the lighthouse. Then . . . things kind of got strange.

Like how?

I don't know. I was seeing things. Things in the water, on the lighthouse.

I sat on his lap, wincing as the cuts on my waist folded and rubbed. I put my arms around him and rested my cheek on his head, rubbing my face in his hair. He was still slightly smoky and funky from the night before, and I could tell by the tension in his body that he was embarrassed. He was embarrassed about what he had been looking at before I came in.

What'd you see out there? he said.

Promise you won't make fun of me.

Of course I won't make fun of you.

Yes, you will.

I swear I won't.

I saw a girl. On Fastnet.

On the island?

Actually on the lighthouse. Like, climbing up the side?

Wait a minute, he said. Tell me exactly what you mean.

So I described to him how I felt during the swim and what I saw.

Killer whales? Are you fucking serious? *Jesus,* Elly.

They are extremely rare, I said. And there is no record of a killer whale attack on a swimmer.

That's just because the water is too fucking cold! Nobody swims in water like that except you!

But the girl, that's the thing . . . I can't understand.

Maybe an effect of light or exhaustion, Fred said. A hallucination. But killer whales . . . seriously, you have to promise me you won't do that again.

Okay. I won't.

Fred squeezed me and nuzzled my neck.

Weren't you scared?

Yes, I said. I was.

I don't know how you do it.

Me either.

You should have told me.

You would have tried to stop me.

Fred took my face in his broad hands and put his nose against mine.

No, he said. I would never do that. I would have helped you.

A note arrived at the pub the next morning, sealed and addressed to me.

E— The fulmars, bonxies, and shearwaters will be filling the skies over the Bill. The hedges will be full of nightjars. Cheers, Seb

Chapter Fourteen

The next week I took morning walks across the bogs of Ballyieragh and along the southern path to the Bill of Clear
to sit with Sebastian and watch the skies. He was there to
catch the single migratory refugee as it beat through the winds to the
island. But when I sat with him in the tussocky grass, cross-legged
and passing his binoculars, Sebastian making notes in his book, he
had a way of making me feel like his attention was never divided.
The conversation was casual, but comfortably steady, and Sebastian
mostly asked me questions. When I talked he would watch me, turning to the sky for a moment, then back, but he always let me play out
the thought until I was done.

I didn't really know what I was doing with Sebastian out on
the Bill, but I did like to hear him talk about birds. When the bird-
watchers gathered in the pub, it was impossible not to eavesdrop.
Bird names sound like the ravings of a madman. Greenshank, chiff-
chaff, firecrest, glaucous gull, teal, wigeon, scaup, shoveler, coot,
kittiwake, and black redstart. Such hallucinatory verbiage, like the
vibrant language of insanity. Sebastian had an endless supply of these
absurdities at his disposal, and he would pepper his sentences with
goldcrest, bonxie, pipit, wagtail, rook, pochard, plover, merganser,
shelduck, turnstone, ring ouzel, wheatear, crake, ruff, brambling,
and lapland bunting.

Fred had this saying he liked to trot out at gatherings with literary scholars. *Literary theory is to writers like ornithology is to birds.* It

was just another way for him to lighten the responsibility, a bullshit way of alleviating the need for an explanation while sounding profound.

Sebastian and I seemed content to respect the relative privacy of our personal lives. One afternoon as we were perched on our usual crag on the Bill, I found myself crossing this boundary.

Do you have a family?

No, Sebastian said, not at present.

Were you married?

No, he said. Almost once. But no.

Brothers or sisters?

I had a younger brother, Mick. He died a few years ago.

How'd that happen?

Sebastian ran his fingers through his hair and leaned over and inspected the grass at our feet.

Look at this, he said. Shrews.

There were a couple of tiny rodents, smaller than my thumb, tumbling among the roots of the thick grass. Their tiny pink faces came to fleshy points, their back legs spinning, crawling over each other.

He killed himself, Sebastian said. Cut his wrists in the bathroom of a chip shop.

We kept watching the shrews struggle.

I'm sorry.

He didn't want our mother, Sebastian said, to find his body. Mick was quite the famous Egyptologist and cryptographic translator, one of the best in the world. He was under a lot of pressure.

I touched his arm, and he turned away from the shrews and looked at me. I had his full face now, that cone of warm, focused attention. He gazed at me like he could do it all day.

My brother was quite a prick, actually. Our father . . . hated the little bugger.

Sebastian sighed, rubbed his hands together.

Is your father still alive? I asked.

No. My father was the sixth Earl of Selwidge. We barely knew him. He left when we were young, went to America.

What was he doing there?

Oh, gambling mostly. He lost everything. Everything he could get his hands on.

More shrews joined the band in the grass. It soon was clear that there were two factions, warring with each other, moving fast, tiny gangs fighting over turf, a patch of grass on a long field that to them must have seemed like the whole of the known world. It was a strange thing to witness on an island with so few animals. There weren't even any insects; the wind was too strong. The flightless animals that do exist there, a handful of rodents and small mammals, all evolved anchoring techniques such as special hooked claws on the forelimbs, collapsible rib cages, spines telescoping to pack the animals into shallow depressions, burrowing abilities like those of moles, shrews, and weevils. Some had spiny jackets of fur, tiny tusks jutting from their upper jaws, flattened tails that could be wedged into cracks, or prehensile tails that could grip rocks or vegetation. Everybody was just hanging on.

In the short muddy yard behind the Five Bells there was a stunted fruit tree of unknown type and origin; early each spring it would produce several odd and singular fruits, like small red apples but perfectly round and with flesh like a pineapple or some other tropical fruit. Sheila served the fruit, simply sliced, in a bowl upon the bar one night each year. The pub patrons lined up to take a slice, eating it quietly and quickly. It was delicious; sweet and subtly sour, like a mango mixed with grapefruit, and the sticky juice remained on your hands for days, no matter how much you scrubbed with soap and water. Ariel tended to the tree, the central part of her nursing involving tying long ribbons of white cotton, old bedsheets torn into strips, to the tips of the thorny branches. The tree had only a few leaves even in the warm months of spring, and the ever-present wind whipped the streamers around in circular patterns of white light, like a storm of snow trapped in a glass.

*   *   *

The next week was the first and last time I saw Patrick drunk. He glowered at a table in the Five Bells, a surly expression on his lips, his hair hanging down over his eyes. He quaffed lagers when they were handed to him but did not enter into the conversation. It was a Friday afternoon and the pub was crowded with birders, builders, woofers, boat crews, and ferry guys mixed together among the small tables and barstools. The other woofers were also drunk but trying to put a good face on things, chatting amiably. I waved to the woofers but stayed by the fire. I sipped a cup of Sheila's mushroom soup and read Cheever.

> When I'm unlucky I get drunk and go to the movies and return to Bristol. The idea is to get away from one place, but I never get away, I never reach another place. I try to struggle with the things that bind me, but I forget the nature of the bonds. I go to the movies. I get up at four and read until dawn. I do everything but the work that I came here to do.

At some point Kieran Corrigan slipped into the bar and was standing at the rail, sipping a pint of stout. Most of the patrons were bird-watchers, so there was no noticeable ripple of identification, but the woofers, most of all Patrick, certainly were on alert. He stared brazenly at Kieran, gripping his glass. The room took on the stale air of anticipation, warming and close, and people shifted uneasily. Akio put an arm around Patrick, squeezing him, whispering something in his ear. At the end of the bar Magdalene was holding Conchur's hand, palm open, and tracing his massive paw with her fingers. His hands were lined with grease and oil, his fingernails beyond recovery. Conchur stared at her, his heavy chin set, and I could see that he was embarrassed. He tried to pull his hand away, but she held on to it.

It's okay, Magdalene was saying, it's okay. My father was a mechanic. I know these hands.

Patrick murmured something to Akio, who released him and turned away. Patrick stood up, leaning a bit on the table, then made his way over to the bar where Kieran was standing. Patrick reached across and gripped the rail next to Kieran and, with his head lowered, began to speak to him in a quiet voice. If Kieran was listening he gave no indication. Patrick grew more insistent, his body lurching a bit, and Kieran stepped back, smiling now. Other people in the bar had begun to notice the confrontation and conversations died down, the patrons nearest to Kieran and Patrick picking up their drinks and moving off. Magdalene still had Conchur's palm in her hands, murmuring to him, their faces close.

Such strong hands, she said.

A mistake, Patrick was saying, his voice rising, you have made a mistake. This island could be completely self-sustaining. You know that.

Patrick was now leaning in close, shouting in Kieran's ear.

But you won't let it happen. What I want to know is why? *Why?*

The pub was now silent. Kieran stood there as if it wasn't happening at all, sipping his pint, setting it on the bar, patting his pockets and pulling out a cigarette, as if he was just a man at the pub having a drink.

You're scared of what he can do, Patrick said. You know you can't stop him.

Conchur, his eyes riveted on Magdalene, said something quick in Irish, and Kieran grunted in reply, a slight shake of his head. Then Kieran straightened up and addressed Patrick in Irish, something that sounded like a question. The other islanders in the bar shuffled and looked at the floor, muttering in Irish. Patrick narrowed his eyes and shook his head. Kieran smiled, as if he'd received the answer he wanted. He set his glass on the bar and placed a bill across the top. Then, the pub still quiet and watching, Kieran Corrigan shrugged on his coat and walked out, Conchur rising, disentangling himself from Magdalene, and following. At the door Conchur stopped and gazed across the crowd. When he found me he paused and wrinkled his eyes, nodded. *You again.* He glanced at the woofers, then back to me, giving me a quick wagging finger, and ducking his head he stepped out the door.

The woofers gathered up Patrick and took him home. They said they laid him down in his little stall in the barn, where he crawled into his sleeping bag and laughed and seemed contented.

In the morning he was gone.

The next day was a Saturday, and in the North Harbor a group of women clustered around the Holy Well of St. Kieran. They had sprigs of wildflowers in their hair and carried baskets of white crepe streamers which they attached to a dark-haired young woman in a wedding dress. Each woman took hold of the end of a streamer until they all radiated from her like the arms of a delicate ivory starfish. The sky was clear and the sun bright and hot on my skin, and the island women reveled in it, taking off their sweaters and rolling up their sleeves. Sheila and Ariel each held a streamer, as did Nora, and they chatted and laughed with each other and other islanders who began to gather. I stood at a polite distance near the Siopa Beag. I know I was a familiar enough presence by that time to cause little interest, but I was still a bit surprised that none of the women acknowledged me.

There was a shout and the creaking of O'Boyle's fiddle and the buzzing chant of a jimby, and a group of men came down the Waist road to the harbor. They were dressed in somber shades of black, coats and pants pressed, some with ties, O'Boyle wearing a black coat and scarf. A man in a suit was at their epicenter and they clapped him on the back as they joined the group of women. He was a gangly, black-haired fellow with the wide mouth and features of a Corrigan. The bride and groom held hands and the rest arranged themselves behind them, the women trailing holding their streamers, followed by the men, then O'Boyle and the hatchet-faced man, who was plying the jimby, his face as expressionless as ever, bringing up the rear. I noticed Dinny skulking about the back in a somber black coat, but he flicked his gaze over me like I wasn't there. A gaggle of young children formed a series of lines at the front of the group, and with a simple hop-step to the whirring jimby tune, they led the procession along the Waist road. Other hangers-on, islanders, a few birders, joined in the rear, so I followed as they trooped up the sloping northern road past Highgate's farm and toward the eastern end of the island.

When we reached the lowlands of Carhoona, near Douglass's Cove, the procession veered off to the left over a stone fence and through a field, the women and girls holding up their dress hems with one hand. In a small depression in the field stood a pond ringed with rock on one side. Before the pond stood two slabs of granite, each seven feet tall, about six inches thick, and a third smaller stone between them, creating a semicircle. One of the tall stones had a roughly bored hole through it, about waist high. The music trailed off, and the procession silently wound itself around the stones in a circle. A group of cows stood at the other end of the pasture, blinking in the sunlight. The bride and groom stepped forward and stood on either side of the stone with the hole. Each said some words in Irish, then they reached through the hole and held hands, prompting the crowd to break into cheers. O'Boyle started another reel, the jimby spun in the hatchet-faced man's hands, the cheers turned into a song, and the procession re-formed and trooped out of the field and down the road to the church, where the priest stood outside in his vestments, smiling broadly, his arms open.

The wedding party filed into the church and everyone else peeled off and wandered away, dispersing across the fields. I noticed O'Boyle sauntering off, playing a slow air on his fiddle. I followed him and called out his name. He spun around, his face lighting up, and I jogged to him and we walked down the gravel spillway to Douglass's Cove.

Not going in for the ceremony? I asked.

Nah. Don't go in much for the Catholics. Besides, the real ceremony already happened.

Those stones?

Yeah, O'Boyle said, Gallain an Chomalain, the pillar stones of Comolan. People been getting married here for four thousand years.

Where'd you go the other day?

O'Boyle stopped sawing at his fiddle and squinted at the ground.

Oh, geez, I was near. The swells were carrying over the bow and the engine got wet. Dinny's crap boat you know.

Why didn't you tell me?

I was yelling, he said, trying to get your attention, but you had your head down just churning away. No stopping you. I was hoping I could hold the position and you'd come by on the way back. But then the salvage boat . . . Yeah, I'm real sorry. Had to get a tow in meself. I was floating around out there for a couple hours.

Tucking his fiddle under his arm, he put his other arm around me, pulling me into his swaying mass, his funky root smell.

We still pals? I'm real sorry, El, really.

Sure. Come over to the Nightjar. I'll buy you a beer. You've never even been to our place.

O'Boyle slipped the fiddle in his rucksack and took out a bottle and offered me a sip.

Seriously, though, I said. I'm starting to take it personally.

Ah, 'fraid I don't get off the island much, he said sheepishly.

Really?

Yeah.

You know they have a ferry, leaves several times a day, goes right by here?

I pointed across to the smudge of the mainland.

Nah, he said. No ferry for me.

When's the last time you were off?

Can't really remember, O'Boyle said.

Really?

It's me home, you know.

Yeah, but don't you ever have a reason to go to the mainland? Just for the hell of it?

Nah.

I grabbed his arm.

Have you *ever* been to the mainland?

Well.

He ducked his chin and snorted into his collar. It seemed an amazing thing to me at the time, but now it makes perfect sense. There was no other world for a man like O'Boyle. All Fred and I had ever done was move from place to place, seeking out something better. Fred and I left places without a thought, then later we would have fond remembrances, wishing we were back there again. We enjoyed this greatly; it was one of our favorite pastimes, this remembering of better times, a mix of imaginative nostalgia and regret. Sometimes I think we kept moving only so that we would always have an idealized memory of a place better than where we were.

I asked O'Boyle about the hatchet-faced man playing the jimby, and he told me that it was Padraig Cadogan, an old islander who had a farm on the southern side of the island. I told O'Boyle I'd seen him here in Douglass's Cove many times just as the afternoon ferry passed, each time taking a picture.

O'Boyle sighed and jammed his hands in his pockets, kicking among the stones by the water's edge. He nodded out at the rocky outcroppings in Roaringwater Bay between the island and Baltimore.

You see that little, low hunk o' rock? Call it Gascanane Rock. Named after Amhlaoibh Gascunach Eidirsceoil, killed at the Battle of Tralee in 1234. The current is extremely strong right there, between that bit and the next bit, called An Charraig Mhór. Lotta ships gone down at that point, trying to navigate into Baltimore. The legend says that a visitor should compose a poem to the rock on the way out to the island, or else you'll founder on the way back.

O'Boyle addressed the rock with an outflung arm:

> O white breasted Gascanane, of the angry current,
> Let me and all with me go past you in safety,
> Stay calm and do not drown me, my secret beloved one,
> And I give you my word that Cleire I will never return.

Nice, I said. You make that up?

Nah, he said. Traditional.

O'Boyle stroked his chin thoughtfully.

Ought to come up with me own, I suppose. Tho' I've never actually come out *to* the island.

And what about Padraig Cadogan? I said.

O'Boyle took a long drink from his bottle and wiped his mouth on his sleeve.

Back when I was just a lad, he said, Padraig had a wife and two kids. Two pretty lassies, ginger like you. This was the winter of 1972, they was maybe twelve, thirteen. Just before Christmastime, and all the kids on the island were set on going to a party on the mainland. St. Mary's parish of Cork had a big festival with singing and treats and such, so pretty much every lad and lass on the island was lined up to go, including ol' Padraig's. His wife helped organize the thing, was one of the chaperones. So Christmas Eve all the kids get on the afternoon ferry to go over to Baltimore, thirty-six kids. Wind was up but nothing too serious, but damned if it didn't start to blow soon as they got out of the harbor. Sky went black and seas came up, no warning. Gale season is always bad, but sometimes we get storms that come out of nowhere. Donovan Corrigan, Kieran's brother, was pilotin' the ferry, a good pilot. Did the route a thousand times. Knows this bay like all the Corrigans, like a map is printed in the brain.

O'Boyle picked up a handful of rocks and started pitching them into the water.

Me mother wouldn't let me go. Didn't go in for Christmas and all that. But a good group of people was right down here, watchin' that ferry, and the sky went dark and damned if it didn't blow the boat into Gascanane there, broadside. Gutted the hull like a fish. The crew never had a chance. It heeled over and went down in thirty seconds. The seas was up to twenty feet by then in the bay, all whitewater and foam. Some say they saw some of the kids up on the rocks, hanging on. But they all drowned, every last one of them. A whole generation, wiped out in one stroke. Kieran's only daughter was out there. Mary. I knew her well. Me and Ariel the only ones who didn't go. The island never really recovered. Padraig, of course, well, he lost everythin'. His daughters, wife. Since then he's been coming out here to watch that last ferry.

*   *   *

That evening I left the Five Bells fortified with cod and chips and a pint of Murphy's and took the seawall path around the Ineer to the Giant's Causeway. I climbed up and over the boulders to the channel between the rocks where the sea fans were thick like forest ferns and starfish lay scattered, rocking in the swells. The cloud cover was light, the sun an angry glow on the water. The story of Padraig Cadogan and the drownings on Gascanane Rock haunted my heart like a shadow. Highgate's children were not on the island that day, Christmas Eve 1972. They were already on the mainland with their mother and so were spared, but this was also the day that Highgate was told that they wouldn't be coming back, the day he was abandoned by his family. He had his own private storm of heartbreak to deal with. I couldn't shake the image of small children clinging to the rock, smashed by icy waves, crying out for help that never came.

I perched on the rocks as the night came on, waiting until I felt fully adjusted, watching the vague shapes of wave crests, the bend of the horizon a faint line of green against the black sky. Fastnet was hidden behind the cliffs of Focarrig and Blananarragaun on the western edge of the bay, the light casting a faint orange swatch across the harbor mouth. The rocks at my feet were swathed in a shimmering foil of light, the effect of phosphorus, tiny organic compounds that drifted into the bay in fluorescent clouds.

The surging power of the killer whales thundering under me, the way they pushed water into bulky moving shapes, the tall black sails cutting through the water.

I didn't have to look back, up the hill toward Highgate's farm; I knew Miranda was watching me. I could feel it in my skin. As I thought of her I felt the deep pocket of fear begin to drain out of me. I knew what she wanted me to do.

*　*　*

I took off my clothes and dove in. The water felt hard and crisp and I came to the surface and swam with my head up, falling into an easy rhythm with the swells, the water flashing with each stroke of my arms. After the initial shock of the cold I could feel my pores shutter and seal and stroking out into the center of the bay I began to warm up. My whole body glowed as the microscopic organisms crushed themselves against my skin. I knew I would have about an hour at the outside before the cold started to cut the blood from my hands and feet. In two hours the delirium of hypothermia would overwhelm my consciousness with a storm of hallucinatory dreams.

I worked my way along the western wall toward the tip of Blananarragaun so I could see Fastnet and the northern seas that stretched into forever. I stayed just beyond the breaks, adjusting my stroke to resist the pull of the crashing waves. I would have to stay close to shore. That was where she wanted me to go.

I made the point of Blananarragaun in thirty minutes, the westerly breeze stronger and the pull of the current forcing me to stay dangerously close to the rocks. The spray made the going difficult without goggles, and I alternated head up and down, taking a half dozen strokes facedown in the black, then raising up to get my bearings. On the small plateau along the finger of Blananarragaun the humped shapes of seals, sleeping. Fastnet was a charcoal smudge with a red eye, the light weakened it seemed by the weight of the night. I treaded water and watched it for a moment, timing the light in my head, watching the sweeping path it created on the ocean. It was a path I had swum once, like a golden road, there and back, almost. Each rotation seemed to make the path cleaner and closer. But then I thought of the immensity of the black beneath my legs, the water that I wore up to my shoulders like a vast dress that had no bottom and no end, and I was terribly afraid again.

There could be a being out there, in the dark, moving through that space, something the size of the island itself, cruising the deeps, displacing black matter like a rogue planet, a brain stem and consciousness buried in thick tons of flesh, a ticking flicker of intelligence between the roots of continents. Or a dense pack of creatures like a silvery emulsion, writhing in fluid shapes, playing out some destiny of instinct that had nothing to do with humans. Billions, more, countless minds, working, thinking, acting, the simple contortions of cellular life, the sublime muscular flanks of whales, the plastic imagination of invertebrates, creating unknown forms.

The milky-white shapes of drowned children in darkness, their arms clutching at the shimmering air above, their silent cries.

Once the ocean was benign and necessary, and now it seemed adversarial, malignant. I was afraid. I treaded water and wept, facing the open sea.

After a while I had to back off the rocks as the current was pulling me south and west, and I decided to turn back to the harbor. My hands were tingling and I had lost sensation in my feet, my legs like kicking stumps. I worked back along the cliffs of Pointabullaun, not far from where Sebastian and I watched the migrating birds, the rocks now on my left, the flashing waves like explosions of white light. I was growing a bit tired and let myself get pushed closer to shore, figuring it would be best to get beached if I lost control of my muscles. I had knots in my forearms the size of apples and my shoulders felt like stone. I felt my jaw shuddering. I had been out too long.

There was a white shadow on the rocks to my left, a shape half out of the water, rolling limply up the slope of a boulder, then back down a dozen yards in front of me. My first thought was a harbor seal, disturbed in its sleep by my splashing and coming to investigate, and I thought it would quickly swim off below me, but the form sank into the water and then rose up in a swell, clearly inert. I didn't have time to fight the push of the wave, and I was picked up and smashed right into it, my right hand slapping on the exposed skin of its back. I shrieked and I fought to get my legs under me. I pushed away and the tender give of the skin and the shape of it up close made it clear that this was a person, a drowned body. It was a man, wearing a collared shirt, the body grossly swollen and mottled, and though he was facedown in the water I could tell that it was Patrick.

I sprinted out and around his body, fighting the urge to scream again. After a dozen strokes I turned and his body was cast back on the rocks, his limbs splayed in unnatural ways, the back humped, legs twisting in his pants like they were on swivels. His bones were clearly shattered by the constant pounding on the rocks, and as he rolled back into the water his head lolled toward me in the moonlight and his face was moving; he was trying to say something to me, as if he was still alive.

Oh, god help me. I can't do this!

I took a few strokes back toward the body, coming closer, within arm's reach. As he settled back into the water and rolled faceup, I could see that his head was covered with swarming clusters of small crabs. They had eaten away his face, filling his eye sockets and hollowed mouth.

I put my head down and swam hard for the inner harbor. My arms were gone at the elbow, my feet lost somewhere in the sea, and I began to feel the shrinking sensation of my torso shutting down. I thought of Fred at the Nightjar, sitting before the peat fire, his glass of whiskey, damp pages of notes on his lap, thinking of me.

I don't know how to explain it except to say that I found something else deep inside, beyond any other pain or anything else I had known. I would make it.

When I finally dragged myself up the mossy steps in the Ineer my whole body was shaking uncontrollably. The air, warmer than the water, felt like a hot blanket and I knew that this meant my core temperature was dangerously low. I felt my nakedness, the tingling of shocked pores dilating, and I cowered at the base of the steps for a moment. I pounded the stones with my hands until I could feel my fingers again and stalked up the steps, flexing every muscle, trying to drive the blood back into my nether regions. I struggled into my clothes, slapping my legs and arms, teeth clacking so hard my jaws ached. I knew that I had to get back to Nora's and warm up fast, and I jogged up the hill with an awkward gait because I couldn't feel my feet. I fell several times heavily on my hands and knees, but since I couldn't feel them it was like some invisible force was catching me just before I hit the ground. When the incline steepened, I set my legs apart and leaned into it, focusing on the fine gravel of the road.

By the time I reached Ard na Gaoithe, my flesh stung with fresh sweat and my face was slick, but I was still shaking and my fingers looked strangely gray and streaked with blood. The light was on in the parlor room, which meant Nora was up reading by the fire. I got through the gate before my muscles started to seize, the cords of my hamstrings going first, tightening up and popping like piano strings. I went to my knees, my stomach and back wrenching me sideways with spasms as I beat on the front door with a numb fist.

When the door opened, a pair of bare white feet, and I grasped an ankle with both hands, sobbing. I heard the voice of a boy call out, a throaty, desperate cry: *Mother! Mother!* Then the pounding of footsteps and Nora's whispered curse and I felt her hot hands on me, helping me up and inside. *Help me, boy!* I felt another pair of hands pulling at me and we were going down the hall, Nora on one side and her son Finbar on the other.

What happened, Elly? she said. Good lord, what is the matter?

My jaws felt like iron but I managed to hiss *hypothermia* through my gritted teeth.

They set me down on the bed and I rolled into a fetal position and retched and coughed up a good quantity of liquid. Finbar stood in the doorway, in his shorts and T-shirt, hair askew, his eyes wide and staring.

We have to get her warm, Nora said. Here, Finn, get a hot bath going! Bring in the heavy blankets from the hall closet.

Nora stripped me down, and because I was too heavy for her she helped me crawl into the bathroom. The tub water was far too hot and I knew I was risking shock, but I flopped into it anyway. There were a few seconds of nothing, then my numb skin warmed, the nerves adjusted, the capillaries popped wide open, and the blood that was gathered in a knot in my torso shot into my frozen limbs. The pain was excruciating, like being set on fire, and I howled like an animal, pausing for breath, then howling again, gripping the sides of the tub, scrambling to get out. Nora to her credit was unfazed and didn't crack. She planted her hands on my shoulder and hip and held me down, turning her face away as I swore and thrashed. In a minute it was over and things equalized and I could feel the pounding beat of my heart in my fingertips and toes and the water in the tub grew cloudy with sweat and the seawater ejected from my pores. I was exhausted and lay back, gasping for air.

Finbar was in the doorway, a stack of blankets in his arms. Nora was talking to me, asking me questions, but I couldn't hear anything except the throb of my heart and the roar of wind and sea. I looked into Finbar's eyes, the deep pools of blue-green, the color of the ocean in the morning, and I could almost see his brain invert itself. Seeing a woman like me, doing what I just did, completely naked and without shame, must have put a mark on that young boy, but what exactly I cannot say.

Chapter Fifteen

I spent about ten hours in bed before I could get upright and eat some soup. Nora sat with me as I ate and told me that the guard had arrived and that Patrick's body was retrieved. She sent a message to Fred that I was recovering fine and would be back soon. The word down at the harbor was that they were ruling it a suicide. The investigators determined he threw himself from the cliffs of Pointabullaun. Nora crossed herself.

The poor boy was heartbroken, she said. There was a note with the body. It was those other woofers, the cute American girls? They broke his heart.

Nora sat with me at the table, stirring her tea, eyeing me with what I thought was nervous concern.

You have to be more careful, Elly, she said. The island does not suffer fools gladly.

Patrick's body was going to be shipped back to his parents in Ohio.

In the afternoon I boarded the ferry for Baltimore and found Stephen-the-fucking-blow-in seated on the aft bench surrounded by a set of stacked crates and luggage. He gave me a grim smile and I sat with him. Roaringwater Bay was rough, and the swells rolled the boat from the side, filling the air with spray. Stephen cinched his hood down and for a few minutes we didn't say anything. I was exhausted and the brisk air felt good.

I'm done, he said finally. We are off.

Do you know who did it? To your mules, I mean.

Them's right there, he said, nodding at the pilothouse.

Two Corrigans were behind the steamy windows, one driving and the other placidly gazing down at us with bulbous eyes and wide, thin mouth.

You see that one in the cap? Eamon Corrigan. Kieran's little brother. 'E's the one, with some others. I shoulda known it would happen.

What are you gonna do? I asked him.

We got a place up in Kerry, Dingle, he said. Beautiful spot on the coast. Had to get out of County Cork. You have to go a hundred miles to escape the Corrigans.

I'm sorry.

It's okay, he said. The missus was sour on the island for some time now. It's better we go.

At the Baltimore dock Eamon Corrigan used the boat crane to unload Stephen's crates. The other passengers walked up the quay, leaving Stephen and me standing there alone. The lights were on in the Nightjar, and I thought about asking Stephen to come in for a bit to talk. I was so tired I could barely stand. Flocks of seabirds swooped in the heavy gusting winds, screaming, calling to each other. When Eamon had gingerly deposited the last crate he stood up and took off his hat and gave Stephen a bow and flourish. Then he stood and gave me a long stare. Stephen nudged me.

This is it, he said. It was nice meeting you, Elly.

He held my hand for a second, about to say something. A small truck was backing down the quay.

This is for me, he said.

Do you need any help?

No, he said. I don't. And you shouldn't besides. You'd be better off not helping.

Okay.

Be careful. You and your husband.

We will.

He stood there, hands in his pockets, sea spray in his beard, as if he expected me to say something. I found myself thinking that he never should have been out there to begin with. The island wasn't for people like Stephen. I sort of shrugged, then turned and walked up the road to the Nightjar.

I found Fred in the middle of a serious bender. I could barely walk right, the skin around my eyes and mouth was chapped and flaking, and he didn't notice. There was a line of dirty glasses down the bar and the floor was muddy. I figured he had heard about Patrick. Fred sat on a stool reading Spinoza and making notes, the jukebox playing Yaz, *Upstairs at Eric's,* at earsplitting volume. The only other person in the bar was Dinny, who sat at a table just looking at me, his white flipper hand around a full pint, a half dozen empty glasses lined up in front of him. I cranked the volume down on the jukebox.

Fred slipped off the stool and shuffled around the bar, holding out his arms like a zombie.

C'mere, he slurred.

What is wrong with you?

What? What's the problem? C'mere.

He clutched me in an unsteady embrace, stepping on my toes.

You feeling okay? he asked. Everything okay? Nora told me about what happened.

I'm fine, I said. Why is there no one here?

And Patrick, Fred said. Unbelievable thing.

I disengaged myself and held him at arm's length. What is happening? Are you pissing off the customers?

He shrugged and rattled the ice in his glass.

Nothing serious. I'm not universally liked around here. Fuck 'em. Dinny likes me.

Fred raised his glass to Dinny, who ignored him.

So you heard about Patrick?

Fred nodded.

Well?

Well, what?

You don't believe he killed himself, do you?

Fred scratched his hip and shuffled back behind the bar. Dinny set his glass down and slunk toward the door.

Later, chief! Fred yelled to him.

Dinny gave us a half wave, his chin in his collar, and tripped over the doormat out into the street. The door swung shut with a bang.

There was a note, Fred said.

But Patrick? I said. Really? You think he would do that?

The guy was eccentric, he said. He was also extremely motivated. Takes a motivated guy to jump off a cliff.

No way, I said.

I told Fred about the incident in the bar with Kieran and the other things I'd heard Patrick say about the Corrigans.

We gotta do something, I said.

But the guard was already here, Elly. They took my statements. They wrote a report, said it was closed. Done deal.

What about me? I said. How come nobody talked to me?

I don't know, Fred said. They never mentioned you. I figured they had talked to you out on the island already. They acted like they had.

Nobody— Listen, this clearly isn't right and you *know* it. We gotta call the police.

And tell them what?

About Kieran, I said. The thing at the Five Bells. The whole story.

Fred poured himself a glass of whiskey and stared at the bar with his eyes closed. My skin tingled with a clammy sweat. He shook his head.

Elly, he said, I don't think that—

Are you kidding me? I yelled. What the hell is wrong with you? Jesus, Fred. The guy was just *here,* in this bar, drinking with *you.*

I fucking know that!

He was giving me this condescending look, rattling the ice slightly in his glass, and in that moment he looked just like his father. I suddenly felt terribly alone.

I walked to the bar and picked up a stack of paper covered with his cuneiform scratching.

What the hell is this for?

It's for the book. Obviously.

He looked at me like I was an idiot. I wanted to hurl something into his fat furry face.

You actually still believe, I said, that you are going to write this stupid fucking novel? You really believe that?

What . . . what the fuck does *that* mean?

It means, I said, that you are the only one in the world who believes you will ever complete the thing. How long have you been working on that? And what have you actually written? You just pile up a mountain of shit, all these fucking little scraps of paper. But you never actually *do* anything with it.

His face faltered. I had hit him somewhere deep inside.

You don't believe I can do it?

No, Fred. *Nobody* does. You've lost it.

He picked up his glass and peered down into it.

You're wrong, he said.

Really.

I still have it, he said.

No, you don't.

I do.

You *think* you have it, I said. But you've lost it.

He bristled, the familiar look, the coming firestorm of argument, the marshaling of rebuttals. Then a tremor ran through his face, and he looked away. I had found a soft part of him and sunk the barb in deep. There was no going back from it. I returned to the island the following day.

The goats always found their order along the slanted fence, their heads held above the angular haunches of their betters before them.

They chewed and bleated and accepted the line with cloudy-eyed nonchalance. When Highgate opened the gate they filed into the feed trough, and after probing the smooth ceramic bowls with their long purple tongues they cocked their heads to allow the blind man to tether them each in her spot. Highgate used this time to inspect the goats, bent from the waist, running his hands over their faces, murmuring to them, feeling their udders, keeping a mental tally of their physical and psychological state.

This is what makes the goat, Highgate said, the most advanced domesticated animal. Their acceptance of the natural order of things. The establishment of this order is nearly invisible. It's like it was always there.

But they aren't born with it, I said. They still have to work it out.

You do have to limit the amount of extra males. But look at the order.

Highgate gestured at Angelica, the lead goat in the pack. She nosed at the feed bowl, a gray-black goat with a white saddle, a massive engorged udder.

It's adapted to milkers, he said. The best milkers lead. Angelica isn't the biggest or toughest goat in the herd by far. They have absorbed what is most important for us and incorporated it into their social instincts. Course goats have been living with humans for ten thousand years. We don't have to tell them who is the best milker. They know.

The wind howled, whistling through the chinks in the stone. Highgate poured feed into each bowl. The food was a simple mix of sugar beet pulp and silage, which kept them passive during the milking. Highgate sanitized his hands and located the buckets in the metal sink, one with cleaning solution and small dried rags along its side, the other empty and sterilized to receive the milk. He hooked the wooden stool with his foot and squatted beside Angelica and went to work. A dirty calico cat crawled under the wall and crouched at his heel.

White breeds are more placid than colored, Highgate said, at least normally. Miranda is obviously an exception. Her mother Lucy has a touch of Saanen in her. Milk genes come through the male line, and Miranda's da was an unregenerate bastard of a British Alpine, more than a hundred kilograms, seven feet tall when he reared up.

What happened to him?

We did him with a bolt gun some years ago, Highgate said. Far too dangerous. Plus he figured out the gates.

What do you mean?

The latch. He worked it out, could fiddle it with his horn nubs and mouth and get the gate open. Once one goat figures it out, that knowledge quickly passes through the herd.

Is that how you normally put down males?

Mostly use a spade, Highgate said. He mimicked an overhand swing.

A good sharp blow to the back of the neck will do it. Nearly instantaneous and painless if done well. Clearly I don't do the swinging.

Which one is Lucy? I asked.

Highgate worked the teats, the milk singing in the pail. The other goats shuffled with anticipation. He nodded at the back of the line.

The runt?

In a way, he said. But a crafty one. Another example of the intelligence of the goat is that they do not equate leadership with quality of life. Lucy is just as happy as any other goat, completely content with her lot. It's a workers' paradise.

Highgate turned the teat toward his foot and shot a few streams in the direction of the cat, who neatly caught each stream in her pink mouth, then he moved the bucket and stool down the line to the next goat.

Did the police talk to you about Patrick?

Oh, yes.

Do you think he did it? I mean kill himself.

Highgate shook his head.

Who can say. The heart of the young is a perilous place. I feel for his parents. I should have sent him home a while back. He'd been here too long. He was holding on too tight.

I thought of Miranda loping across the night fields, the way she stepped up and over fences like a man. How she watched me in the Ineer from the top of the hill. I wanted to know if it was her deformity that made her that way, or if the aberration was merely the focusing agent of her strange psychology. I asked Highgate what he thought.

He paused, holding Nai's teats over the pail, the cat obediently stationed at his heel. That strange ever-present grin, the line of even white teeth, at times seemed more like a grimace than a sign of happiness.

Miranda is the master of her own station, he said. There was a time, back when she was young. Our relationship was different.

He shot the cat another stream and then began milking into the pail.

I gave her a lot of special care early on. She was imprinted on me to some degree, followed me everywhere. Treated me like I was her mother. But when she started walking and moving across the island . . . well, it was expected.

Are you sad about that? I said. Do you wish she stayed here, with you?

Highgate shook his head.

Never. Not at all. She has special abilities, gifts. Why would I want to hold her back? I guess she is like my child, in that way. She is loose upon the world and that is as it should be. I feel for Patrick's parents. A terrible thing, to have your child pass before you.

He switched teats and pulled thin jets into the pail, the milk foaming.

I should have protected Patrick.

What could you have done?

Highgate stopped milking and turned to me.

I should have protected him. All of us. He did so much here. We could have helped him.

Highgate stood and flipped the stool against the wall, sending the cat scrambling. He picked up the milk pail and opened the chute latch.

Unhook them for me please, he said. That's enough for today.

* * *

Then I got drunk with Sebastian at the Five Bells.

I feel heavy, I said. On the earth. Sort of swollen, large. Clumsy. I don't know how to explain it.

His eyes were placid, gray-blue, unblinking. His fingers rested lightly around his pint glass, motionless. I didn't know if he wanted me to continue. I shrugged and set my elbows on the bar and drank my hot whiskey.

And in the water you feel light, he said.

Yes.

Buoyancy. Weightlessness. It is a pleasant sensation.

Yeah.

How much do you weigh?

Are you kidding? You can't ask me that.

I'm a biologist, he said. I'm allowed. In the name of science.

I looked at my hands, curled on the bar, the long bony fingers. I had wrists like a longshoreman's, corded with veins, my forearms like hams. I closed my eyes and felt the density of my bones. I was suddenly tired and wanted to fall down right there, just let myself go. I felt like I was going to go through the floor. I could still feel Patrick's slippery skin on my fingertips, the taut weight of his body. I raised my drink and downed it, which made me think of Fred for a moment, and I laughed hard and loud at this embarrassing irony.

What?

I was thinking about Fred. My husband.

Your husband is a lucky man, Sebastian said. You must be well loved.

What? Why?

He turned his glass on the bar a few reflective revolutions, fingering the condensation.

Because people fall in love with you, Elly. It's plain to see. People fall for you everywhere, people you don't even know.

I shoved him with my forearm.

Stop it, I said. That's ridiculous.

No, Sebastian said, it's not. You create love out of nothing, every day.

The next few minutes seemed like scattered images, full of sensation. Sebastian was helping me through the door, my feet like lead,
and I remember the powerful surge of stars, popping like flashbulbs
in the sky, and the roar of wind and ocean that wrapped around my
head like a blanket. I was leaning into him, enjoying the feel of his
shoulder, his hand around my elbow, my cheek on his collarbone. He
smelled like the sea, raw, and briny, or maybe it was just the air, but
it was wonderful and I drank it in. When we came around the Ineer,
that beautiful bowl shimmering with night and stars, I asked him to
go for a swim with me.

No, no, he said. I'd drown. I'm a bit tipsy, and you certainly are too.

I'd save you, I said.

He laughed.

I suppose you would.

Don't be afraid.

I was hugging his arm to my chest, our faces close together, the
wind pushing my hair over both of our heads. Below the seawall the
water thundered and trickled off the boulders. I wasn't thinking
of anything but how I wanted his body next to mine, to kiss him
deeply. I wanted to hold him in the leaping sea, for him to feel my
strength.

Too cold, he said. We'll freeze to death.

No, I said. We won't.

Sebastian looked up the hill where the faint pinpricks of Nora's
place shone, the road a faint ribbon of gray, the sedge and heather on
the black hillside shifting in the wind.

I'd die, he said. I'm not like you.

I fell into his chest, my face on his neck. I remember my lips
under his chin, the smell of lime and wool, the faint stubble on his
face. I held his lapels in my hands, bunching them in my fists. I think
his arms were around me, at least it felt like they were. I can't be
sure. I may have only imagined what I had played out in my mind
a hundred times. It was quite familiar to me by then, so I would
not be surprised if I was fooled by my own longing into thinking
that Sebastian embraced me that night, rather than merely bracing

himself against my lurching body or gingerly holding me off in a gentlemanly fashion.

The next few minutes are unclear, but we were walking up the hill. I remember feeling the burn in my legs, and when I looked up the road, it seemed as if it pierced the night sky like a glowing arrow, as if it passed into the stars.

Then we were at Nora's gate and I was sitting on the stone wall, feeling sick and leaning my head between my knees. Sebastian was standing in front of me looking out over the fields.

What the fuck is *that*?

Sebastian pointed up the hill to Knockcaranteen and the wind turbine, his face screwed in confusion. I got to my feet, and I could see that he was pointing at a tall, loping figure, coming down the road toward us at terrific speed, a hundred yards and closing. It throbbed and contorted with unknown motion, but it came on fast and I clutched Sebastian's arm and screamed, partly in terror but also partly in relief that this confrontation was finally going to happen and that someone was there with me. We huddled by the road as she came closer. But she was moving too fast, something was not right, the movement was too smooth and at twenty yards I could tell it was not Miranda. It was Finbar Cotter, shirtless, standing on his pedals, pumping his bike down the road like a ghoulish apparition. He flew past without a glance in our direction, his thatch of hair slicked back with sweat, his torso ropy with ribs, tendons, and blue veins, a steady *creak creak creak* of his crankshaft the only sound. When he hit the crest of the next hill, the road down to the Ineer, he folded into a tuck and dropped like a stone into the black void.

Bloody hell! Sebastian said.

I sat down on the wall and hid my face in my hands. I felt terribly sick.

A light in the house came on, from the upstairs, Nora's bedroom. My scream must have woken them.

I have to go, I said. Thanks for the drinks.

I went in the door without looking back and felt my way down the dark hallway with both hands, dragging my fingertips along the paneling, knocking down the series of framed Irish Tourist Board posters which fortunately did not shatter on the carpet. I locked my door with the skeleton key and got in bed, taking my clothes off under the duvet. I heard some creaking of footsteps in the house, the front door opening, more creaking of stairs, then silence. There wasn't anything to do. I didn't feel that I would be hideously embarrassed in the morning. Rather I was thinking that when I saw Finbar coming toward us I did not think of Fred. I did not wish he was there with me. In fact I wanted no one else there more than Sebastian.

Chapter Sixteen

Fred was using a small cave along the southern cliffs that led to the old beacon as his smelting site to make the metal for his Time Travel Wish Fulfillment project. In the morning I made a couple bacon sandwiches and a thermos of coffee and brought it out to him. He spent most mornings at the site working on the project before the pub opened. At this point I didn't even know what he was making.

The cave he'd selected was really just a shallow depression a couple yards deep where Fred had located some veins of iron ore and he determined it would be easier to smelt it on-site using a small furnace he'd built with stones as opposed to dragging it off somewhere. The process also created a lot of heavy, rank smoke that wouldn't go over well in town. You could smell it from a quarter mile away, and the black smoke swirled in the heavy sea winds, pushed against the cliff face and driven in every direction.

That morning Fred was outside the cave sitting on a campstool, stripped to the waist, staring at the glowing furnace, his upper body striped with soot. Dinny Corrigan squatted on a stack of firewood reading a thick paperback novel. Pickaxes and hammers were propped against the cliff face with a wooden box of charcoal bricks, a stack of limestone rubble, and a small blanket with gnarled nubs of black rock.

Fred stood and took the sandwiches and coffee gratefully, tossing a sandwich to Dinny, who acknowledged me with a nod before returning to his book. I sat on the ground next to Fred and watched the furnace while he ate. It clearly was not going well.

The reducing agent, he said, isn't working properly. We need coke. This charcoal won't cut it. I've already tried several types of peat. I'm changing the project, anyway.

Yeah? How?

Gonna make something else, something more practical. A fire-arm. A gun.

Dinny chuckled, and we both stared at him for a moment. Fred shrugged.

Easier to do, he said. Don't have to worry about the electronics. I can't build a circuit out of this shit. Better choice anyway. If you were to go back in time.

The day was clearing, the sky rolling back to the east and creating a pristine expanse of sky over the Atlantic. A crowd of seagulls so thick it created a shadow bunched over the water just off the cliffs; a pod of whales perhaps.

I'm gonna go back out to Clear, I said. While the weather is holding up.

Sure, Fred said. I got things to work on here.

Come with me. The weather is perfect. We'll have a picnic.

Fred gazed at his furnace. Dinny watched us carefully, his white flipper hands held as if in prayer. A few wispy ropes of scar tissue climbed out of his collar.

That would be nice, Fred said. Dinny, watch the furnace for me? Another few hours, then just bank it down. Tomorrow I gotta locate some sulfur.

Dinny nodded and went back to his book.

We ate cold pasta and drank two bottles of white wine on a grassy bluff overlooking Pointabullaun, my favorite view of the Atlantic and Fastnet. It was hard to pull my gaze away from it.

I still can't believe, Fred said, that you tried to swim out to that fucking thing.

Can we not go back to Baltimore? I said. Just stay here?

I wish, he said. He pried up a piece of shale and stood and whipped it off the bluff into the water below.

So, he said, I called the police yesterday.

What?

I reached up and pulled him down by his belt loop.

Yeah. I told them everything that you told me. I told them . . . we don't think Patrick committed suicide.

What'd they say?

They said they'd create a file and look into it.

Did you say anything about the Corrigans?

Sort of.

Was there . . . any reaction to that?

Hard to say. Probably nothing will happen.

He lay back on the grass and I rolled over and grabbed him around his middle.

Hey, I said, I really appreciate that.

I put my cheek against his and we watched the sky, the tall grass rushing around us like fire.

You know how when you are a kid, Fred said, how it seems like life is just an unending series of moments like this?

I'm not sure what you mean.

You are always having to leave places, he said, to do something else. Whatever it is that you are doing, whatever it is that you want to keep doing, it has to end. And it ends for reasons that don't make any sense. Like, why *do* we have to leave? Ever?

The blue bowl of the sky was endless. Like lying on the bottom of a pool, a thousand feet down and looking up.

People have jobs and things, I said. Responsibilities.

Still. What would that be like if you were a kid and instead of being yanked away from everything you actually could just stay? If your parents just said, okay, we'll stay? Always?

That would be pretty excellent, I said, I have to admit. But you'd quickly be vagabonds. Hobos wandering the streets.

Fred propped himself up with one arm and looked at me. The wind tore at his shaggy hair.

Seriously, Elly, how hard would it be? I mean for us to be able to always stay, and still lead some semblance of a normal life? You mean we couldn't figure it out? Bullshit. It could be done.

Well, that would likely be one spoiled kid.

Maybe, Fred said. Or maybe he'd be the most well-adjusted kid in the world. One that never knew the constant, needless defeat of his desires. Instead of a long series of failures he would know only the joy of contentment? Is that possible?

Maybe. It would help to be rich. Really rich.

Exactly, Fred said.

He lay back on the grass and put his hands under his head. I snuggled into his armpit and closed my eyes. I could see it coming.

We could do that, Fred said. What if . . . if Ham comes through with that money, like he says . . . we could do it.

I tried not to stiffen or give some sign of alarm. I thought of deep blue water and sky.

Wouldn't that be something?

Yeah, I said. It would.

I mean, if we had a baby.

Yeah. We'd have to actually have the baby, first.

Do you want to?

God, I don't know. I know that I don't want to have a baby because Ham wants us to.

Me neither. But I want to anyway.

It's not just the money?

Oh, Elly. Of course not. That's just extra. That just makes it easier.

You don't even know where he is, I said.

Oh, I do, Fred said. I can see him right now. He's swimming in a pool of water in the sky. He is tall and beautiful. A redhead like you.

I meant Ham.

Oh.

I mean, we don't know what is going on, with Ham. Where he is. True.

Or if he'll have any of that money. It seems to come and go for him, right?

Yeah, Fred said. Probably a bad idea.

The sun was warm on my face and I closed my eyes and let them soften to fiery orange. The waves crashed on the rocks. The wind twisted the grass into insistent shapes. I held on to him.

When Fred and I first moved to Burlington I taught swimming lessons at the YMCA as something to do and a way to augment our income. It was Fred's idea, trying to help me use my natural talents for some kind of potential career. Teaching small children, the Water Babies classes, was the most unnerving and difficult for me. Not difficult in that they had trouble learning to swim, as they often took direction and were less afraid of the water than older kids or even adults, but there was always that desperate fragility in their persons that I could not shake. I would hold them on the surface with one hand, their glistening bodies twisting and thrashing, their enormous bean-shaped heads, brawny little torsos, and spinning red limbs. I didn't know how to talk to them so I mostly gestured and demonstrated by pantomime, which seemed to effectively hold their attention. Perhaps they were mesmerized by the odd sight of this woman, gesticulating and moving her arms, like some kind of silent clown act. I have never known how to deal with small children, but it was more than that. Their innate density and power, like a small sun, a compression of so much life, seemed to me like a dangerous, weighty package. A baby seemed like the opposite of space and broadly disseminated life, like the inverse of the open sea.

Chapter Seventeen

Kieran's guesthouses and the new pub were nearly complete. The grounds were churned with thick black mud, the builders skulking around smoking cigarettes in the shadows of the various construction vehicles that were scattered like the husks of dinosaurs. They watched me walk by with an unsettling concentration. I gave them a tight wave but nobody blinked. The tall, narrow guesthouses formed a line that nearly bisected the Waist, the pub and restaurant abutting the road and cutting off the North Harbor from the Ineer. They were painted the bright colors favored in rural Ireland—deep reds, a royal blue, lemon yellow—and they were staggered at different heights and with different façades to give the impression that they were built in different decades, with tall casement windows, heavy oak doors, and faux slate roofs. The pub had a wide, double-door entrance, and there would be a large restaurant area, a wooden deck that overlooked the Ineer and also had a vantage over the North Harbor for cookouts in the summer. A gazebo in front would hold an ice cream stand for tourists. They wouldn't have to trek all the way up to Highgate's farm.

Nora stayed upstairs or in the parlor, not greeting me at the door. In the morning we had painfully cordial exchanges as she served breakfast.

Why don't people like us here? I asked her. I mean Fred and me.

She was standing in the doorway to the kitchen and I immediately regretted asking. She was one of the few islanders who treated me kindly, and I didn't want to lose that. I owed her for what she did for me the night I found Patrick's body.

You don't know, Elly, she said. That's not how it is.

Nora maintained something like a smile. She kept looking back into the kitchen, as if checking something on the stove.

You're right, I said, I don't know anything. I'm just trying to understand.

You shouldn't worry about this, she said. I'm afraid I've got the kettle on the hob. Do you need more toast?

I can't seem to get a straight answer, I said. Only a couple of people will talk to me. Some people are real friendly, like you of course, but still, there's this feeling. I can't explain it. It's bad in Baltimore, with Fred. Nobody comes to the pub.

Her face worked and her eyes drifted away to a spot over my head. She didn't want to say what came next.

We keep to our own kind, she said. Just the way of things.

But you helped me before. You know me.

Please don't ask me about this. There are some things that cannot be explained. There are things about this island that even we don't understand.

She turned away and went into the kitchen.

Standing in the road in front of Nora's I saw a man perched in a window in the old lighthouse up the hill. He was wearing a long coat, and what surprised me most was that I didn't think you could get inside the lighthouse as the entrances were all gated and locked. His face was behind a giant camera lens levered on a hunk of stone, pointing in my general direction. I figured that he was a birder, likely trying to get long shots of Fastnet. I waved to him. After a moment he raised his head from the camera and held up a hand. We stood there for a few moments, our hands raised. I turned and went down the hill.

Clear had always felt lonely, but now I desperately wanted to see a kindly face. I crossed the western plateau and through the boglands to O'Boyle's caravan. His new house now had three standing walls, a washbasin, an old bureau, an expensive-looking leather arm-chair, and a gleaming stainless-steel gas barbecue grill in the yard. But still no roof. Smoke puffed from the chimney of the caravan so I took the path down into the gentle depression in the bog. Across the way by the northern cliffs, toward Dún an Óir, I saw another figure, standing in the waist-high bracken, a black silhouette against Roaringwater Bay, watching me approach. Another birder? It was not Miranda, I could see that right off. When I stopped and shaded my eyes she quickly turned and I could tell it was a young woman. She disappeared behind the rise toward the northern cliffs.

O'Boyle was lounging on the couch in a pile of blankets and drinking tea, sleepy and content looking. There was the close, sweet aroma of bodies.

I saw a girl up on the hill, I said, to the north. Wearing a cloak?

O'Boyle leaned forward to pour me some tea. He was a bit sweaty.

Ariel, he said. Havin' a cuppa wit me.

Really.

Yah. Nice lass. Known her since she was a babe.

How old is she?

Oh, she must be something like thirty-five by now.

That's impossible, I said. She can't be a day over twenty. She looks like a teenager.

Clean livin' I suppose. Island living.

Wait, how old are you?

O'Boyle grinned and stood up, slapping his belly. He was wearing an old flannel shirt and gym shorts, and his erection was painfully obvious.

Thirty-nine, he said.

I stood up and stared at his face. It was worn, but unlined, the skin taut, his eyes rounded and bright. I didn't believe him and I told him so. He shrugged and scratched himself and ambled into the kitchen. Perhaps his sense of time had become warped because he never left the island. Perhaps an island year was a different unit of measurement.

Ariel was born here too?

Oh yah, O'Boyle said. She goes back, well, back as far as I do, that's for sure. Our people . . . have known each other for many centuries. More tea?

He was taking something that looked like dirt out of a small pouch and pressing it into a tea diffuser. The kettle was whispering on the hob. The caravan rocked with buffets of wind. I looked into my cup. There were bits of flotsam and I could dimly discern a small pile of twigs on the bottom.

No thanks.

Your man Fred still in the cave, working at the forge?

Yeah, how'd you know?

Dinny told me.

Really. Didn't know that guy even spoke.

Not much, O'Boyle said. But he comes around, has a can or two. He's a good lad all considered.

What happened to him? I mean his hands, the scars.

O'Boyle slouched on the couch and frowned into his sagging belly. A thin patter of rain rang on the sheet metal roof of the caravan.

An accident, he said. On the salvage boat.

Conchur's boat?

Yeah.

Was there a fire?

O'Boyle shrugged and stared into his teacup. We sat there for a few moments listening to the rain.

Dinny used to be a talkative chap, O'Boyle said. Talked plenty. Sometimes . . . he talked too much. He used to work the ferry, other jobs on the mainland.

For Kieran?

Yeah. One day, 'bout four years ago, Kieran puts him on Conchur's crew. They head out the first day. They had a couple boats then, smaller ones, and Dinny was driving one of them, him being Kieran's nephew and all. That night his boat comes floating into the South Harbor, all afire. A ghostly sight. It just drifted in, full of flames, and beached itself on the rocks. Dinny was still on board, alive. They didn't find him until after they put the fire out and drug the boat up. He was badly, badly burned. I was there when they pulled him out, blackened and arms and legs drawn up. Looked like a burnt spider. Hands, legs, most of his body. A real mess. His boots were melted to his feet. Some kind of accident. The rest of the crew got off on Conchur's boat, but Dinny was trapped belowdecks.

O'Boyle sipped his tea, swallowed.

'E never said much after that.

That night I slept fitfully, everything seemed uncomfortable. I lay in bed with the mental image of a tangled knot of springs and wires, all twisted and straining around some central force, the whole spiny mess about to explode and fly in all directions.

The Spring Regatta was held every year in April to mark the beginning of the tourist season on Cape Clear. The Ineer was packed tight with yachts and sloops from all over Europe, and in the Five Bells they were four deep at the bar, the stone patio serving as the dance floor, and O'Boyle and a few others played all hours of the day and night.

Fred closed the bar and we came across on the sailboat with Bill and Nell. We had a thin stream of people coming through on their way to the island, stepping in to have a pint while waiting for the ferry. But they didn't stay long.

Fred had assumed a consistently belligerent manner with customers, as if each one who came in was a kind of intrusion. On the bar he had long, narrow hunks of iron ore, and in between pulling beers he was trying to bore out the barrel. In a large bowl-shaped stone he had powdered charcoal that he was grinding with a piece of granite, the handle wrapped in seaweed. A wooden box held chalky hunks of sulfur that made the bar smell faintly like rotten eggs. In the alley behind the bar he had a six-foot pile of manure mixed with potato peels, leaves, and other food refuse. Twice a week he went out and poured a bucket of his urine over the mixture. In a few weeks he'd be able to extract the potassium nitrate, or saltpeter, to complete his gunpowder recipe. None of this was helping business, but Fred didn't seem to care. He shrugged off anything I said about it, maintaining that we only needed to hang on until the summer season. His book would be finished, he said, and he could devote himself fully to the business. I didn't believe him.

By this time we were lucky to have sex more than once a month. In the beginning of our marriage Fred was so desperate for me that he would actually pine and beg for my naked body, to have his hands upon me, to be inside me. Now we mostly had brief, awkward encounters, mechanical in tone, that seemed to make Fred more relieved than anything else. I did not fake or overplay my enjoyment of these acts, and Fred seemed fine with this as well. I wondered if he had grown tired of my body, that what had attracted him to begin with was the strangeness of my size and shape, and after time I merely became ugly to him. I would lie in bed at night, Fred snoring beside me, and touch my arms and stomach, feeling my skin, the thousands of tiny bumps. I didn't know how it felt to him.

That heat Fred had for me, was it displaced somehow or alleviated at some other portal? I never felt for a moment that Fred would cheat on me with another woman, rather I suspected mostly that he was cheating with himself. I do not know which is worse. There is a lot to be salvaged in being displaced by a fantasy, a memory, a projection of the mind, rather than an actual person. But I was a real body, here, waiting, and to be left aside for a thought was another kind of unpleasantness that is difficult to consider, now, after all that has passed.

It was a bright and sunny day, though the winds still tore through Roaringwater Bay. The boats that made the journey actually under sail, as we did, did so reefed and lashed, and Fred scrambled about the foredeck as Bill bellowed commands from the cockpit. I hadn't been on the sailboat with them in a while, and Fred attacked lines and rigging like an old salt, hauling away and swinging around the halyards, grinning at me like a fool. Some part of me was reluctant to have him on the island. Clear had become a kind of private kingdom for me.

We had chilled oysters with hot sauce and great mounds of Sheila Flaherty's potato salad, apparently made without mayo or mustard, bound together by some other ingredient I could not name. The Five Bells patio was a babel of languages, the yachting set in their linen pants pouring liberally from magnums of champagne, birders with their lenses askew across their chests, imbibing, always with one eye to the hillsides. Fred slipped off with the woofers and came back goofy-eyed and chatty, massaging my neck and telling me how much he loved me. I watched Bill, one arm clamped around Nell, the two of them beaming as they watched the furious activity of the harbor at sunset.

There were several especially large sailboats drawn up at the quay, and people sat on chaise lounges on the teak decks with cocktails and glass bowls of peeled shrimp. A three-masted schooner at the far end of the dock flew a large American flag, the deck oddly empty. It was the same sailboat that we'd seen anchored behind the Calf Islands when Bill attempted to sail us out to Fastnet. I saw a tall man emerge up the steps from the cabin, adjusting a camera bag and putting on a pair of sunglasses. He turned to take in the scene up the hill, and the afternoon sunlight fell on his face. Sebastian. He stared for a moment, but I do not know if he could pick me out in the crowd.

Later in the Five Bells we got drunk with the woofers. I was tired and sort of half listening to their talk, watching the windburned tourists at the bar feeding each other drinks, resisting the urge to go outside and walk down to the Ineer to see Fastnet. Fred, Gus, and Magdalene were bent over a scrap of paper. Fred was making a list with a pencil, tallying a set of numbers.

This guy owns a chain of pubs, Fred said, all through County Cork. I'm talking like forty pubs. He loved the stuff. The cheeses especially. People love the organic thing. They may not give a shit in places like Baltimore, but in the cities it's all the rage.

No way we could produce that, Gus said. Too much.

See, this is how you do it. You give them everything you got. Then if it sells, they will front you the money to expand. A kind of partnership.

Are you serious? Magdalene said. Is this real?

It was Patrick's idea, Fred said. I just happened to meet some of these guys through Murphy's. I think it could work.

The American girls, Stacy and Sara, were whispering to each other. They looked sorrowfully drunk.

Stacy put her arm around her friend in consolation, and I realized in that moment that it hadn't been Patrick digging out an unattainable romantic vision of love, rather it was Sara who had fallen for *him*. The girls held hands and looked into their empty pint glasses. They still thought that he killed himself. I wanted to reach out across the table and touch their faces, say that I was sorry. I wanted to tell them that Patrick did not kill himself, that he did not throw himself off the cliff. I know this because I was in the water that night with his body. I was there because he had to tell me.

After midnight we were in the Five Bells on the bench by the fire. I was nearly asleep, resting my head on Fred's shoulder. Fred was still high and lecturing the woofers on some matter of Herman Melville. *There are some enterprises in which a careful disorderliness is the true method.*

I felt a touch and Ariel was standing there, one of her gecko fingers on my wrist. She could stand beside you and you would still not know she was there. It was as if she had no discernible presence, until she wanted to. She gestured to the patio outside.

You should see this, she said.

We all tumbled out onto the near-empty patio illuminated by sputtering tiki torches. The band was winding down, clearly exhausted, and the only pair on the dance floor was Bill and Nell, dancing a rather formal waltz. The moon hung over the waters of Roaringwater Bay like a watch on a chain, the streak of buttery light stretching into the harbor mouth.

He does it every year, Ariel said.

Her globed eyes flashed in the torchlight. The song ended and Bill went over and engaged in a short discussion with the band, and they nodded and smiled and took up their instruments again for one more. As they began to play Bill took his wife into his arms and held her close, Nell burying her nose into his chest with obvious delight.

I forgive you,
'cause I can't forget you
you've got me in between
the devil and the deep blue sea

It's their wedding song, Ariel said. Every year he has it played for the last song.

We watched them stagger along the patio's edge, two people who spent so much time in each other's arms.

Ariel sighed and hugged her thin arms. It isn't often you see a love like that, she said. It's a rare, true thing.

The woofers wandered away, despondent, crawling under the hedges to sleep. Fred put his arm around me, cigarette clutched in his teeth. He was golden from the sun and wind, and his teeth were strong and white in the moonlight, and we watched the old couple stretch out that moment. Bill and Nell were really lost in each other, edging around a few square feet of flagstone, and as the song ended Bill bent over his wife like an aging willow. They were lucky people. I turned to say this to Ariel, but she was gone.

I am grateful that Bill and Nell got to share such a moment, over and over, that brought the past and present together with such sincerity and joy. I wish I had the words to tell it.

The wind shifted and brought the smell of cattle and bramble wrapped in the salty Atlantic, the smell of the west. I could feel it on my back, the warm wind of America, coming across all that expanse of blue, a breath or exhalation, and the remaining pockets of illumination slowly faded out, all the cities of America, in the house of my parents, Fred's father, in the homes of everyone we ever knew.

Fred chucked away his cigarette, angrily. His eyes were wet with tears.

That has to be, he said, the most romantic fucking thing I've ever seen in my life.

The days began to warm, and the howling wind turned to the steady pounding gale that was springtime on Cape Clear. Fred went back to Baltimore to open up the pub and I spent another few days on the island to swim. I promised Fred that after this I would spend more time at the Nightjar to help with the spring crowds that were due to descend upon us. It was a struggle, however, and I spent much of my time circling the Ineer, an eye to the open ocean, or sitting on the seawall watching the slender line and flash of Fastnet. Each strobe of the light was like a heartbeat. There was something so attractive about swimming such a long line in deep water, all that open space on every side. The sensations of my body, that tiny speck of gristle moving in its spasm across such a vast space, gave me a feeling of incredible power and utter insignificance. There was great comfort in this. Maybe it's like a kind of reverse astronomy, the inverse of stargazing. This is something Fred would have been able to put a name to.

I could feel Miranda up on the cliffs, watching, and one evening I saw her standing on an outcropping, her white hair whipped by the wind. I held up a hand, but she only turned and disappeared into the heather. I knew what she wanted me to do. But I just couldn't do it.

A few days later when I got off the ferry in Baltimore and came up the quay the air was thick with nightjars soaring through the dark, silent as moths. They came up from the harbor in waves, sweeping up the street and rising at the last moment over the storefronts, working through the streetlights and signs with a few turns, searching out the insects. Fred was hosing down the floor and squeegeeing the water out onto the sidewalk. He was humming some kind of Irish tune, bobbing and shuffling his bare feet. Under the streetlights I could see he was still smudged around the neck from his forge and his shorts were stained with black handprints.

Put that down, and come out here for a second, I said.

I put my arms around him and kissed him on his furry face and he murmured his appreciation. He was drunk, with a three-day musk on him.

Look, I said, pointing at the birds flashing in and out of the light. Our namesake.

Fred squinted into the lights, hands on his hips.

Nightjars, I said. They're feeding.

Ah.

If you look close you can see the mouth gape, I said. They can unhinge their jaws, almost like a snake, fly wide open and funnel the insects right in.

We watched their graceful turns and quick arcs, their long tails rippling with each quiet beat of their wings. Fred looked out over the harbor, the faint lights of Sherkin, shimmering.

Who told you that?

About nightjars?

Yeah.

I read it somewhere. They also have special feathers that allow them to fly without sound.

Fred put his arm around my waist and gave it a squeeze. We stood there quietly for a few moments and watched the birds swoop and feed.

That's pretty cool, he said. It's a good name for a pub, either way.

Yeah, it is.

I love this place, he said.

I know.

It's like a new world, he said. I don't know what I would do without it. I think maybe the Nightjar saved me.

It's our world. It saved us.

I love you, he said.

I love *you*.

Not as much as I do.

Oh, I think you are wrong.

Fred turned me in his arms and we rubbed noses.

No, my husband said, this is one thing I'm sure about.

We clutched each other in the hallway, shuffling on the floor, Fred kicking over a stack of books as he fumbled with my shirt buttons. His breath was hot and sharp with whiskey, his beard scratching my neck and chin. I clutched at his broad back with both hands. I wanted to lie down and have him loom over me, to fill me entirely, to blot out the world. On the bed he peeled off my jeans and buried his head in my crotch, and I saw clouded shapes in my head. Something was forming, a shape gathering in the dark knot of Fred's hair as he clutched my ass and put his tongue inside me. I was dreaming of an animal, an animal rising up between my legs, as Fred was putting my knees over his shoulders and entering me, his eyes wide and mouth hanging open. I shuddered with the fullness of him, cried out, and pushed myself up to meet him. I grabbed handfuls of his chest hair, put my fingers through his beard and into his mouth. I felt swallowed up, as if I was being consumed by an epic force, and warmth spread up my spine and took my brain in its hands and held me, carefully cupping me like a small bird. I held on to him.

Chapter Eighteen

O'Boyle was sitting on the edge of the quay, his fat bare legs dangling, sandals hanging from his toes. I crawled up the slick steps, stripping off my goggles and cap. He grinned at me and swigged from a can of Old Peculier.

Oi, a good one?

Yeah, I said. Good time.

Stayin' in the Ineer these days?

Yeah.

I stretched my arms over my head, bending side to side to loosen up. I had finished a few quick laps across the inner mouth of the bay, just enough to saturate me. I wrapped myself in a towel, and used another to dry my hair.

Like a drink? O'Boyle said, pulling another can of beer from out of his pocket.

No thanks.

He cocked his ear for a moment, like he was listening to something, then sighed and looked at his hands.

I have to ask you something, he said.

Yeah?

You've seen her, he said. The one who walks Highgate's fields at night?

You've seen her, too?

You know . . . where she lives then?

He gave me a shaky grin.

Where she lives?

Yeah, O'Boyle said, Highgate hasn't . . . he hasn't shown you where she lives?

He tried, I said, but she didn't want to meet me yet.

I opened my gear bag and took out my jeans, sweater, socks, and shoes. I sat next to O'Boyle to dry my feet.

But, you have a general idea, yeah?

Why don't you just go ask Highgate?

O'Boyle crumpled his beer can and kicked his legs on the quay, looking down in the water.

'Fraid I can't do that, he said.

Why not?

Highgate doesn't like me much.

Really?

Yeah, well, the dogs definitely don't like me.

Why not?

O'Boyle stood and cracked the fresh can of beer.

You wanna come back to the van for a smoke?

It was still early, not even noon, and the clouds were streaming in from the sea to the west, low and purple, which meant heavy rain.

You have anything to eat? I said.

I make a wicked grilled cheese. Plenty of lager.

The rain thrummed on the roof of the caravan, the shifting wind causing the plates and glasses on the table to wobble. I picked at the crusts of my grilled cheese, made with heavy soda bread and hunks of Irish cheddar. The ground outside the window was already a giant mud puddle. His new house now had the skeleton of a roof, a door cutout, and a small wooden gazebo to one side. Through the door you could see a sodden leather armchair and an iron bed frame with an ornate scrollwork headboard. The barbecue kit in the yard had an orange sheen of rust. O'Boyle tidied up around his hot plate, washed his hands, and handed me the glass pipe and lighter. He was such a slovenly fellow, yet remarkably fastidious in the kitchen. The hash in the pipe looked like tiny squares of chocolate, but it tasted like deep earth.

You've spent a lot of time with Highgate, eh?

A bit, I said. He's an interesting guy.

That he is.

What's the problem?

O'Boyle stretched and shrugged.

Usual blow-in stuff, he said.

The smoke pooled on the roof of the caravan in shifting shadows. The gas lantern on the table began to fluctuate and flicker, and I knew that I was getting high.

Like what? I said.

You know, mainlanders comin' in and trying to change things. Thinkin' they know how the island should be run.

But Highgate is running a fucking organic goat farm! I exploded. You of all people . . . I would expect that you would be supporting such a thing.

O'Boyle swilled his beer.

It's not that, he said. Sure, the organic farming thing is fine. But Highgate has a way of getting people stirred up. He thinks he knows how things are supposed to be.

But, who cares?

This is an old place, O'Boyle said. Older than any other part of Ireland. This is the first giant's tear, the first to rise from the ocean. There are things here that are older than any of us.

I couldn't help but laugh. O'Boyle looked cross.

I'm sorry, I'm sorry. I think I'm high already. I got it, older than all of us, the giants, I got it. But really, you're talking about Kieran, right?

The flickering light showed only half of his generous, ogre face. He smiled wanly, and put the pipe to his rubbery lips.

Tell me about him, I said. And about you.

Why?

I want to know.

If I do, will you take me to her? If I tell you everything?

Miranda?

Ah, he said. Miranda. Yes, Miranda.

I slouched down in the chair and squinted at rain spattering on the window. The light in the room seemed to be draining out, and I was having trouble thinking. *Do me a favor,* Highgate had said. *Keep Miranda a secret.* Why? What did it matter?

But I don't know where she lives, I said.

You have a good idea, yes? A general approximation? You can show me?

Tonight?

Yes.

Why?

Because we can help you. Because I'm going to tell you what you want to know. Now listen.

O'Boyle's mother was a woman known simply as Maeve, who in her final years lived in Coosadoona, in the ruins of the Dún an Óir, the Castle of Gold. She was known in her youth as a great beauty gifted with an ethereal singing voice. For many years she had assisted islanders with herbal remedies and sung strange airs that no one could identify at weddings and funerals. She was unmarried when she gave birth to O'Boyle, and she never identified the father. Just before the birth she received a visit from Father Cadogan, a stately man much cherished by the parish. An hour later he fled her rude hut with his cassock torn and cursing under his breath.

Soon after O'Boyle was born, Maeve began to drink, starting at daybreak and continuing until she collapsed in the ashes of the hearth, the mewling baby latched at her breast. She began to rant and claim that she talked with the spirit of her sister who had died many years before. Maeve's sister had wandered off from her cottage when she was a teenager, and was missing for a month. A group of islanders, led by Kieran's father, finally found her in a cave on Blananarragaun cradled in a nest of auks and storm petrels, her skull picked clean.

Maeve said that her sister came to her in daytime dreams dressed in a white shift, the collar ringed with blood, a screaming blizzard of snow in her wake. Her sister told Maeve the future. Her visions always contained ashes and smoke, fire, raw earth, deep tombs of rock, and always death, but not the transfiguration of a watery death, a passage through to some other state, the prevailing vision of death on islands like Clear, but rather the eternal tomb of the soil.

At some point in her madness Maeve seemed to forget her son was there. As a toddler O'Boyle roamed the cliffs and shorelines like a feral animal, scavenging for bird eggs and tubers. He took to lurking outside the pub, ferreting through the garbage and listening to the traveling buskers through the window. The island women eventually gathered the boy, and an old woman named O'Boyle who lived on the exposed moorland of Ballyieragh on the western cliffs took him in. O'Boyle took this woman's name and she left him her cottage and land. Flat broke and without a vocation, O'Boyle sold the land to the Corrigans soon after his mother's death and took up living in the caravan.

A few months before Maeve died she locked herself in the old castle, refusing to come out or to take visitors. She said that her sister told her she must die there. When they finally broke in the door after many weeks of silence, they found her moldering in the corner, covered in a fuzz of mossy toadstools. On the castle walls she had scratched with chalk in letters a foot high:

Insa Chonair chlúthair ar thaobh na gréine,
sea a dhein Ciarán Naofa ar dtúis a chill

In cosy-sheltered Comar on the sunny side,
Holy Kieran first built his church.

Then in English she had written:

A brave vessel, who had, no doubt, some noble creatures in her,
Dashed all to pieces. Oh, the cry did knock against my very heart.
Those blown in on the easterly winds, they will sink them all.
The blind priest, animal spirit, the cliff walker with cloven feet,

Night swimmer, who watches the drowned and the yet unborn,
All will lament as the great eye is swallowed by wind and water.

I was drowsing on O'Boyle's reclining chair, the caravan dim. As he talked, his dark shape hunkered over the table, I had half dreams of fish people in the waves of the Ineer, elfish children scurrying around Fastnet Rock, I saw Highgate standing on a windswept cliff, inches from the edge, his arms outstretched to the sea, the giant turning arms of the wind turbine above him. The drumming on the roof had stopped, and the only sound was the gurgling, ticking noise of the island draining, the water pouring through the vast honeycomb of limestone bedrock. The air in the caravan was fetid and close and I asked O'Boyle to open a window.

What time is it?

Just past four, he said.

Really? Was I asleep?

No, he said. I've been talking a long time.

Do you mind if I take a nap?

O'Boyle got up and brought me a bottle of water and a thin wool blanket. He spread the blanket over me, tucking it under my chin. I was warm, and the chair felt unbelievably soft. My muscles felt like melting butter.

What about Kieran? Aren't you going to tell me about him?

Yes, I will. And then we will go.

I was rapidly falling into a quiet hole, my body letting go. I closed my eyes.

Where?

O'Boyle's voice sounded like it was coming from far away, like it was echoing down a long tunnel.

To Highgate's, he said. To see Miranda.

I had a dream that I was lying in a shallow pool, a muddy bottom, with twigs and leaves floating in the brackish water. There was an intense pressure and my stomach began to twist and swell, growing larger, and I sat up and gripped it with my hands. It was perfectly round like a snow globe, and inside I could see a rounded bay, like the Ineer, full of beautiful blue water, ruffled to whitecaps in a gentle wind. In the water were hundreds of moving things, swimming at the surface and below, and as my stomach grew I could see that they were faces, human faces, all paddling and stroking around, moving among each other in a kind of choreographed mix. They were all tiny children. Then the figure of a man rose up, an old man in a cassock with a wooden cross on a leather thong around his neck. He waved his hands over my stomach and everything went black.

I awoke in the dark, lying in my bed at Nora's. I was in my underwear under the covers and my body felt sore and wracked like I had swum for miles in heavy chop. A shadow crouched by the bed, and by the smell and the breathing I could tell it was O'Boyle. He was crying. I sat up.

What? What is it?

Oh, Elly I'm sorry, he blubbered.

What?

He wiped his face on his arm, rubbing it back and forth like a dog.

What did you do?

You never meant anything, O'Boyle said, you never meant anything but goodness to me. I knew that once you saw her out on the rock. We knew you would come.

What are you talking about?

Fastnet, he said. You saw her, on the tower. Elly, I'm sorry but it was the tea that first time. You wouldn't listen to me. The second time . . . I couldn't save you. Nobody could. But she was protecting you. Otherwise—

You drugged me? I said. Why? Why did you do that?

We had to do it, he said. You don't understand. You don't know what he can do.

O'Boyle stood and shuffled to the door. When he opened it the

light from the hall revealed his face wet with tears. He was covered
in mud and brambles, his pants torn.

I'm sorry, he said. You never meant anything but goodness.

In the morning I packed up my bag and walked down the hill to
the South Harbor. The ferry wasn't due for another hour, so I sat
on the seawall of the Ineer and watched the swells roll in and push
themselves up the stones. I wanted to leave, to get back to Fred and
the Nightjar, to take a long shower and then sit downstairs at the
bar with him, a cup of coffee, and his scribbling, listening to music
we both loved. I couldn't bring myself to go back up the hill and to
Highgate's farm.

Time passed, and in the North Harbor the ferry came and went.
Why would O'Boyle want to find Miranda so badly? Had I led him
to her? I would at least go see Highgate, make sure everything was
okay. Maybe it would be nothing, and I wouldn't have to tell him
what I had done.

I know how this sounds, now. I'm not proud of it.

Highgate seemed happy to see me. He had been out in the fields
tending to the new kids and his fingers were cramped up with cold
and we sat down in the living room to warm up. I stirred the peat fire
and adjusted the damper.

Wonderful to have you here, Elly, Highgate said.

I was dunking a biscuit in Akio's milky-weak tea when Gus burst
through the front door.

Ravens, he yelled, the fucking ravens!

Highgate leapt from his chair, hands tucked in front of him like a
boxer. The dogs were already at the door, setting up a low whine, hair
raised. Highgate moved to the door, and by the time I got outside he
was sprinting down the back fields to the sea, the dogs flanking him.
The sun had broken out of the clouds for a moment, and the air over
Roaringwater Bay was dazzling. At the first fence Highgate took

a few long strides then stepped up and over, cut right, and headed north, skirting the heavy section of undergrowth and bramble. He must have counted the paces to the fence. The old man was *moving,* outpacing the dogs through the heavy grass.

We hustled after him, and when we came around the bramble rise to the north field Gus drew up, pointing into the sky. Heavy black shapes moved in slow concentric circles, broad-winged ravens, a couple dozen or more descending and ascending like a silent black funnel to the ground. The wind shifted and howled, impossibly hard, and I instinctively put my hands to my ears, and the harsh overcast sky and bright colors made everything lose focus and telescope like a flickering filmstrip: white flashes on the ground, Highgate in his parka glistening wet in the patches of sunlight, the dogs leaping around him. A kid struggled on its side, its face a gory mess of blood and bone. Gus shouted something to me I couldn't hear in the buffeting wind. Highgate knelt on the ground, his hands searching the goat's body. The dogs kept a tight circle around him, their eyes pinned on the cone of ravens that screamed and banked over the blind man's bowed head.

Gus and the woofers worked quickly to gather the other kids and got them back into the barn. Back at the house I waited in the living room while Highgate and the woofers disposed of the body. I could hear them murmuring in the kitchen, something like a prayer. Highgate shuffled in and joined me on the couch, kicking the stove with his bare feet to determine if it was hot. I scooped some peat out of the bucket and arranged the flue.

Sorry you had to see that, he said. It is a rare thing.

How can you stop them?

You can't, he said. You can only hide the kids, hope the mothers protect them. The problem is that the ravens work in pairs; one distracts the mother while the other goes after the kid. They always attack the eyes, blind them first, so they don't know where to run. But a whole flock . . . that just doesn't happen.

He took off his hat and ran a hand through his white hair.

They are harbingers, he said. It's been many years since they've come. The old islanders called them the messengers of woe. Something else is on its way.

What?

The stove hissed as the draft was sucked across the coals. Highgate set his tea down on the table with a rattling hand and turned his sightless eyes to me. He looked genuinely afraid.

I had a sudden image of O'Boyle, standing among broad leaves and engorged blossoms, the sky a cloak of glistening stars. It wasn't like a remembrance, more like a scene played out in my mind. He was in a small valley with heavy vegetation, and I could smell the intense odors of foxglove and ragwort, the musk of goat. O'Boyle turned and said something to another figure standing nearby. A woman, wearing a large man's coat, her long hair wet and hanging down the back, her hands shaking. There was no wind, and the powerful animal smell hung heavy in the air. I could hear the faint plink of water dropping into a pool. I couldn't see her face.

It was me.

There were others there in the dark, other men moving around us.

You need to go, Highgate said. Get back to Baltimore, your husband. I'm afraid they are going to come for you, too.

He knew.

The wind rattled the phone booth behind the post office. I had to use my flashlight to see the numbers on my phone card and to dial the sixteen-digit number to reach my parents. A man answered. His voice was strangely electronic, and for a moment I wasn't sure if my parents had gotten a new answering machine. But then the voice paused and was obviously waiting for an answer.

Hello? Dad?

Yes? the voice said.

It's me, it's Elly. Can you hear me?

There was a cloud of static and then the line became clear. It was my father.

Something terrible happened, he said. Your sister . . .

More static like an electronic sea.

. . . done it to herself like that. We don't know what to do. Your mother . . .

Hello, Dad? You're breaking up.

My mother got on the phone. She was crying.

Hello, Elly? Oh, my goodness, you wouldn't believe it. Have you been watching the news?

No, Mom, what's going on? What happened to Beatrice?

Your sister . . . hospital yesterday, but no one really knows . . . fires across the river and the smoke you wouldn't believe . . .

Mom? Are you guys okay? Is everyone okay?

Yes, yes, she said. Don't you worry. We're fine.

PART III

A POEM

My sense of morality is that life is a creative process and that anything that chafes and impedes this forward thrust is evil and obscene. The simplest arrangements—trees, a line of bathhouses, a church steeple, a bench in a park—appear to have a moral significance, a continuity that is heartening and that corresponds to my whole sense of being. But there are speculations and desires that seem contrary to the admirable drift of the clouds in heaven, and perhaps the deepest sadness that I know is to be absorbed in these.

⊗⊗

We rise from sleep all natural men, boisterous, loving, and hopeful, but the dark-faced stranger is waiting at the door, the viper is coiled in the garden, the old man whispers lewdly to the boy, and the woman sits at her table crying.

⊗⊗

How the world shines with light.

The Journals of John Cheever

The final event of the contest, the poetry reading, took place at the Old Crown and Anchor in Cork, a giant pub with a stage and seating for a hundred. The three finalists stood on the stage along with the president of Murphy's, who was wearing an improbably green stovepipe hat. The first three rows were taken up with media and the podium had a dozen microphones sprouting from the front like a bouquet. Fred was glowing, seemingly expanding every moment with power. He was in his element. Fred always had the ability to transmit emotion in a glance or steady gaze. It was part of the secret to his strange charisma.

The others had come to the podium clutching sheaves of notes, sweating and mouthing their memorized lines. Fred bounded up and swept the crowd with eyes that shone like a funnel of light, over the guests, other contestants, the judges, until his eyes rested on me. He paused a moment, swallowed, his eyes softening slightly.

Shy one, shy one,
Shy one of my heart,
She moves in the firelight
Pensively apart.

She carries in the dishes,
And lays them in a row.

To an isle in the water
With her would I go.

She carries in the candles,
And lights the curtained room,
Shy in the doorway
And shy in the gloom;

And shy as a rabbit,
Helpful and shy.
To an isle in the water
With her would I fly.

He was reading it to me. I wanted to reach out across the room and hold him. I could feel his heart steadily thrumming in my ears like the sea.

The day following 9/11 Fred retreated into his office with a few bottles of whiskey. After he didn't come to bed the first night I knocked softly, and when no one answered I opened the door. Fred was in his underwear, huddled at his computer with his headphones on, rocking back and forth, making a strange low moaning sound. The only light was the flickering blue of the computer screen. The desk and floor were covered in paper; Fred had taken his novel manuscripts out of their boxes and strewn them all over the room, as if he was looking for something. I closed the door and went back to the bedroom and crawled into our bed.

I didn't see him for three whole days. There was evidence in the kitchen, food left on the counter, empty bottles, that he emerged sometimes in the night. I figured I would let him go. On the fourth night he woke me when he crawled into bed. He was naked and urgent for me and we made love quickly. Afterward we lay on our backs in the dark, listening to the whir of the ceiling fan, the house settling.

Duncan Avery is dead, he said.

I know. It's terrible.

It should've been me.

It doesn't work like that, I said. If you are to blame for his death then we are all to blame. For all of them.

How?

Every decision can be traced forward to some tragedy. You know this. The world doesn't end at our fingertips. We affect the world every moment.

Fred turned to me and put his lips against my ear.

I can't shake it, he said.

You will. You have to.

Something will happen. Something good.

We will make it happen.

I hope so, he said. I . . . don't feel alive.

I wrapped myself around him, pressing us together.

You are alive, I said. You are here with me. And I am so grateful for that. If it had been you . . . I'm happy it wasn't you.

It feels wrong, he said. To be happy that it wasn't me. It feels wrong to be alive.

The next morning Fred got up early and burned all of his writing, his novels, everything, in the fireplace. I was awakened by the smell, and when I came in the living room he stood in his bathrobe before the fire as the flames roared up the chimney. The heat was incredible, and Fred's body was slick with sweat, his eyes bloodshot. Outside charred paper and flaming bits of pages fell like snowfall, catching on the trees, falling in the yard, drifting out over the lake.

Fred! What are you doing?

He tossed in a fat stack of paper and the fire whooshed and sparkled.

I never had a real story to tell, he said. Until now.

He walked over to me and kissed me on the forehead.

I'm fine, he said. It's over.

Then Fred showered, shaved, put on a suit, and went into his Burlington office.

A few weeks later his father Ham came buzzing low over the trees in his seaplane, looking for a place to land. Within the year we would be living on the Irish coast, an outpost at the end of the world.

The afternoon after the incident in the school bathroom I met my sister Beatrice at her car for a ride home like usual. Her face was sullen, inert, in a sort of frozen state, and it was so striking that I was scared to speak and we drove home in complete silence. When we pulled into the driveway, Beatrice asked me to wait a moment, still holding the wheel, staring through the windshield at the garage door. Finally she turned to me and in her face, just for a second, I saw an expression of such sorrow that I had never seen up to that point in my life. It was a look of mourning, as if she had been abandoned here, alone. Then covering her face with her hands she burst into tears. Beatrice leaned over and I held her as she sobbed in my arms, but she would not say what had happened to her.

That evening at dinner she had to be asked twice to pass anything and she stirred her pasta around her plate. Her presence made us all feel clumsy and irritated.

What on earth is the matter with you? my mother said with a note of exasperation in her voice. Will you please straighten up?

Go to hell, Beatrice said, her face calm. *All of you can go to hell.*

The next morning at swim practice my teammates doggedly stripped down to their suits, staggered out onto the deck, cursing the cold tiles, the cold water, the coming hour and a half of toil. I had slept little, but everything seemed in sharp focus, the fluorescent lights casting us all in stark relief, standing at the pool edge, our sleepy coach scratching a workout on a portable blackboard. The other girls huddled together, arms crossed, sullen-faced, shivering. I flung myself into the air and attacked the water. Our coach always worked us hard but I went at the timed sets like a frantic machine, coming in way under the interval, lapping the other swimmers in my lane, slapping at their feet so they would get out of the way and if they didn't I swam over them. At the end of the last set I was panting like some kind of hysterical animal, my chest heaving, my skin blooming with flowers of blood, and my arms felt hard as iron. My coach knelt by the pool in his flip-flops, his jeans wet to the knees, and gave me a small pat on the shoulder. Everyone else was out of the pool, standing there, looking at me. My goggles were fogged but it didn't matter; they looked like ghosts on the edge of a deep wood. I was fifteen years old.

I went down and pushed off the wall and dolphin-kicked halfway across the pool and exploded into butterfly, tearing through a two hundred. I finished hard into the wall and immediately vaulted out of the pool as I could feel my muscles about to seize. I was crawling on all fours on the tile in a world of smoke. On the deck there was a white bucket with a twenty-dollar bill in the bottom. If you filled the bucket you got the money. I grabbed the rim with both hands and heaved everything I had. My body was convulsing, and I buckled over into a fetal position, my bladder spasmodically releasing. I covered my face with my hands and wailed. An indoor pool is a world of echoes, and the sound was deafening. I didn't care about anything.

You see that? my coach said.

He was standing over me, addressing the rest of the team.

That's what it takes, he said. To win. *That* is what's required.

Until now I have never told anyone other than Fred the story of what happened to my sister, or how her life seemed to spiral away from her that day. Her last year of high school was a calamity of conflict, long hours of shouting at my parents, a sudden change of friends, quitting the field hockey team, staying out all night. Her face became hard, her voice cold and sarcastic, and she bickered with me over nothing at all. For so many years all I wanted was to be more like her. All my young life I had lived happily in her shadow. And then she drifted away to a place I couldn't find. It was like a great light had gone out, and as I moved into adulthood the world seemed cast with a silver glow, rippling like water, something always slipping furtively away just out of the corner of my eye.

Beatrice began bartending in ski towns and waiting tables at summer resorts, and rarely called our parents, who became like lost birds, wandering around the house in a daze, unable to comprehend what they had done.

Two years after she left home, when Beatrice was twenty, she called my mother one night, laughing hysterically into the phone, to tell her she was pregnant. It was well after midnight, and I heard the strident tone in my mother's voice in the kitchen. I crept out of my bed and watched her shout into the phone from the darkened doorway, the echo of my sister's tinny laughter filling the room.

We didn't hear from her until four months later. She called late at night again, and this time I answered the phone. She kept pausing to talk to someone else who was there with her. In the background I could hear music and shouting, the clink of glasses.

You all should be happy, Beatrice said. You all got your way.

What do you mean? I said.

The baby's gone, she said. Done.

What? How?

Don't be an idiot, Elly, she said. I lost the baby. Had a fucking miscarriage.

She covered the phone for a moment and I could hear her arguing with someone.

Do you even know what that is? she said.

Yes, I said.

You don't ever want it, she said. I wouldn't wish that shit . . . You *don't* want it.

There was a crack in her voice and she covered the phone again.
Beatrice?
A muffled sob. A woman screamed with joy in the background.
Yeah.
Are you okay?
Oh . . . fuck, Elly. Listen. I gotta go.

Heartbreak is often described in stories as something like getting hit in the chest with a heavy object, a kind of blunt trauma of the heart. For me it is more like the furtive scraping of a branch, as if someone were digging around my ribs, poking about looking for something soft to stab. A finger rattling around my spine, unexpected but always present, like a dry cough. Its touch is dead-dry and without feeling, like something without a human concern, the passionless expressions of lizards and stone.

The man who died in Fred's place fell from the eighty-sixth floor of the World Trade Center. Duncan Avery clung to the smashed window frame with a group of people until the heat became too intense. He spoke with his wife on his cell phone just before he fell. He told her that he was sorry but that he had to let go.

The Averys lived in Jersey City with their three small children. His wife, Marie, was a pediatric nurse who one Christmas gave us a baby blanket she'd knitted, the pattern a pale green shamrock on a field of blue. It was shaped like a lopsided hourglass. Fred had it folded neatly in an old seaman's chest. Marie told Fred she hoped that it would bring us luck, that it would bring us healthy children.

Chapter Nineteen

The builders came in first, skulking off the street, the rain running off their clothes. They spread out around the room, a couple by the fire, a few others drawing up to the bar. Fred poured them lagers and they sat in their squinty groups, sipping their beer and muttering in Irish. We had a half hour till closing and we didn't have any other customers. Fred went back to reading while I went in the kitchen and made up a couple of turkey and cucumber sandwiches. I had an hour of Patty Griffin in the jukebox, the entire *Flaming Red* album, and in the kitchen I heard the steady thump and swing of "Tony" warming up as the door opened again, the sound of rain and the sea, then silence again save for the music.

When I came into the main room there were two men in ferry gear, one of them Eamon Corrigan, standing inside the door, shaking off their wet jackets. Fred set his book down and stood behind the bar, smiling gamely, waiting for drink orders. I set the sandwiches on the bar.

What'll it be, gents? Fred said.

The Corrigans looked around for a moment, taking in the surroundings. I put my hand on Fred's arm.

Hey, I said to him, I think we ought to—

One of the builders at the bar reached over and flipped the plate of sandwiches across the room, shattering it against the wall.

What the fuck? Fred said.

I had an idea that maybe we could back out into the kitchen, lock the door, escape into the back alley. Eamon Corrigan stepped forward, his survival suit crinkling. He had that wide, gap-toothed Corrigan smile of a child, his black hair wet against his forehead.

What? Fred said. What is it?

Fred's chest was heaving, his breath coming fast. Eamon muttered in Irish, and a builder at the front door flipped the open sign around, and turned off the main room lights. The only light came from out of the kitchen and Fred's reading lamp behind the bar. The builders gathered around us.

What do you want? Fred said.

The door opened with a whoosh of air and water, and Conchur stooped under the doorframe. Water came off his oilskin trench coat in sheets, and he took off his hat and scratched his head with a distracted air, as if he had just come in for a beer. When he saw me he gave me a nod and an almost apologetic expression.

You left your big anchor at home, mate, Eamon said. Now you are *fucked*!

Then Conchur came across the room and Fred and I stepped back, but Conchur shot a hand over the bar and had Fred by the shirtfront. I grabbed Fred's arm but Conchur yanked him forward, dragging both of us across the bar. A couple builders peeled me off my husband, pinning my hands behind me.

Conchur held Fred at arm's length, the entire front of Fred's T-shirt balled in his fist.

Get off me!

Fred twisted and wrestled with Conchur's wrist.

I'll call the fucking police!

Fred took a long, looping swing at Conchur, clipping him on the chin. The builders squeezed my arms tighter.

'E wants a bit, does 'e? one of the builders said.

Fuckin' blow-in, Eamon Corrigan said. You and the blind man, a couple of goat-fuckers, are ye?

I'm gonna call the guard! Fred yelled, his face wild with fear.

Eamon stepped behind Fred and swatted him across the back of his head.

You stupid fuckin' Yank. We *are* the guard!

Stop! I screamed. Please!

Conchur grinned at my husband, gathering more of his shirt into his hand, getting him tight, and drew a fist back by his ear.

You ready for this, mate?

I remember the sound of the rain drumming on the windows and Patty Griffin singing, the sour beer smell of the pub, how the light from the docks outside glistened on the yellow survival suits of the Corrigans.

Then Conchur hit Fred square in the face, crunching his nose, and my husband groaned and tried to turn away, putting up his forearms as Conchur began to repeatedly punch him, even and steady like a piston, hitting Fred in the eye, the forehead, the temple, the ear. He dropped him to the floor and Fred curled up, trying to protect his face. I began to struggle with the builders holding me. I probably outweighed both of them, but they had hard, cruel hands, practiced to violence, and they cranked my wrists behind my back until I was on my knees, crying out in pain. A shadow hurried by the front windows. *There were people just outside, going on about their business.*

I began screaming. Conchur knelt and straddled Fred, pinning his arms down with his knees. Fred's face was a smear of blood and saliva, his cheeks and forehead blotchy red and swelling. Conchur began to smack him hard with his open palm, side to side. Fred was crying as he turned his face away from the blows, an awkward gasping sound I had never heard my husband make before. He looked at me for a moment, and in his eyes I saw his anger and frustration, and behind that, something larger and more hurtful to us both.

When they left I crouched on the floor cradling his head as he covered his face and wept. After a while he stopped and I looked at his face, lightly touching the swollen parts, and he asked me if it was bad and I said no, it wasn't so bad. He asked me if I was okay and I said I was fine. Then he said he didn't want me to look at him anymore, so I turned away.

We locked up and went upstairs. I stood outside the bathroom as he washed his face, not knowing what else to do. I heard running water, then the small grunts and gasps as he dressed his wounds. I thought of him standing at the sink in his underwear, fingers of dried blood matted in his chest hair, his eyes in the mirror. What was he thinking, what did he see there? I would never know.

Are you okay? I said through the door. Can I help?

No, he said. Please, let's not talk about it.

Okay. I'll be in the room.

I lay in bed in the darkened room, and after a long time Fred came out, holding a damp towel full of ice to his face. He stood there a moment, his silhouette against the hall light.

Do you want me to turn on the lamp? I said.

No, he said.

He got into bed and arranged himself carefully on his back, still holding the ice to his face. I moved over to him and he put his arm around me and I rested my cheek on his chest. Fred gave my back three little pats, like he always did.

What are we going to do? I said.

Nothing, he said. Let's just sleep.

The next day when Fred went down to open up the bar I sat at his desk and watched the fog burn off Baltimore harbor, the moored boats emerging one by one like returning sentinels. On the computer was a list of dozens of folders containing hundreds of files with fragments of language, poetry, soliloquies, titles, names, locations, long screeds about religion, culture. I clicked a couple.

You have no idea what loneliness is. Consider the Galápagos tortoise, June of 1937. A tortoise nosing its way around the island falls into a deep rocky crevice, getting wedged facedown. Moisture collects at the bottom in a pool, inhabited by a weedy mold and blind amphibians, so the tortoise is able to remain nourished. A Galápagos tortoise can live for more than a hundred years. That tortoise is still down there, facedown in the black. No one knows that he is there and there is no hope of salvation. He can only eat and survive and think his lonely turtle thoughts, long grasses, the sound of wind, the dream of being naked in the sun. Get ahold of yourself for fuck's sake.

If you had a million years it wouldn't matter. Be glad you don't. Giving cut flowers to another is such a powerful expression because they will die, very soon. Put them in a nice vase, give them water and light and perhaps stroke a stamen or two at midnight. They will die knowing they meant something, and that is all we are trying to do here.

Take solace in this; your cares may not be original but they are universal. And seriously, which is more important?

You know when you have the image of something in your mind, but when you go to do it you can't make it right? It just doesn't match up? There is only one problem in this life and this is it.

One folder was simply labeled "Images." I opened it. Inside was a series of pictures, a long sheet of thumbnails, images of figures, human figures. I didn't really want to see the particular species of pornography that my husband was so absorbed with, but I clicked on one image anyway and it expanded to show the edge of a building, a black-and-white photo, a cluster of people in the windows, and a blur of movement halfway down, out in the white space of the sky. It was a woman, her skirts billowing, her arms slightly bent and gesturing out, like she was holding an invisible dancing partner.

They were all pictures of people falling. People falling from buildings, bridges, many falling from some unknown source, the picture just of a body in the air, in flight. The first grouping was a series of photos from something called the Triangle Shirtwaist

Fire, grainy black-and-white photos of women jumping out of windows, their faces composed, most clutching their pocketbooks, some chastely holding their skirts down as they jumped. Most seemed determined to land feetfirst, as if they would dust themselves off and walk away. Others were more contemporary, people falling from suspension bridges, a whole series from the Golden Gate Bridge, the Eiffel Tower, skyscrapers, the burning towers. I scrolled through the thumbnails for a minute, but there was no end. There were thousands of them.

Downstairs the bar was empty, sunlight pouring in the windows, the jukebox blaring Neko Case. Through the kitchen I could see the back door open and Fred in the alley, sifting through his manure pile with a rake. He was shirtless, a pair of baggy shorts, barefoot, and the hair spread off the top of his chest like flames. He carefully lifted a bucket and poured urine over the mound, singing along.

Does your soul cast about like an old paper bag?

Out in the street Kieran's builders were jackhammering the sidewalk, the street full of lorries and dust. It was an impossibly sunny day. The builders followed me with their ferret eyes, a small knot of Corrigans on the quay, shopkeepers, tourists, it seemed everyone was watching, waiting to see what I was going to do. I ran down to the ferry pier to the pay phone and called my mother. I entered my card number and the call connected, but there was no ringing, just a strange dull buzz. After a few moments I heard a voice on the other end, distant and faint. Hello! I said. Is it you? The phone booth was vibrating with sound, and I gripped the receiver, and pounded on the glass. I couldn't hear what they were saying. It was a voice that sounded like my mother, but it could have been anyone.

Chapter Twenty

Fred was determined to stay open, and he didn't hide his injuries from anyone. I wasn't sure he was going to be able to bear it. He threw open the doors to the Nightjar and stood out on the sidewalk, his face a swollen, scabbed mass of purple. One eye was nearly shut, the whites of his eyes streaked with blood, his nose cracked, and the nostrils stuffed with bloody wads of gauze.

Only a few weeks left till summer, he said. If that is the best they can do, then we'll make it.

Bill came over as soon as he heard, and the two of them commiserated together at the end of the bar. Bill was clearly upset, and they had a whiskey together. I drank hot tea and rubbed Fred's sore neck. He had a hunk of black walnut behind the bar that he was whittling into a stock.

Look, Bill said, I live out there, with them. I can't get into this.

No problem, Fred said. I'm making my own gun anyway.

Bill forced a barking laugh, and Fred scowled at him. He didn't understand that Fred was serious.

Keep the chin up, Bill said. All will be well.

He finished his drink in an uncomfortable silence, muttering excuses, had to get back to the island, Nell, et cetera, and as he left he gave me a look of consolation.

I'll be back, Bill said. Count on it.

*   *   *

After he left Fred set his whittling down and searched the bruises on his face with his fingers.

Why is it, he said, that the only friend I have is that old hack?

Don't do that. Bill is a good person.

And then there's Dinny, Fred said. Good old Dinny. Barely said a fucking word to me. Probably best friend I got.

When I looked at his face a kind of resentment took root deep inside me. I wanted to let it go and merely be in love. It seemed like so many miles and years had passed since I wept in front of open, raging fires, shaking with desperation and desire for his presence. Where did that go? How does a love that strong and demanding abandon you? I watched him grimacing as he touched the blackened and swollen parts around his mouth, and what I felt then burrowed into my heart like some groping mechanical parasite, spinning in the scoop of flesh, building a hard shell around it, putting in anchors.

There's me, I said. I'm your best friend.

He dropped his hands and his face softened into a close-eyed smile. C'mere.

I went behind the bar and stepped into his arms. I kissed his face lightly.

We're gonna make it, he said.

Can we sell? Can't we sell the place and get out of here?

I'm not leaving, Fred said. Not yet.

He turned away from me.

But we can just *leave,* I said. That's what they want.

Do you want to go?

I didn't know what to say. The truth is I didn't. Despite everything I still felt there was something left to do.

I'm gonna take care of it, Fred said. I promise. Please. I need this.

I wasn't sure if I trusted him. His inner chamber of secrets was deeper and larger than I had imagined, and I felt shut out and deceived.

Okay, I said.

*   *   *

In the late afternoon Fred closed up the bar and we went for a walk up to the Baltimore Beacon. On the streets everything seemed to proceed as normal, the usual blank faces and empty stares. Nobody said a word to us.

The old Baltimore Beacon was a nesting place for nightjars, and at dusk the air was thick with their silent winging, a vortex of them circling the pointed peak. They began to roost there more than a hundred years ago, when the beacon was lit by an oil burner refracted through glass, drawing insects from all points as well as ships, and the nightjars still began their evening feeding there, a fruitless hour of trolling the windblasted bluff before they turned en masse and headed for the lights of the harbor, marking their passage with their mechanical trill, a call more like an electric vibration than a living song. During the day they clustered about the base of the lighthouse, small lumps of mottled gray blending with the lichen-covered rock. When you stepped near them they emitted a short croak and then unsteadily took to the air. If the insects are plentiful and available, the nightjars will feed until they are gone, gorging themselves to the point of exhaustion, and they drop out of the sky like furred stones. The nightjar will literally eat itself to death.

We sat on a thick tuft of grass overlooking Roaringwater Bay and passed the flask back and forth, Fred grimacing as he sipped through his scabbed lips. Off in the west the low horizon was lined with black clouds a hundred miles across.

Looks like a gale, Fred said. Just what we need.

Beyond Sherkin the hazy image of Clear glowered in the fading light. I thought of Highgate walking the cliffs, sniffing his way. Was he looking for Miranda? Did he know what I had done?

These storms, Fred said. Every day is like a new world out here.

He squinted into the sun and tipped the flask.

When I was out there swimming, I said, near Fastnet, it changed so quickly. The water, the sky, everything. Like the closer I was to the lighthouse, the worse it got.

Remember that sailing trip, Fred said, with Bill? That was crazy.

Yeah, just like that.

Do you think Highgate has something to do with this?

With what? Conchur and those guys?

I don't know, Fred said. Do you think we just got caught between them? Highgate and Kieran?

I knew exactly what he meant but didn't say anything.

The woofers are always at the Nightjar, Fred said. I helped Patrick with supplies. He just wouldn't back down from Kieran. And then I basically told the guard that we think Kieran had him killed. It wasn't just about the farm, Patrick was protecting Highgate. You know his wife and kids left him? He found out on Christmas Eve?

Below us on the rocks the gulls were screaming, beating their wings, preparing to take flight. Fred offered me the flask but I waved it off. He shrugged and took another pull, wiping his mouth on his sleeve before continuing.

Patrick said something terrible happened that day, that Highgate felt responsible.

My heart spun in my chest and I ripped up handfuls of grass.

The ferry, I said.

What?

That's when the ferry went down. A huge storm came up, real quick, while the Corrigans were taking the island children to a Christmas party on the mainland. The ferry hit the rocks by Douglass's Cove. They all drowned. Kieran's brother, his daughter. O'Boyle and Ariel hadn't gone—they were the only kids on Clear.

My god, Fred said.

I know.

He took another drink and again I waved it off. The narrow jut of land that we sat on seemed to thin and the sea dropped away to a great distance, like we were perched on the edge. Was it getting darker? Some kind of rising horror was placing its cold palm on the back of my head and I shivered, my skin flexing and tightening. The drowning children, this tragedy following Highgate's heartbreak. As if his sorrow made the seas rise up in consolation. In the Five Bells Patrick had said that Kieran was afraid of Highgate, *afraid of what he can do*.

I leaned into Fred and held on. How could that be true? How

could Highgate have done it? As soon as this thought flickered across my brain I had an unsettling feeling that someone was watching over my shoulder, just out of sight, like when Miranda watched me swimming in the Ineer. I knew that if I turned I would see someone, but not Miranda. I didn't know who it was. I was afraid to look.

Fred was silent and we sat for a moment watching the setting sun over the water. He turned to me but I couldn't look at him.

I want to tell Ham we want the money.

Oh, Fred. I don't know.

Look, if we have the money we can do whatever we want. We can start over, or go somewhere else. We can do it right this time.

But, a baby? I said. We . . . can't do that, not now.

Why?

The sun was melting into the horizon, falling next to the rounded hump of Cape Clear. The trail of light traced its way past Clear, Sherkin, through Roaringwater Bay and to the cliffs of Baltimore. For a moment the water had that familiar, comforting look, like if I could hurl myself into its depths I would find solace. I thought about Miranda, swaying on the hillside, her hoofs buried in the soft grass, the wind tossing her mane and tickling her beard. Watching my small shape, thrashing about in the Ineer, swimming to Fastnet.

I can't, I said. Oh, Jesus, Fred. I can't do it.

Fred drained the flask and coughed. He had tears streaming down his face.

It doesn't matter, he said. Fuck it. What does it really matter?

The next morning Fred was working on the flint ignition mechanism for his handmade gun. The metal tube that he had forged in the cave was lying on a piece of cloth. He'd managed to get a smooth bore and had a rough stock and handle carved and bound with metal staples ready to attach. His shaggy hair was over his collar and he had cryptic layers of words scribbled on the backs of his hands with a black marker. It was going too far. I was going to say something, but when I came in Fred tossed an envelope on the bar.

Slipped under the door earlier, he said.

I felt my body contract for a moment, then the swelling hum of blood to my face. The envelope was slightly damp and unopened. On the front it said: "for the big ginger lass" in a rough hand. Clearly it was not from Sebastian.

Inside was a Polaroid photo. It was taken from Douglass's Cove, facing east toward Baltimore across the Gascanane Sound. The Polaroid man with the little dog: Padraig Cadogan. The light was weak and gray, like it was taken in the early morning, and the distance made the image vague, but I could make out the blocky black stern of Conchur's salvage boat. It was close to the black rock of Carrigmore and a small boat was pulled up and three men in storm suits were huddled around something, a white form on the rocks.

Fred was standing behind me, looking over my shoulder.

What's that?

I started walking toward the stairs. Why did Padraig Cadogan send the photo to me? Why a photo of the same rock where his daughters and nearly all the island children drowned? On the bottom of the photo was the date. It was taken that morning. On the back: "Christmas Eve 1972." The day Highgate was abandoned on the island by his wife and family, the same day the ferry was lost.

I heard O'Boyle's voice in the dim light of his caravan, reciting the words his mother had scratched into the walls of the ruined castle:

Night swimmer, who watches the drowned and the yet unborn,
All will lament as the great eye is swallowed by wind and water.

I don't know what would happen if I lost her, Highgate said. *I don't know what I would do.*

Oh, dear God.

I checked my watch. It was ten till noon. The next ferry left in five minutes.

Hey, Fred said, what's going on?

I'm sorry, I said, but I have to get out to Clear.

I ran upstairs to get my parka. I opened my duffel bag on the bed and ransacked the bedroom looking for something but I didn't know what it was.

Fred was standing in the doorway, his arms outstretched.

What the hell? Elly? What are you doing? Bill is bringing the boat in. I thought we might hang out.

I'll be back this evening, I'll take the six o'clock back.

What the fuck is with that picture? Who sent you that?

A man named Padraig Cadogan. You don't know him, it doesn't matter. I have to see Highgate. I have to show him this picture.

Why?

I'll explain when I get back.

Fred followed me down the stairs, a bar rag in his hand, his forehead knotted in confusion. It was a look of distrust. His face was bruised and swollen like that of an aging boxer after a bad fight. He didn't understand that I felt I only had a small chance to make it right. He didn't know that it was me who brought this on us.

I'll come with you, he said.

No. They won't let you.

Through the window I could see the ferry was tossing off the lines to depart. I dropped my bag by the door and stepped into his arms and hugged him tight.

But you can't go alone, he said.

I'll be back.

I released him and went out the door and across the street. When I reached the quay I turned back and Fred was standing in the doorway, his T-shirt rippling in the breeze. He held up his hand. When I left he must have still thought it was his fault, the pub, the Corrigans, everything.

That was the last time I saw my husband and I carry that heavy stone in my heart every day of this life.

*   *   *

The ferry was empty other than two Corrigans in the pilothouse. I stepped on the boat and they immediately motored out, as if they were waiting for me. As we came around by Gascanane Rock, I barely had the guts to look. It was difficult to make out at first, but there was something white lying on a flat piece of black rock, and as we passed I had a clear view.

It was Miranda, splayed out on her back, her limbs bent out to her sides and nailed to the rock with long ship bolts. Her fur was shocking white, almost clear, and the lines of her body in that position made her seem like something not of this world. Her rib cage was split wide open, the ribs visible and purple organs glistening. A raven perched on her head, feeding on the flesh of her snout, her eyes empty black hollows. A couple more ravens on the rocks nearby, preening their shining feathers.

One of the Corrigans stepped out of the pilothouse with his hood up. He cupped his hands around a cigarette and leaned back against the bow, facing me. When he lifted his head I could see the squared glasses and wide mouth, cigarette dangling. *Kieran.* He gazed at me, the smoke streaming out of his nose as we swung along the north side of the island. I looked away, my hands in the pockets of my parka, clenched tight. I had a deep, cramping sensation in my stomach, and I stared hard at the cliffs of Cape Clear. I was searching for a figure on the cliff top, but no one was there.

The black line of clouds that Fred and I had seen yesterday advanced on the island like a swelling curtain, moving with visible speed. The ferry fought through the high swells and charged into the North Harbor. Even in the sheltered harbor the water was white and tossed and the wind whipped foam into the air and carried it off into the hills like giant clusters of soap bubbles. A small group of people queued on the quay, bundled up and carrying bags and packages. As I came off they streamed onto the boat. Sebastian was at the end of the line, his leather satchel and binocular case strapped on his back. When he saw me coming off he stepped out of the line.

You are going the wrong way, he said.

His smile was tight. He was trying to be calm.

I can't, I said. I have to do something.

Listen, this gale is going to do some serious damage.

This island has been through it before, I said. It's not going any-where. I just have to run one errand.

Okay, he said. I'll go with you.

Sebastian gripped my arm and pulled me away from the small crowd. He quickly scanned the pier.

There's something I have to tell you, he said.

He fixed his eyes on mine, his irises flexing and widening, his mouth going soft.

No, I said. I can't do this, not now.

Wait, he said, it's not—

Please just help me, I said, my voice cracking, *please.*

There'll be another ferry, he said. Where do you need to go?

Up across Ballyieragh, by Lough Errul. I need to go see someone.

Let's cut through by the bird observatory, Sebastian said.

We headed up the hill behind the old ruined church and west along the cliffs of the north side of the island. The sea was deep black and the coming clouds from the west were shutting over the sky like a lid. The waves boiled around the rocks at the bottom of the cliffs, the swells already more than ten feet, thundering against the island.

In another couple hours, Sebastian said, we'll want to be off the island. Or dug in somewhere, high up.

We came along to the finger of land that held the crumbled ruins of Dún an Óir, the Castle of Gold. Sebastian stopped and used his binoculars to scan the ruins.

I thought I saw something moving in there, he said.

I thought of O'Boyle's mother locking herself in the castle, scrib-bling on the walls her portents of doom. The land bridge was washed away, and to get up there you'd have to do a serious bit of climbing over boulders and sea.

That's a bit odd, Sebastian said, lowering his glasses. A group of birds, taking refuge. Can't tell what kind.

Let's keep going, I said, his caravan is just up over the next hill.

O'Boyle's new house had been dramatically improved, all the walls, door, and windows in place, a new sloping metal roof, the concrete chimney already belching smoke. The old caravan was squashed flat like a cockroach and had been dragged off a ways toward the cliffs. A steely, slanting rain, smelling of seawater, began to fall. We cinched our parka hoods around our faces.

Wonderful, Sebastian said. I hope this person owes you money.

We came down the hill toward the house. The windows were blazing with light, and I began to try to formulate what I was going to say. In the large window by the front door we could see a lamp on the kitchen table, a warmly lit scene that reminded me of the opening of a play. O'Boyle pulled out a chair and sat down, setting up a teapot and a couple of mugs. He was wearing a clean white shirt and smiling and laughing about something. He reached across the table and took hold of Ariel's hands. She was wearing a strange kind of crown of sea nettles on her head, a simple green dress, her head bowed, a smile on her lips. The fire flickered in the background, and I could smell roasted meat and potatoes.

They held each other's hands across the table, and I thought of that moment back in Cork, before all this started, when the winner was announced. When Fred turned and knelt before me, seized my hands in his, his face afire with joy. *It's really happening!* he said to me, *we did it, this is really happening!* The world spun around us like we were the only thing that existed, just for a moment.

I watched the two of them in their small circle of light. The wind shifted and pushed the rain sideways, burning my eyes with sea salt. Sebastian cursed and held his arm in front of his face.

Quaint, Sebastian said. We going to the door? Getting bloody soaked here.

No, I said. I'm done.

Seriously? Then let's get back to the ferry.

He took my hand.

The black wall of clouds had now overtaken Fastnet, and the thin finger of light seemed pathetic under its immensity. What could

I possibly say to Highgate? Would one more betrayal somehow assuage his grief?

Okay, I said, let's go.

We cut back south to the rim of the Ineer, to follow the path that led to Kieran's construction site and the Waist. The Ineer was frothing and rolling; sets of ten-foot waves thudded into the stone quay. The rock beach was already stripped bare to naked stone, and as we neared the cliff we could see the long black form of some enormous marine animal being pounded against the rocks at the foot of the cliff.

Bloody *hell,* Sebastian said. That's something you don't see every day.

What is it?

I leaned into the hill, away from the cliff, clutching handfuls of grass. I was too afraid to get close enough to the cliff to look down. Sebastian crawled on his hands and knees to the edge and peered over.

Not sure. Maybe a basking shark. Or pilot whale. The thing is *huge*.

He lay down and hung his head over the cliff, using his binoculars.

Christ almighty, he said. It's a goddamn killer whale. Poor bugger is beaten up pretty bad. He's gonna be torn to pieces in a few minutes.

Fastnet cast its pale eye across us and I thought of that day in the sea, the girl scaling the side of the lighthouse. Fastnet would hold; it had been through many storms and surely some worse than this.

By the time we made it across the Waist and to the North Harbor, the ferry was already docked and a few passengers were queued up to board. The Corrigans were in their bright survival suits, scrambling over the deck, and in the pilothouse Kieran was listening to the radio and eating an apple. He rapped on the glass and Conchur stepped out of the forward hatch. He was the only crew member without a survival suit, instead clothed in dun-colored overalls and a black watch cap. A fresh wound ran from his chin to one ear, a ragged tear of skin, crusted with dried blood. Conchur dropped the gangplank, and the passengers began to board. Sebastian and I joined the back of the line. The rain turned to sleet, sharp and painful, and a collective murmur rose from the small crowd and everyone cinched up their gear a bit tighter. I pulled my hood low, following close behind Sebastian, my face nearly into his back.

I was hoping that they wouldn't recognize me, or that perhaps they would just let me go. This was a foolish hope. When Sebastian and I reached the gangplank Conchur put a forearm in between us to block my way. I didn't say anything, merely looked up at his face. Up close the wound along his jaw was gruesome, a deep, jagged furrow. *Miranda.*

With a quick shove Conchur pushed me off the gangplank onto the quay, and I fell backward, sitting heavily on the wet concrete. On the boat Sebastian reached back for me and spun around in alarm as Conchur hauled up the gangplank chains in one fist, slamming the latch home. Kieran gunned the engines and the ferry lurched away from the dock.

Sebastian went to the rail and looked at me, astonished, and I saw him measure the widening distance to the dock, his hands tightening, one leg starting to come up, then relaxing as the gap quickly stretched six, ten feet. He began to search frantically through his pockets for something. I tried to smile at him, to show him it was okay, that he shouldn't worry or cause any trouble, but I could feel my face sliding apart and I know I must have looked awful, sitting on the wet dock. Conchur took hold of his arm roughly, saying something to him, and two other Corrigans stepped up beside him. Sebastian held up his hands, saying something in reply. Conchur nodded, and Sebastian dug into his coat pocket and pulled out a small piece of paper. He held his other hand out, as if to say, this is all I've got. This is it.

The boat was nearly twenty feet away now and Conchur released him. Sebastian balled up the piece of paper and stepping into the throw he launched it at me, a bug in the wind. It was knocked down a few feet from the quay, dropping into the tossing water. I crawled to the edge of the dock on my stomach but couldn't reach it and without thinking I slid into the water. The water was cold, colder than I had ever felt before, zeroing in to my bones, and I flailed awkwardly at the paper. When I had it in my hand I turned and hauled myself painfully onto the dock.

Sebastian grabbed Conchur's arm and said something to him, pointing. Conchur shook his head and shrugged him off. Sebastian began shouting to me, pointing up the hill, his voice lost in the wind and sea. He was pointing toward Highgate's place.

I unrolled the wet wad of paper in my hand. It was a business card, a cloudy insignia and contact information already blurred beyond recognition. On the back something was written in pen but as I tried to wipe water off the card came apart and the wet lumps fell through my fingers.

The ferry turned out past the protective wall and was immediately smashed with waves, driving it backward. In the steamy pilothouse I could see Kieran flailing like a marionette, steering and correcting. Once he pointed the boat into the waves and got on the throttle the ferry began to chug away, rising and falling in the swells, toward the lights of Baltimore. Sebastian was crouching in the back, clinging to the rail along the transom. He gave me a long wave, from the shoulder, insistent. I waved, again trying to tell him I was okay, his staring face shrinking as the ferry lurched toward the mainland.

I was alone. Random debris flew about the harbor, empty wooden pallets skipping across the quay and crab pots and fish traps tumbling off their racks and into the sea. Froth from the water whipped up over the docks and mixed with the flying materials, creating a low, foglike layer of wind-driven flotsam. Whoever was left on the island would be battened down. I thought about Nora's, or going up to Nell's place, but it was Highgate who'd told me he'd take me in. I knew he wouldn't leave.

I would call Fred and tell him everything. I would tell him that I was wrong, and I would do whatever he asked. I only wanted to get off that island, out of Ireland. We would start over, start a family, and the sudden thought of a child filled me with a glorious kind of relief, like I was released from a net, like I was saved from drowning.

When I reached the top of the hill I could see the glowing white farmhouse on the far slope of Highgate's fields. I cut across the middle of the island, taking the footpath to the post office and the phone. The sky was roiling, black and skeins of purple, and in the darkness of the trees surrounding the post office I found the phone booth and slipped inside, the pines bending and cracking, pawing at the glass. I could barely see the numbers but I somehow made the call to the Nightjar. Fred answered quickly. His voice was thick and urgent. The static rose and swelled with the wind.

Elly?

Fred, I'm sorry! I'm still here—

Why didn't you get on the ferry?

I couldn't get on—

Are you safe? I looked for you—

I'm sorry, they wouldn't let me—

The phone line was fading in and out, and Fred was shouting something unintelligible. Sea spray was blasting through the cracks in the booth and shingles were ripping off the roof of the post office like playing cards.

Listen to me, he said, stay where you are. I'm coming . . .

No!

We can make it . . . North Harbor . . . Bill and Dinny. Wait—

Fred, don't! You can't!

Get to high ground, he said. Just hold on.

Then the line went dead.

The rain came sideways, indistinguishable from the sea spray. The tall grass was flattened and slick, and I had to crawl over the low stone fences that whistled like a deranged chorus as the wind tore through the gaps. To the west, in the teeth of the storm, the ocean was firing over the cliffs of the Bill of Clear and Ballyieragh in tremendous walls of water and mist, the winds pushing it across the island, and seawater fell from the sky in heavy sheets. I came up along the northern cliffs, to my left Roaringwater Bay and to my right the broad ascending fields of Highgate's farm. I cut up a goat path directly toward the house. When I came over the first rise I could see it, the white house glowing faintly, the windows now dark. The fence gates were open, the goat house door was banging in the wind, and I ducked in, figuring Highgate might be there hunkered down with his animals, but it was only full of whirling dervishes of straw, the packed dirt coming loose and spraying like a sandstorm. In the muddy yard there were a few black clumps on the ground, some kind of small animal, that definite inertness of death. I staggered over to one and nudged it with my foot, bending to see it clearly. They were ravens, six of them, crumpled in various poses as if they had been mashed in the air and flung to the ground.

I found the door and pounded on it with both fists. I tried the handle and found it open so I pushed inside, closing the door behind me. It was near-total darkness inside, the smell of peat fire, human feet, and goats. I could see the faint gray outline of the door into the kitchen straight ahead and the steps upstairs to my right, and I waited a moment to let my eyes adjust.

Hello? I called out. Anyone here?

A low shadow moved into the kitchen doorway. A deep guttural growl, the flash of animal eyes. A bolt of lightning lit the room for an instant. Hector, the old dog, crouched, hackles raised, long teeth bared. I turned and my hand found the knob and I spun out into the roaring wind and slammed the door behind me, pulling it tight. I leaned against the door to brace it. There was a moment of silence and I had just begun to relax when the full force of Hector came slamming into the door. His muzzle smashed through the small window at the top, snapping savagely at me, and I stumbled back and fell in the mud. The door held. Hector stopped snapping, and as I watched, his snout poked around, sniffing hard, then withdrew.

I picked my way back through the yard, stepping around the dead ravens. I stopped to rest on the stone wall, watching the water thrashing in the bay. A flicker of light caught my eye. Down the sloping fields, a figure stood on the cliffs at a small point that jutted out into the water.

It was Highgate. He stood tall with his back arched, his toes right on the cliff edge. His cap was off and his white hair and long beard flowed over his shoulder. He stretched his arms out to the western sky as it roared, and great crooked spires of lightning thousands of feet long reached down and churned the foaming red sea.

I ran for Ard na Gaoithe. I still had a key to Nora's place and it was one of the highest points on the island. I passed through the top of Highgate's fields and made the road at the base of Knockcaranteen, where there was a deep thrumming sound, cutting through the howling wind. The giant wind turbine at the top of the hill was lit with a hellish blue-white light, spinning with terrific speed. Water streamed from the blade edges, trailing in long glistening threads. The turbine groaned in great metered wails of screaming iron, bolts popping like gunshots, the blades beginning to wobble, oscillating back and forth, still rotating impossibly fast. Ripples began to wrinkle the middle of the tower as it twisted. The concrete blockhouse at the base seemed to vibrate, its windows flashing white, thick channels of blue electricity escaping and arching through the barred windows and door, where they climbed the tower like ascending snakes or corkscrewed themselves into the earth with smoking fury.

To the west the stacked waves like rolling mountains stretched across the horizon. They reached Fastnet Rock, towering as high as the lighthouse, incredible waves a hundred feet or more. They swallowed the fist of rock and the finger of stone and the baleful light was eclipsed, then glowing faintly through the wall of water like an underwater eye. The wave passed and the light streaked again across the island, once, twice, three times, until the second line of waves swept over the lighthouse and Fastnet went dark.

The next few minutes were a blur of slogging through grassy fields, pelting seawater rain, howling winds. I crawled like an animal over fence lines. My mind went inert, some kind of survival mechanism, and all I saw was the ground in front of me, the hazy outline of the hill, the spinning sky. I kept going.

When I reached the top of the hill by Ard na Gaoithe, I looked back east, toward the mainland. A few lights winked in Baltimore. Somewhere out in the black among the churning rock and sea my husband clung to a boat, coming to save me.

For a moment I felt as if I could summon up everything inside of me, all the love, the hope, the regret, the forgiveness, that I could use all of this to burn hot and bright, like a beacon splitting the sky. I watched the water and dreamed him going back, turning around, at the quay and hustling up to the Nightjar, soaking wet and grimly concerned, but not really worried, thinking of a nice drink to shake off the cold. I would survive. He had to know that.

The island shuddered as the mountains of water crashed into its foundations.

I closed my eyes and saw myself flaring up, rising like a column of fire. I prayed to the sky, the earth, the sea. I sent everything I had into the world.

Epilogue

In June the sky above southwest Ireland cracks wide open like a bowl of endless blue. The winds that just a month before held the icy sting of the Northern Atlantic now seem to carry the warmth of the Gulf Stream and all the wafting scents of the flora of the islands, a sharp, clean smell of distant lands. The fields of Cape Clear explode into green, the ground still saturated by the deluges of spring, and the gorse sheds the rusty sheath and goes gray-green, growing a few inches a day. You can almost see the island swelling up, rising out of the water. The tourists, Irish and English mostly, the whole decidedly western European, arrive with the fresh air and sunshine, and the Ineer becomes crowded, the stone quay lined with pale Scandinavians swathed in sunblock, children swimming in the blue-green water, the visibility so acute in the sunlight that you can see to the bottom, forty feet down. So much laughter. Even the strands of kelp that wind up from the depths seem to twist with delight.

They found Bill Cutler's body on the rocks under the western bluffs that lay just below his house, as if his body was trying to return home. There was a service at the church. I didn't go. I couldn't face it. In my mind I can see Nell's small lined face, stricken with anguish. She would never come back from it, and for her final years she would shut herself up in the house that Bill built, the draft whistling through the stone walls, looking out over the western reaches that claimed her husband.

Dinny Corrigan was found the next day clinging to some boulders along the western cliffs, naked and blue, but alive. He was transported to a hospital in Cork and was never seen again.

Fred's body was never found, and some part of me is glad for it.

When I returned from Ireland I moved in with Beatrice in Arizona. Our apartment complex has a pool and I float in it at night, staring up at the stars until Beatrice comes out and starts throwing things at me: balls of paper, bottle tops, empty beer cans. She is pregnant again, and she doesn't sleep much at night. It's the gunsmith's baby, but he split to Alaska to build a log home on a homestead and trap game. When I come in I fix large bowls of heavily buttered popcorn and Beatrice and I watch sitcoms together on cable while the crickets tune up and the night closes in with its warm blanket.

I never swim in the ocean or any other natural body of water. I spend a lot of time in the pool here in Phoenix, swimming endless laps at the YMCA, listening to the dull crunch and hum of my body under the blazing sun.

In America everyone seems to be shouting at each other through a globe of thin glass, a muted, distant feeling. Everyone seems so angry and suddenly vital, but you can't hear what anyone is saying. I go for a lot of walks through our part of the city. The lights are dimmer, fewer people on the streets, and in the evenings the bored waiters lean against the windows and smooth their aprons.

I have a job at the community college teaching literature classes, but it is only a matter of time before I am fired. The faces and gazes of the students, which used to be like figures in a painting, now come off the page, right at me. They really see me. I assign them nothing but Cheever, and they respond with some curiosity but mostly indifference. I ask them to write about their experiences with the stories, but they have realized that I don't care if they ever turn anything in, so I get little. Despite this, they all show up for every class. I don't know why they come. I mostly have them read passages aloud, which they seem to enjoy. I read aloud too, and I cry sometimes. I am not ashamed of this.

Fred's father gave me all the money anyway. I was floating in the pool one afternoon when the shadow of his plane came rippling over the water in a dark flash. I knew it was him before I even opened my eyes. I watched it go into a steep bank, circling around, a little red plane with jaunty white stripes on low-slung wings, like an old crop duster. I stood up and waved as Hamilton Bulkington came low over the apartment buildings and palm trees. By the time I dried off and changed clothes he was waiting in the lobby of our building, wearing a rumpled suit and carrying his valise, a deep set of creases above his eyes and a damaging turn of mouth. He was the closest thing to Fred left on the earth. I held him for a long time, and he patted my back and murmured into my hair.

I'm sorry, Elly, I'm so sorry.

I know that he wasn't apologizing to me, but to his son.

I didn't want the money, but he pleaded with me, saying Fred would want me to have it. Of course that is true, so I accepted it.

Ham took off an hour later, coming by to circle the pool with artful dips, and then he put the nose of the plane into the blue sky and climbed into that open space until he was just a speck of dust.

Back in the apartment at dinner I put out plates, knives, forks, spoons, napkins, and fill our glasses with ice water. Beatrice cooks pasta tossed with spinach and olive oil and sprinkles our plates with cheese. She wants to name the baby Antonio, for no real reason other than she thinks it sounds romantic, like someone in a novel.

Beatrice is due this April. I can feel it happening already. I am tending some kind of powerful love, working it like a small fire. I have all the money set up in an account in his name, waiting for him. He will never know want or the need to leave, he will always be able to stay right where he is, where he belongs. When we sit on the couch watching TV, I put my hands on Beatrice's belly and wait for him to move. I can feel him in there, spinning and dreaming, swimming in the sea that never ends. I cannot wait to hold him in my arms.

My parents call me occasionally, and leave long messages on voice mail, but they know I'm all right. It's not like I'm making a new life for myself in Arizona. It's more like a half-life, part of a life I already had, but it is my own. Today, in this new life, my love rises like the trunk of a great silver oak, crashing into the sky with the sound of the sea.

Sometimes I have dreams of St. Kieran, in his wool cowl and thorns, standing waist deep in the ocean. I am floating before him, like I am already dead, the night sky spread above us. For an instant he looks like Fred, and every time I have a straining moment of hope, but then his face clouds into that of a stranger, a man who has been dead for hundreds of years. St. Kieran puts his rough hands on my stomach, touching me gently, and the moon winks out and I know that I will float like this forever.

This is the only story I will ever tell.

Acknowledgments

Much of my research for this book consisted of time spent gamboling around Cape Clear, Sherkin Island, Baltimore, Skibereen, and surrounding areas, hanging out in pubs, talking with locals, taking lots of long walks. I also used many books, including *Cape Clear Island: Its People and Landscape,* by Eamon Lankford, *The Natural History of Cape Clear Island,* by J. T. R. Sharrock, *Swimming to Antarctica* and other books by the great Lynne Cox, Charles Sprawson's beautiful literary history of swimming *Haunts of the Black Masseur,* the books of Chuck Kruger, as well as several well-worn maps of Clear and Roaringwater Bay. I appreciate the general welcoming spirit of the denizens of Clear and their forgiving nature as I often blundered through their pastures and paddocks in my island roaming. Special thanks to the Cape Clear Island Co-Operative, An Siopa Beag (best food on the island), Ard na Gaoithe and Eileen Leonard, Ciarán Danny Mike's Pub, Cotter's Pub (best pint on the island), the gracious Mary O'Driscoll, a friend to all the writers and artists that blow through, Joe Aston and Gannet's Way on Sherkin Island, the Harpercraft store, Club Cleire, and especially Ed Harper's goat farm. Ed can tell you everything you need to know about raising, breeding, and milking goats, and a lot of other things besides.

I was fortunate to meet (and race with) the legendary open-water swimmer Ned Denison, of County Cork, who supplied me with various bits about swimming in the waters off Ireland. Thanks to him and all the Cork Co. swimmers I spoke with during my participation in the Beginish Island Swim. I also received valuable training and coaching help from the Dallas JCC Masters Team, Scott Eder, and Brian Loncar Racing in Dallas. As far as I can determine, no one has ever swum from Cape Clear to Fastnet and back.

Good parts of this novel were written at Yaddo and the MacDowell Colony, and I am grateful for my time at these wonderful places. I would like to thank J. L. Torres, Michael Carrino, Bruce Butterfield, and the English Department of SUNY Plattsburgh. Kjell and the racing crew of the J/105 *Freya* on Lake Champlain, and Phil, Amber, Ty, Amy, and all the rest who taught me to sail, and to Roland for taking a total unknown rookie out Soling class racing. Also thank you to the Arts and Humanities Department at the University of Texas at Dallas for their support of my research.

I am indebted, as always, to the short stories, novels, and journals of the great John Cheever.

I would like to thank once again my agent, Alex Glass, and Trident Media Group, and I am so fortunate to work with the best editor in NYC, Alexis Gargagliano. Thanks to all the folks at Scribner for their support, my longtime readers Mike Mannon and Seth Tucker, and lastly my wife, Stacy, who spent the last eight years hearing me talk endlessly about this place and this story.

About the Author

Matt Bondurant's second novel, *The Wettest County in the World* (Scribner, 2008), was a *New York Times Book Review* Editors' Choice and one of the *San Francisco Chronicle*'s 50 Best Books of the Year, and is currently being made into a film by director John Hillcoat, starring Shia LaBeouf, Tom Hardy, Mia Wasikowska, Gary Oldman, and Guy Pearce. His first novel, *The Third Translation* (Hyperion, 2005), was an international bestseller, translated into fourteen languages worldwide. A former competitive swimmer and collegiate water polo player, Matt has competed in numerous long-distance swimming races, including the Beginish Island 4-Mile Swim off the western coast of Ireland. He currently lives in Texas.

www.mattbondurant.com